PENGUIN BOOKS

I BELIEVE IN ANGELS

Patricia Wendorf was born in Somerset, but just before the Second World War her parents moved to Loughborough, where she still lives. Her first two novels, *Peacefully in Berlin* and *Leo Days*, received excellent reviews, and the Patteran trilogy established her as a well-loved writer with a unique voice. She is also the author of *Double Wedding Ring*, based closely on the history of her own family in Somerset, and *Lives of Translation*, both of which are published by Penguin.

Patricia Wendorf has herself been diagnosed as having thyroid cancer, and this is strongly reflected in *I Believe in Angels*.

Patricia Wendorf

I Believe in Angels

PENGUIN BOOKS

PENGUIN BOOKS

Published by the Penguin Group
Penguin Books Ltd, 27 Wrights Lane, London W8 5TZ, England
Penguin Books USA Inc., 375 Hudson Street, New York, New York 10014, USA
Penguin Books Australia Ltd, Ringwood, Victoria, Australia
Penguin Books Canada Ltd, 10 Alcorn Avenue, Toronto, Ontario, Canada M4V 3B2
Penguin Books (NZ) Ltd, 182–190 Wairau Road, Auckland 10, New Zealand

Penguin Books Ltd, Registered Offices: Harmondsworth, Middlesex, England

First published by Viking 1994
Published in Penguin Books 1995
1 3 5 7 9 10 8 6 4 2

Printed in England by Clays Ltd, St Ives plc

Come to the edge
No, we will fall.

Come to the edge
No, we will fall.

They came to the edge,
He pushed them, and they flew.

Guillaume Apollinaire

everything whatever.

In the early mornings Amy walked in St Gilda's Gardens, which had a bandstand, a bowling green, a miniature lake and rockery, and a carillon of bells. Within the Gardens there was a café, the doors of which opened outwards on to a small paved square where stood white chairs and tables. Beside the square there was an aviary.

She sat in the sunshine of late September drinking lemon tea and watching the imprisoned birds. The grass grew long in their enclosure; there were sawn-off branches set in concrete to make convenient perches. The budgerigars and zebra finches seemed content, but the parakeets were restless. They hung on the wire mesh, suspended by their tiny feet, looking enviously at the sparrows pecking at crumbs underneath the café tables, unaware as yet of the black cat which watched from the forsythia bushes. When Amy could no longer bear to watch she turned her chair towards the flower-beds. The trees were in their final gold; the horse chestnuts shed their fruits, much to the delight of small boys. Between the branches she could see the red roof of the library.

Three months ago she would not have lingered in the café. There would have been Aunty Belle's letters to be posted, her library books to be exchanged, her favourite paté to be bought at the delicatessen. As Aunty Belle so often said, Amy did everything for her and Mimi.

Well, that was all over now – Amy no longer did anything for anybody. It had taken a lot of getting used to. Idleness. Just sitting in the sun. Watching the birds.

*

Amy had lost a summer. Mislaid a season. Could not seem to recall even one of that year's misty June mornings or hot afternoons. Not a single deep-blue evening. She came back to the normal world in the first week of September, except that normality must now be redefined. Presented with the fact of her continuing survival, life itself would need to be evaluated. She was becoming aware that she had, in the past few months, learned a new kind of thinking. As her strength returned she began to walk alone in unfrequented places, or to sit in almost empty cinemas, not watching the performance but pondering somewhere far back in her head the curious turn events had taken. She concerned herself endlessly with debates that would never be resolved, arguments she could not win; and all the time she consciously avoided the old temptation to anticipate the future. The recent treachery of her body, once experienced, must henceforth be respected. For Amy sickness had never been an option. It was Aunty Belle and Mimi who enjoyed ill health.

She stood up abruptly, scattering the sparrows from underneath the table, further alarming the parakeets who relinquished their hold on the wire mesh and retreated to the safety of their concrete-rooted perches. Amy watched them thoughtfully, and then began to walk away towards the green wrought-iron gates.

When she reached the bridge which spanned the stream she stood for a while, taking in the vistas of the grouped trees, the colours of the flower beds, the antics of the wild ducks and pigeons. In the first weeks of her homecoming she had sometimes needed to lean against the stone parapet, waiting for the trembling in her legs to pass. Now, she could walk without pause, past the smooth green velvet of the Bowls Club's rinks, to the wooden benches that faced the bandstand. Here she experienced as always a curious pleasure at the bandstand's shape, and the little flight of stone steps that led up to its round raised platform. She associated the structure with military music played by men who wore dark blue uniforms and peaked caps, although, to her knowledge, she had never witnessed such a performance. Today the bandstand was occupied by art students from the University who found it a convenient vantage point for sketching. She glimpsed the girls' long dark skirts and fringed jackets, their artfully tousled hair; the boys' cropped heads and deliberately ripped jeans. They were a merry bunch. As she walked away their laughter rang out like half-remembered music, and Amy smiled for the first time in many weeks.

She had found the lump on a Friday morning. Sitting with friends in the Patio Café, looking at the aviary birds, she had, while taking off a gauzy scarf, touched the skin of her neck and there it was, the size of a small egg, nestling cosily and half-concealed behind her collar-bone. She remembered the way her fingers had explored the smooth hardness of its contours. She had glanced swiftly around the familiar faces and was thankful that among the chatter no one had noticed her gravity, her stillness. For a week she had done nothing, had inspected her neck night and morning, willing the lump to disappear. But from the moment of discovery there had been an inevitability about it. Standing before the bathroom mirror, head and neck held stiffly and inclined slightly forward, the thing was hardly to be seen. But when she tilted her head backwards the lump appeared, like a full moon rising.

Her first hospital appointment had been reassuring. The consultant was a young man, the friend of a neighbour. It came out in conversation that Amy's neighbour had attended the doctor's recent wedding. This fact seemed to make a link between them.

The examination had been thorough: three-quarters of an hour of questions, a lot of peering and prodding, all with reference to her thyroid gland. The lump had been touched and looked at briefly, and then ignored. She had been sent to the pathology department and given a blood test. She had also been referred to another city hospital, where a scan of her neck was to be taken.

Amy was vague about scans. She supposed the procedure to be a sophisticated sort of X-ray. When Lali phoned to inquire about the hospital visit Amy said, 'Nothing to worry about. They're investigating my thyroid gland. They seem to think it may be a bit dodgy.'

'Are you quite sure, Mum?' Lali worked in hospital administration and medical persons in Amy's opinion had a tendency to be dramatic when it came to diagnoses concerning family members.

'Perfectly sure,' she said, 'and anyway, a peculiar thyroid gland could account for the under-the-weather feeling I've had lately.'

'I didn't know you'd been feeling poorly.'

'Well, not ill. Just tired. Don't worry, love. It's all being sorted out.'

Dominic, the younger of her twin sons, drove her to the hospital where scans were taken. She had worn the new blue silk dress and matching high-heeled sandals; had her hair set especially for the occasion. She felt nervous but cheerful, as if she were going to a garden party given by someone of elevated social standing. She talked so brightly and distractingly to Dom, that on entrance to the hospital complex he missed the sign which indicated the Radiology Department, and needed to go round again.

The scanner was housed in a dimly lit room which held a bed, several monitoring screens, and other gadgets to which she could not put a name. She had been told to remove all her clothes and put on a gown of some light and blue material, rather like a dishcloth. She lay on the bed, her head tipped uncomfortably backwards, her shoulders raised on pillows. A film of jelly-like substance was spread across her throat, and an object rather like a hand-held hairdryer was passed back and forth across her neck. If she squinted sideways she could just see the screen which showed an oscillating pattern of light and dark splodges. In the round black area which she supposed must be the lump there were tiny movements which seemed to cause concern to the operators of the machine. The procedure seemed to take a very long time. Amy grew bored with squinting at the screen, and began to think about Dom, left sitting in the stuffy heat of a hospital corridor.

When she at last emerged he said, 'What now?'

She shrugged. 'Yet another appointment. Next week at our local hospital. I'm to go on Thursday. For the results.'

Michael had worn silk socks. He bought them six pairs at a time from an exclusive little men's shop in Knightsbridge, two pairs of navy, two black, and two dove-grey. Amy had always seen Michael's predilection for fine fabrics as a sign of his inborn good taste and superiority. It even gave him a kind of glamour in her eyes, set him apart from the undiscerning males who made do with Terylene or nylon. Chris and Dom wore socks of thick white cotton, sporty items which had logos in strong colours printed on the ankle and around the rib. When her sons brought their washing home, Amy felt a rare sense of recklessness and freedom as she thrust their tasteless choices into the machine.

If she had been asked last year whether she was contented with her life, Amy would have answered yes. It would have been a lie, but the questioner could not have known that; would have seen only what Amy intended to reveal.

There must have been a time when it had started to go wrong. Michael, to be fair, had never actually said she should handwash and iron his expensive socks. It was one of those things that was never talked about in their sort of marriage. But Amy had known from the beginning that he had standards higher than her own.

There had been a morning – just hours before Michael's

disappearance – when, standing at the ironing board in her white and scarlet kitchen, Amy had switched the iron to 'high' and rested it gently on a dove-grey sock, then watched with awful pleasure the scorching and shrivelling of the delicate fabric. She had rushed to open doors and windows in an effort to dispel the resulting stench, and then had hidden the widowed sock at the bottom of the spare-room wardrobe.

The house was too big. As always on her return from the park, she found the sight of its exterior, its red-bricked, sash-windowed aspect, repellent and curiously threatening. Amy had lived the first years of her life among buildings of mellow golden stone, many of which had mullioned windows, cottage gardens. She half-remembered honeysuckle hedges; wallflowers which actually grew from crevices in walls; lanes in which the trees leaned inwards to form a canopy of green. In this city of her adoption, this alien place of flat landscapes which gave no views, St Gilda's Gardens was one of the few areas of visual pleasure available to her.

She went into the house through the front door, removed her shoes and placed them neatly with her coat in the down-stairs cloakroom. She went back to the door and closed it almost without sound, as if, upstairs, little children might still be sleeping. She paused in the hall, allowing the quiet of the rooms to settle around her. Once inside the house, Amy could imagine herself to be anywhere she chose. She had taken care to make a home of tranquillity and charm to which Michael would always want to return. She had tended the house as if at any moment, night or day, every inch of it was liable to be subjected to his critical inspection. His taste was for pastel colours, soft green carpets, lamps on low tables, diffused light. She found herself, even in the weakened state of her convales-cence, washing up and drying her single cup and saucer immedi-ately after use; observing the mindless rituals on which her domestic life depended. Except that, as Lali had long ago remarked, Amy was no longer in a domestic situation. True domesticity, she had discovered, required a minimum of two persons in order to be valid: and Michael had gone.

She sat down in the gold velvet button-backed chair that had once been his special place; it no longer faced the television set, but was turned towards the glass doors which faced the garden. Beside the chair Amy had placed a low wide table which held the telephone, her reading glasses and current library book, a radio, a box of Turkish Delight, a carton of rainbow-coloured tissues, a nail file, and her vitamin tablets. The clutter, so abhorred by Michael, gave her a certain satisfaction. She had recently added a footstool and two wool-embroidered cushions to the chair, which ruined utterly the elegance of the room. In the first months of her convalescence Amy had shut down her thinking mechanism, had bidden her head to be quiet while her body attempted to heal itself. But now, in the autumn of the year, with the fall of leaves to the bare earth, she found memory returning, slowly, like blood flowing back into an unused limb.

Amy did not want to think about her husband, had in fact managed quite successfully, she believed, not to think about him in the four years of his absence. Now, when her body hovered so precariously between past weakness and returning strength, he came pushing back into her thoughts, demanding a consideration he surely did not merit.

He had never missed that pair of socks, which for Michael was an indication, she supposed, of his state of mind when he did his packing. He had chosen his hour of departure well. It seemed to Amy at the time that he had come home and found his shirts freshly laundered, hanging creaselessly on hangers, his socks folded neatly into pairs, his Y-fronts as snowy white as those in the TV commercials, and decided that he might as well go while his clothes were clean. While she had been spending her regular Tuesday with Aunty Belle and Mimi,

PATRICIA WENDORF

vacuuming and dusting her aunts' small house, changing sheets and pillowcases, making up a list of shopping, Michael had removed all his personal belongings, and driven to a flat on the far side of the city.

Amy had come home that night through an October dusk, driving slowly; she recalled how the smell of garden bonfires had reminded her of her own strange unpremeditated act of arson. She had deliberately switched her thoughts back to Aunty Belle, who complained that day of swollen knee joints and a painful shoulder. Perhaps Amy should have called the doctor. But her aunt did not like doctors. She had parked her car underneath the street light and looked towards the unlit windows of the house. Michael was not home yet, and just as well, since supper would be late that night.

She found it particularly painful now to remember how she had come back thankfully to her own kitchen, which at first glance looked exactly as she had left it: the ironing board set up beside the window, the iron left on the drainer to cool, the pot of chives still wilting on the window-sill for lack of water. She kicked off her shoes and filled the kettle without at first noticing the absence of the piles of neatly folded laundry, or the empty plastic hangers thrown anyhow across the kitchen table. She had not for a moment believed that Michael had put away his shirts and underwear. It would never have occurred to him to do so. The absence of the Anglepoise lamp that had been her last Christmas present to him had been the only further confirmation she needed of her husband's departure. She had not bothered to check drawers and wardrobes.

That evening she sat for the first time in the gold velvet chair that had been exclusively his. She felt no surprise, no sharp pang of betrayal, no sense of shock. What she had experienced was a deep internal aching, in the region of her throat, as if the bruise of an old loss, a long-ago desertion, had somehow been reinflicted, just as she had always known it would be.

8

The removal by Michael of one particular object from the house seemed like theft to Amy. He had taken the blue Lalique figurine from the cabinet which held her little collection of coloured glass. Even now, after all this time, just to look at the space where the figurine once stood had the power to wound her. It was almost as if it had been Lali herself that Michael had stolen.

Her third hospital appointment had been early in July, and with a senior consultant. Amy had worn green, a light summer suit with crisp white lapels and matching strappy sandals. She combed her thick black hair hard back from her forehead and secured it with a jade clip. The skin of her face had darkened as it always did in summer, so that even the expensive suit, the broad white streak in her hair, the careful make-up, could not quite disguise her look of 'gypsy'.

The day had been humid, airless. In the Outpatients Department all doors and windows stood open to the noise of traffic. According to the notice-board in the waiting area, her consultant's clinic was already running one hour and twenty minutes late. Amy sat down with Dom in the red-seated chairs beside the tea- and coffee-bar. They drank tea and ate chocolate biscuits they did not really want, just to pass the time, and observed the progression of patients as they were called from waiting area to chair-lined corridor, only to wait again before entering the consultant's room.

Amy recalled the operators of the scanner, and their low-pitched anxious exchanges. As if he had caught her thought Dom said, 'It'll be all right, you know.'

'Yes,' she answered, 'of course it will.'

She studied Dom's profile, the sweep of his thick dark hair, so like her own. She saw his shoulders twitch, his fingers linked in a familiar restless movement. Life had not yet taught him to be resigned, patient. She hoped it never would.

She sensed his concern for her and wished there was some

way that she could spare him this particular worry. But perhaps after all it would turn out to be an unnecessary scare. She imagined them leaving the hospital together, laughing over coffee and cream cakes in the Patio Café, the lump declared innocuous and safe.

She said, 'Is it very inconvenient for you, taking all this time off work to ferry me to hospitals?'

'Of course it's not inconvenient. Chris can manage quite well on his own for an afternoon.'

An hour passed, and still she was not called. She looked at her wristwatch. 'This must be very boring for you. Why don't you go out for a bit? Nose around the shops or something? We could be here for hours yet.'

He stood up. 'Well, if you're sure. I need to do some shopping. I won't be too long.'

He walked away, tall and thin and handsome, and two young nurses smiled sweetly at him as he passed them by.

So long had Amy sat in the red-seated chair, that when her name was called at last she did not hear it. It was the lady who dispensed drinks from the tea-bar who leaned over and said, 'I think you're wanted, dear. It must be your turn.'

Amy followed a nurse down a corridor which was carpeted in green. The chairs in this area had green seats. She sat opposite a poster which gave advice to diabetics.

Nurses ushered patients through mysterious doors. Amy heard the polite, impersonal greeting repeated to each one as the doors closed. 'Good afternoon. Well – how are you? Do sit down.'

She wondered what she should say when it was her turn. 'Very well, thank you' hardly seemed appropriate in the circumstances. 'Bloody awful' would be equally misleading. 'Terrified' would be the most honest answer.

She removed her jacket, touched the jade clip which secured her hair, checked her make-up in her compact mirror. Her features were drawn, her skin sallow underneath the tan. Just sitting in a hospital waiting-room had made her look ill. Dom was correct, of course. Everything was all right, really.

The nurse in the green dress called her name. Amy rose, and together they entered the consultant's office. She was, she now realized, his final patient of that long, hot afternoon. He did not bother with a greeting, but muttered, 'Sit down, won't you.'

Amy sat. She watched his large clean hands open up her folder and withdraw five slips of flimsy printed paper. He studied each one. 'Good,' he said. 'Very good. Your blood tests were all clear.'

Amy remained seated. The consultant stared inquiringly at her. She began to realize that this was all he had to say. That he expected her to leave.

She said, hesitantly, 'What about my scan results?'

He did not say, 'What scan results?', but the question hovered, ballooned above his head. He turned again to her file, which contained only the five test results, and the notes made by the previous doctor. He said to the nurse, 'Where are the details concerning Mrs Sheldon's scan?'

'I'll make inquiries, sir.'

He turned back to Amy. 'Perhaps you would care to wait outside.'

The traffic in the corridor had lessened. Only a few people still sat in the green chairs. The rows of empty seats made Amy feel uneasy; it was like lingering unnecessarily in a theatre once the performance was over and the audience departed.

The nurse came back. She said, 'Are you quite sure that you had a scan, Mrs Sheldon?'

Amy said, smiling, that it was not an experience she was likely to forget. She gave the name of the hospital, the date and time. The nurse went away; Amy waited, minutes lengthened.

From where she sat Amy had a clear view of the anteroom which led into the consultant's office. It contained a desk and chair, a filing cabinet and a telephone. At the desk sat a middle-aged lady in a grey dress, who was not a nurse. The telephone rang, and almost at once the secretary turned to look at Amy, then she picked up a pen and began to write, and Amy knew that her scan was the subject of the phone call. The writing went on for a very long time. In answer to a question from the nurse, she heard the secretary say, 'Tell him I have the results now, but I need to transcribe them into longhand.'

The muddle over the scan had not improved the consultant's temper. Amy sat down without waiting for his invitation. From the window behind him, sunlight caught the gleam of gold from the man's heavy rings and wristwatch. He shuffled the papers back into her folder and laid both his hands upon it, as if the elusive answers might again go missing.

He said, 'It would seem that your scan results give some cause for concern.' He spoke reprovingly, as if the unfavourable news was somehow her fault. He began to talk about hot and cold thyroid nodules, about multi-nodular tumours; about the necessity of their immediate surgical removal. Especially in her case.

Amy thought, but did not say, but the blood tests were all clear. Then she thought, but I might have known that I could never be that lucky. Her fear of surgery, of a knife cutting into her flesh, was so great that she could barely voice the question. 'Do I really need an operation? Isn't there some other way?'

'No,' he said, 'you really need an operation.'

'So are you telling me that I have cancer?'

'No, I am not telling you that you have cancer. It could be an adenoma.' He paused. 'I am making an emergency appointment for you to see a surgeon.'

She had never heard of adenoma, and in any case she did not want to believe this cold disinterested man. 'I don't want surgery, doctor.'

He leaned forward, both hands flat upon the desk, and Amy was reminded of a judge about to pronounce sentence.

He said, spacing each word so that she could not possibly misunderstand, 'My advice to you is this. Get that lump removed from your neck – before it kills you!'

The surgeon was only marginally older than Chris and Dom. The appointment with him had been written on her card in red ink. His examination of her was thorough and performed at first in silence. When he started to ask questions she heard herself, by means of optimistic answers, attempting to influence his final diagnosis.

She said, 'I feel extremely well. Not in the least bit ill.'

He said, 'We need to operate. Quite soon. As quickly as possible. Within the next week or ten days.'

'I don't want surgery.'

He did not look at her. He said, 'I can't force you to have an operation. But that is what you need. Urgently.' His glance flickered briefly in her direction; he opened a red-covered diary and studied dates. He said, 'I'll see you in hospital – next week.'

She walked back to where Dom sat beside the coffee-bar. Her steps were short and careful. In her head denial raged. She truly did not feel ill. She had felt ill, last month, last year, but that had passed. It was only a lump, for Heaven's sake! They were all behaving as if she might die at any moment. There were surely more life-threatening conditions? She halted beside the diabetic chart. Well, her pancreas at least was in perfect working order. Also her heart and lungs, and all her other bits of vital equipment. Bloody doctors! What did they know?

She stood before Dom. He looked at her face and did not speak. She said, 'Operation. Next week if they can fit me in.'

*

Shopping for the items listed in the hospital's information leaflet had been done in the company of Lali, who rejected Amy's shabby summer nightgowns and inadequate wrap, the sponge-bag with the broken zip, and the balding furry mules. Her mother's standards had clearly slipped in the years that she had lived alone.

'I should have thought,' said Lali gently, 'that someone who makes pure-silk, hand-sewn lingerie for a living would have set aside a few choice creations for a special occasion.'

'And what special occasion should I be anticipating at my age?' Amy had asked her. 'A second honeymoon is highly unlikely. The milkman is the only male who sees me in my dressing-gown these days, and all my meetings with him take place on the doorstep.'

They shopped for cool cotton nightgowns made pretty by frills at the neck and hem. A blue silk kimono and matching slippers were luxurious and bought to give her courage. Lali filled her new sponge-bag with soaps and sprays that smelled nice.

In the evening of that same day Amy climbed the stairs that led up to the top of the tall house. She opened the dormer window of her workroom and looked out across the Gardens, the bandstand, the copper-domed carillon of bells. Her head felt light and empty, and unreal. She clenched her fists, pressing the fingernails into her palms so that she might feel the pain and know that she was still Amy. She had not allowed herself to think about cancer, but now the awful word edged sideways into her mind and she felt the world tilt. She spoke the word softly into the darkening night, rolled the horror of it on her tongue and then fought the need to scream and weep, to smash and rend. She saw her life spinning out across the treetops, the power no longer hers to make decisions, to have control, to plan. She thought about cancer now – what she knew about it, the things she had heard people say. It was always fatal. It was an invasion which could not be halted. She began to test out certain words which until this moment had possessed no meaning for her. Surgery. Radiation. Chemotherapy. She had a picture of herself: stripped of her identity, no longer a person, no longer Amy – devoted mother of her children, faithful niece of Aunty Belle and Mimi, wife of Michael, who had left her – but a body in a blue gown made of dishcloth fabric, a throat from which 'a lump must be removed before it killed her'.

Amy stood very still beside the open window, knowing that she had reached a point of crisis from which there might be no turning back. Very slowly she unclenched her fists, feeling the imprint left by her nails in the soft palms. She waited, as if for a message, so that she might know what she should do. Her head began to turn around, to look back into the room, and with that movement came a calmness, a knowledge that she was still herself, that control had not altogether been taken from her.

She moved to a light switch, and at her touch reality returned. She saw the stacked bales of coloured silk, the carded lace, the half-sewn garments, lying just as she had left them on the work table. She began to move among the precious clutter of her daily occupation. There were garments to be completed, deliveries to be made, a bridal trousseau to be given its final trimmings. She studied the order book, made calculations. A week, the surgeon had said, maybe ten days. If she started working early every morning there should be time and to spare. She lifted a hand to her throat; she had asked Lali what precisely was an adenoma. A tumour deriving from glandular tissue, Lali had said. A benign – therefore harmless – growth.

The dependence of her aunts had been a gradual matter which increased with the years, as they lived on, triumphantly, into great age. They appeared not to hear when Amy complained of feeling unwell. They regarded her still as the girl she had once been.

There had been mornings last winter when Amy had gone into the overheated little house, carrying bags of heavy shopping; she sat on a kitchen chair, her head bent low, fighting faintness and bewildering exhaustion. The aunts, busy filling fridge and cupboards, had waited patiently for Amy to recover sufficiently so that she might make their morning coffee. She had seen her own indisposition as being of slight importance when measured against their frailty, their partial loss of sight and hearing. She thought she understood their refusal to accept help from anyone but her.

Their expectations were not unreasonable. Amy owed them a debt which could never be repaid. To tell them now that she would have to be absent from their house, their lives, was not an easy thing to do.

She said, 'I've had some tests done at the hospital. It seems that I need an operation, my thyroid gland has to be removed.'

Aunty Belle said, 'You never told us you were ill.' There was as much resentment in her tone as if Amy had deliberately lied about her state of health.

'But I told you,' said Amy. 'I mentioned several times in the past year that I was under the weather.' Under the weather was a favourite euphemism of the aunts which, in the past, had covered any disability of theirs, from a hangnail to a sleepless night.

'Well, what exactly is wrong with you?' Aunty Belle demanded. Mimi, seated at the far side of the table, sat in an attitude of silent terror, her coffee-cup not quite at her lips.

Amy prevaricated. 'I'm not really sure. You know what doctors are. They never tell you anything, do they?'

'Yes they do,' her aunt said. 'Don't tell me you're going into hospital without knowing why! How could you expect us to know that you were ill, if you never tell us anything!'

Mimi spoke at last. She said gently, 'What's wrong with you, Amy?'

Amy said, 'I think – they think – that I've got cancer.'

She sensed their fear and anger. From their pinnacle of advanced age, from their state of infirmity and need, her illness must, she thought, appear to them as a wilful desertion which, with forethought by her, might have been avoided.

She gazed helplessly at the two faces, puckered and dismayed, like those of bewildered infants. 'I'll contact Rose,' she said. 'Rose will be only too happy to come over. She's always asking if there's something she can do.'

Rose was a distant cousin whom Amy knew only from phone calls, or accidental meetings in shops or in the street. Rose had always said when speaking of the aunts, 'I feel that I should do more for them, but it's difficult to see quite what I could do. Now remember, Amy! You must let me know if there is any way in which I can help you out!'

Aunty Belle had been very angry when Amy had once suggested that Rose might do a little of the shopping, a few chores. Even now, faced with Amy's imminent departure into hospital, she said, 'Oh, we couldn't possibly put upon Rose. She has a very important job in the city, and then there's her charity work. Oh no. That will never do.'

Amy said, 'I don't see that you have any choice. Lali says I might need to have treatment after the operation. In any case I shall be convalescent for quite a long time. I am,' she said, as pointedly as she could manage, 'no longer a young woman.'

She saw the incomprehension in their eyes at this last statement. They would never see her as being other than Amy young, Amy willing, Amy whose function was to keep them safe in this, the twilight of their days.

Aunty Belle said, 'There's no need for you to telephone Rose. I can manage to do that much for myself.'

Amy never wept. She supposed that as a child she must have cried, but had no recollection of so doing. She would feel a heaviness behind her eyes, an ache deep in her throat, but no tears came.

She drove away from the cluttered little house, from the two women who were the only family she had ever known. Never again would she enter cheerfully and be welcomed warmly; she was swept by a sense of desolation so bitter that it was no longer safe for her to drive. She pulled into an empty space between parked cars, switched off the ignition, gripped the steering wheel until her fingers ached, and waited for the trembling bout to stop.

Failure, she thought. The story of my life. Letting people down, and even if I get it right, I never get it absolutely right. In the first months of Michael's absence she had worn, instead of her nightdress, an old pair of his blue pyjamas which he had failed to take with him into his new life. She had lain on his side of the wide bed, the pyjama jacket wound tight about her body, the faint scent of his cologne still clinging to the silk. She had not allowed herself to think about him, for as the aunts had always said, there is no use crying over spilt milk, and what is to be, will be. She had thought instead about Christopher and Dominic and Lali, who were his children; and hers. She carried a photograph of Michael in her handbag, a snapshot taken years ago of a young boy, grinning widely, his hair tousled, a spaniel puppy in his arms.

She had concealed Michael's defection from the aunts over a period of time. Since they rarely left their house, and never visited Amy, this deception had not been difficult to maintain. When Christmas came with its unavoidable once-yearly meetings, she had been forced into confession.

It would have been easier to tell them the bad news while they were on neutral ground. She had imagined taking them back to the cosy red-plush restaurant where they had so often enjoyed ordering their favourite dishes. On the day before the outing they would summon the hairdresser to the house, have their hair shampooed and set into tight curls. They would dress up for the occasion, put on necklaces, rings and brooches, apply rather too much make-up. It would have needed only a glass of sweet white wine to make them merry. In the festive atmosphere of the little treat, between dessert and coffee, Amy could have slipped into the conversation that she and Michael were no longer together. For had she not, on other occasions, informed them in this same propitiatory manner of other crises in her family? After lamb and mint sauce she had broken the news that Chris and Dom were cohabiting with the ladies of their choice. Roast pork and apple sauce had been the sweetener which had made it easier for Amy to tell them that Lali and Tim were about to set up house together, without, as Aunty Belle said later, benefit of clergy. But Belle and Mimi in the past year had moved into yet another dimension of their great age. The flowered-silk dresses now hung unworn in the wardrobe. The necklaces, rings and brooches stayed in their velvet-lined boxes. The aunts wore everyday frocks and comfortable slippers, and hardly ever applied lipstick. When Amy had suggested lunching out – a special treat – they had declined.

She had given their house its pre-Christmas, extra-thorough cleaning, had hung fresh white nets at all the downstairs windows – as they said, without the nets they might be in danger of being spied upon by strangers. As she vacuumed and polished Amy tried out in her mind a dozen different ways of saying, 'Michael has left me.'

In the event they had made it easy for her. As she sat with them one morning, drinking tea and eating biscuits at the kitchen table, Aunty Belle said, 'We've made out our Christmas present list. Take it with you when you go. We decided on everyone's gift, except for Michael. What do you suggest?'

Amy said, 'Michael won't be spending Christmas with us this year.'

Mimi fitted a cigarette into the ivory holder that Amy remembered from her childhood. She lit the cigarette with a kitchen match, inhaled, and then blew smoke inelegantly through her nostrils. Aunty Belle made her customary exaggerated waving motion at the blue wreaths from Mimi's Senior Service.

Mimi said, 'What's happened, Amy?'

'He's gone,' Amy said. 'We don't live together any more.'

'But where?' Aunty Belle demanded. 'And with whom? And what about the shop? However will you manage?' She paused to breathe. 'You must have done something awful, Amy. No man leaves his wife without a very good reason.'

Amy thought fondly and disloyally of Uncle Ken, who in 1939 had volunteered to sail to France with the British Expeditionary Force, rather than stay safely at home with Aunty Belle. Amy had loved Uncle Ken, but it was only at his funeral that she had realized how much. She said, 'I don't know where he is.'

'But how are you managing?' asked Mimi.

'A sum of money is paid into the bank on the first of each month.' Amy tried to smile. 'It's hardly enough to pay the bills. If I want to keep my car I shall need to get a job soon. As for the shop, Michael's partner Freddie is there on weekdays. He and Michael travel around to antique fairs most weekends. Or so I am told.'

Aunty Belle said, 'I simply don't understand you. How can you sit there and talk so calmly about your broken marriage?' The aunts were avid readers of romantic novels, in which heroines blushed and heroes were silent and manly.

Mimi said, 'I'm sure it's just a petty misunderstanding, dear. Men can be very silly sometimes, we just have to be patient with them.' She blew a perfect smoke-ring. Amy watched it float across the kitchen to hover in the corner where the fridge stood.

Aunty Belle said, 'What reason does he give for going?'

'I haven't asked him. As I said, I don't know where he is.'

The smoke-ring disintegrated high up near the ceiling. Amy had set her teacup down very carefully into the saucer. Weariness engulfed her. She felt that without enormous effort she might never rise from her chair, leave the kitchen, resume her life.

She said, 'Michael went because he wanted to go. The reason doesn't matter.' She had picked up the pad on which the Christmas list was written, reached into her handbag for a pen and then scored a single heavy line through Michael's name. One less to shop for that year. A minimal lightening of the burden.

Preparations for going into hospital began with a large un-zipped holdall set down in the middle of her bedroom carpet. Into it she tossed those items which she considered to be essential to her comfort. A couple of Dick Francis novels, a spare pair of reading glasses, a book of crossword puzzles contributed by Chris. She added at intervals an elaborate manicure-kit, a birthday gift she had never used; notepaper and a batch of unanswered letters, a tube of peppermints and the dog-eared photograph of Michael as a boy.

She rose early every morning and sewed until her fingers and her vision were no longer capable of effort. She embarked on a systematic cleaning of the house. If she died, Michael would be obliged to return home. He would see then that she had done her best. She mowed the lawn and weeded flower-beds, proving to herself that the possession of so much energy indicated good health.

It was in the loose hours of late evening that Amy was wide open to fear. She stood in the workroom checking and recheck-ing finished garments, nervous that haste had made her stitch-ing less than perfect. Before getting into bed she would tip out the contents of the holdall, count them over, assess their value to a bed-bound woman. In the end she always tossed the whole lot back into the bag. Rather safe than sorry, she echoed Aunty Belle; always better too much than too little.

On the day before she was due to enter hospital, Amy

delivered to her clients every single promised garment. She tidied her workroom, sent out bills, wrote cheques.

She visited Aunty Belle and Mimi. So acute was their discomfort in her presence that they forgot to offer her tea. She saw their lost reproachful looks and there was nothing she could say.

'You forgot to bring our lamb chops on Friday,' said Aunty Belle. 'We had to open a tin of salmon for our Sunday lunch. You know we always like lamb chops on a Sunday.'

'But I thought,' said Amy 'that cousin Rose would be doing your shopping now. You should have phoned her as you said you would. I'm sure she wouldn't mind.'

'Oh,' said Aunty Belle, 'we couldn't possibly telephone Rose about lamb chops. She is a very busy person. She has more important matters on her mind.'

As Amy left them she was conscious of their withdrawal from her. It was as if she had already died and they wished to be left alone to mourn her.

Her admission to the City hospital had been arranged for the last day of July. She woke very early on that Monday morning, took her first cup of tea up to the workroom and watched the sun come up between the branches of the trees. She managed for some minutes not to think about the next few hours. She thought instead about her garden: the need to purchase new bush-roses; of bulbs to be autumn-planted for next spring's flowering; of honeysuckle that would need to be trimmed back, of geranium cuttings she would take.

The unusually orderly workroom had a dispirited appearance; everything in its place, and a place for everything, which reminded her inevitably of Michael. She wondered if he knew that she was considered by the doctors to be very ill. She opened a drawer and gazed at the spools of coloured thread, graded carefully according to their shades. She closed the drawer and moved back to the window. Lali would have told him.

Michael and Lali lunched together on a regular basis. She had once come upon them unexpectedly, sitting at a blue-clothed table in the Copper Kettle Café, so deep in conversation that they never noticed her peering in at the window, even though she made no effort at concealment. She stood on the narrow pavement, jostled by impatient shoppers and rendered immovable by rage. She had actually grabbed the handle of the café door, determined to confront them, but the anger had seeped away; she swallowed her pain and walked off into the snowy afternoon.

She accepted on that day what she had never before cared to face. Lali had secrets. For all her charm and open manner, there were many things her daughter did not tell her. Lali told her private thoughts and feelings to her father; to Michael who had left Amy, taking with him the Lalique figure. Lali, she now realized, believed that Michael's desertion of her mother was all her own fault, and Amy wondered why it had taken her so long to face the truth about all this.

She passed the Copper Kettle on subsequent Thursdays and Michael's car was always parked close by. She tried to imagine their conversations. 'And how is your mother?' Michael might ask.

'Oh, she keeps busy,' Lali would say. 'She's got this little sewing business now. Hand-stitched lingerie for the rich and infamous. Glamorous creations; not at all Mum's style. But she's quite the businesswoman these days. Doing awfully well!'

They would smile contentedly at one another across their toasted sandwiches and coffee and go on to discuss those subjects nearer to their hearts.

Christopher and Dominic admitted to passing Michael on the street without a nod or word of greeting. They returned their father's gifts at birthdays and Christmas, unopened. This partisan behaviour gratified and yet alarmed her. She spoke to them about it. After all, she said, he is your father. But they had smiled and patted her shoulder and said that she was not to worry about it, they would deal with Michael in their own way. After a time the cards and gifts no longer came.

Sometimes she projected her present problems forward into a possible future. Supposing the children married, had children of their own? How would family matters be arranged then? What did estranged parents do in such situations? Would the separate warring factions stand on opposite sides of the church or registry office? Would grandchildren need to be visited by appointment so that Michael and she could avoid an embarrassing meeting? These dilemmas settled into her mind and simmered there for hours, sometimes for whole days. She often thought, when delivering some intimate garment, that the client would be amazed and disconcerted if she knew how many of Amy's unsolvable problems had been stitched into its fabric.

She took one lingering look around the workroom and then walked swiftly through the rest of the house, closing windows and shutting doors. It was rather like her usual nervous countdown before going on holiday, but without the promise of a pleasant destination.

The zip would not close on the bulging holdall but she could not bring herself to leave a single item behind. She dragged it downstairs, bumping the bag on every step. Down in the hall she stood before a full-length mirror and studied the lilac linen dress, and matching shoes, the amethyst ring and earrings. She tucked in a loose strand of hair and had a fierce longing to pull out the restraining purple clip, to substitute golden hoops for amethysts, the tailored dress for one of gaudy swirling colour. She moved closer to the mirror, tipped her head back and studied the smooth round lump that rose up from beneath her collar-bone. She touched it lightly with one finger as if contact could tell her what went on underneath the skin. Through the glass panel of the front door she saw Dom's hand poised to ring the bell. She smoothed her features into a smile of welcome and went to let him in.

The drive to the hospital was just like any other journey she had made in Dom's car. She knew that when he was alone he drove very fast; with her seated at his side they drove sedately through the heat haze of the summer morning. She barely registered the quiet streets, the shady gardens. They talked about matters unconnected with her physical problem. She inquired about Chantal and thought there was a certain reservation in his answer, but it hardly seemed the moment to pursue the subject of his partner's well-being, when she was herself the cause of so much anxiety for him.

She said, 'We're much too early, you know. I would rather not get there a single minute before I absolutely have to.' They were passing a café.

He said, 'We could have a coffee here, if you like?'

Unlike the Copper Kettle with its blue cloths, these café tables were covered in red-check. They drank strong hot coffee out of flower-painted mugs. Dom's wrist was positioned so that he could check the time without appearing over-anxious.

He said, 'Chris will come with me to visit you tomorrow night. He gets a bit emotional on these sorts of occasion –' Dom floundered, not quite knowing how he should continue.

'I know,' she said. 'He'll be fine once the operation is over. Tell him not to worry about it. Tell him that I understand.' Her last experience of hospital had been at the twins' birth. Her state of terror then was equalled almost by her state of terror now. She remembered ward sisters in white starched aprons and elaborately goffered caps; terrified probationers who seemed always on the verge of tears; a regime of prison strictness with visiting husbands being reprimanded for sitting on the bed, and the babies she had laboured long to deliver being taken from her for extended periods of time, without any explanation. She looked at Dom and remembered his birth, twenty minutes after that of Chris.

She said impulsively, 'When you were born you caused me not a single pain.' She touched his hand. 'Thank you for being with me now.'

He smiled, wanting to keep the moment light. 'I'm only coming along to view the nurses. They tell me the most attractive ones work on the surgical wards.'

Driving into the hospital car park, registering her arrival at Reception, walking up the stairs with Dom carrying her hold-all, was like entering a bare and functional hotel. The entrance to Ward Forty-Seven was through white painted swing-doors, and it was now that reality surfaced and she was forced to admit that this nightmare was actually happening to her. The fear which had lain just below the level of her conscious thinking seemed to shake itself awake, to heave and rise and flood the cells and pulses of her body. As if from a great distance she heard Dom say, 'Good morning, nurse. Name is Sheldon. My mother requested a private room.'

The nurse was alert, efficient, pretty. She consulted a typed list, and placed a tick beside Amy's name. She said, 'We have no vacant amenity beds, I'm afraid. In any case, it's not usual for surgical patients to occupy private rooms.'

They were standing beside the nurses' station, a sort of three-sided office area which held telephones and files, and the inevitable computer. Amy heard a young nurse say into a phone, 'She's had a restful night. Her condition is stable. Yes – you can visit any time after two this afternoon.'

Dom and the nurse began to walk away and Amy followed on legs that felt as fragile as spun glass. She was aware of space and light, of sunshine slanting down from long uncurtained windows on to a yellow floor. On the edge of her vision women in dressing-gowns moved carefully and slowly. She was aware of their interested scrutiny but did not return it.

The nurse and Dom had halted beside a bed that stood in a corner at the very end of the long ward; from it Amy would have an uninterrupted view of the doors which led into day-room, lavatories and bathrooms. She would be as far from the observing nurses in their station as she could wish to be.

'Your mother can get unpacked,' the young nurse said, 'and

into her nightie and dressing-gown. Doctor will be along to see her in about fifteen minutes.'

She spoke to Dom as if Amy were not present, or severely deaf. As she walked away Amy saw her glance back and smile at Dom across her shoulder. Amy noted his answering grin, and wondered again about Chantal.

He said, 'Do you mind – about the amenity bed?'

'It would have been nice. However,' she tried to sound confident and blasé, 'it will only be for a few days.'

'Yes, of course it will. You'll be out of here in no time.' They gazed at each other across the uncreased counterpane and regimented pillows. Dom's face had the hunted expression of the departing guest trapped on a railway station.

Amy said, 'You really ought to go now.'

He came to stand beside her; he kissed her forehead. 'Chris and I will come tomorrow evening.' He walked quickly away and did not look back.

She had not known how much she wanted to be on her own, until the amenity bed was denied her. She had looked forward to a small white room in which her terrors might go unobserved; a nun-like cell where the lump and she could fight a private battle. She pulled the sprigged-cotton curtains close around the bed. Their six-by-five feet of inadequate privacy could not possibly compensate for a solid door which could be closed.

She unpacked the holdall into the shelves and compartments of a bedside locker. She hung her towel on a rail, and her sponge-bag from a hook, then placed her books and reading glasses beside a water-jug and tumbler. She undressed and put on a new nightdress and the blue kimono. Since there was no place to store the clothes in which she had arrived, she stuffed them into the holdall and wedged the bag into a space between the locker and the wall. She climbed into the narrow bed, carefully, so as not to crease the bedspread.

The sheets felt slippery and cold; in spite of the heat of the day she shivered. The pillows at her back were hard and lumpy. Tension stiffened every muscle in her body; her eyelids felt like corrugated cardboard, making it difficult to blink. There were sounds beyond the curtain: the squeak of rubber wheels, the flushing of cisterns, the rattle of china.

The girl appeared without any warning sound of footsteps. She came through the curtains, holding out her right hand. She said, 'I'm Joanna.' Her clasp was firm and warm. She sat on the chair beside the bed and consulted the clipboard which she carried. Her bunches of reddish corkscrew curls were tied back with blue ribbons; her scrubbed face glowed with perfect health. She wore a long white cotton coat over a blue dress, and a gold crucifix hung on a chain around her neck. She looked about seventeen years old.

She glanced up from the form which was fastened to the clipboard. She said, 'I'm your house doctor. I shall be looking after you on a regular basis. Now, you are Mrs Amelia Sheldon, aren't you? Fifty-eight years old?'

'Yes,' said Amy.

Without a hint of any wish to flatter she said, 'You look considerably younger.'

They began the game of question and answer which was to become the main preoccupation of that curious day. Amy was wheeled like an invalid to the X-ray department and the room where electrocardiograms were taken. Her pulse and blood pressure were checked a dozen times. The lump was never referred to by anybody. Throughout that morning she continued to claim a state of total health.

Since she had been absent from the ward when the menu cards were being filled in, a nurse had made Amy's lunch selection for her. She had not expected to be hungry in this place; the curtains around her bed had been pulled back and she watched with keen anticipation the arrival of the metal wagon which contained hot food. As it trundled slowly down the ward, she caught the mingled aromas of macaroni cheese and shepherd's pie, two kinds of soup and a choice of puddings. When it came to her turn she was already faint from hunger. She watched for the contents of her tray and saw that it contained a sandwich.

'Light diet only for you, dear,' said the student nurse. 'Operation in the morning.' Amy examined the soggy bread and slimy lettuce, the wafer-thin slice of tomato. The crusts alone were dry; she dissected them carefully and ate them. A thimbleful of lemon mousse was her ration of pudding. The cup of tea which followed was extremely good. She again felt fit and strong, and energetic. Her fellow patients were pale and heavy-eyed; they gave her a limp wave of the hand as they passed by on their way to the bathrooms and dayroom. Some leaned on walking-frames, others trailed tubes and drips. Nobody approached Amy's bed. She selected the new Dick Francis and put on her reading glasses, but all she could think about were the four words spoken by the little nurse: 'Operation in the morning.'

The surgeons appeared in reverse order of their rank. As the food wagon squeaked away down the ward, the curtains were twitched closed around the bed and a tall, very thin young man sat down beside her.

He said, 'We met last week, in your local hospital.'

She nodded.

'Your first operation is scheduled for tomorrow morning. It will be of an exploratory nature. If it proves necessary we shall have to operate again.'

She said, 'There's no need to pussyfoot around the subject. I know I have cancer.' She had not expected that she would be able to say the word. She almost smiled at the shocked expression in his eyes.

He said, 'Who told you that you have cancer?'

'I don't need to be told, I just know it.'

He looked uneasy. 'There is nothing in your notes to indicate malignancy.' Amy felt sorry for him then. He looked so very young, and one's own mortality is always hard to come to terms with.

'Don't worry,' she said. 'I'm not an hysterical woman. Whatever you find – I want to know *all* about it.'

He went away grim-faced, and she suspected that her behaviour was not that of a normal docile patient.

The senior man appeared with an entourage of six medical students, four boys and two girls who must only recently have exchanged their school blazers for white coats. The top man stood at the foot of the bed with his acolytes ranged on either side; the flowered curtains billowed out behind them. It was not until all were in position that he asked Amy's permission that they might stay. She leaned back against the lumpy pillows. She said that they were welcome to observe whatever it was he had come to do. After all, this was a teaching hospital, and they had to start somewhere.

He had come to lecture. He began by saying that they should pay close attention to her case, since they might rarely see its like in a lifetime of surgical practice. Amy obliged him by performing her party trick of tipping her head backwards so that the lump rose prominently into view. She was told to maintain this position so that guesses might be made as to the lump's size. A figure of three centimetres by three centimetres was their collective decision. He talked for another ten minutes using very long words. When he questioned them on matters concerning the thyroid gland it was only the girls in the group who attempted to answer. He then nodded briefly in Amy's direction and thanked her for her cooperation. The students backed out between the curtains, clearly embarrassed by their lack of thyroid knowledge. Amy was left with the new information that her lump was a surgical and medical curiosity. The top man's voice, audible beyond the curtains, had aroused the interest of her fellow patients, and they came to sit companionably on her bed. She was no longer the newcomer, an apparently healthy woman with no visible impairment. She was the possessor of a lump, which had just been prodded, measured and evaluated by the top man. Her lump was a jewel of indeterminate carat and unknown value, and gave her credibility. She mentioned it off-handedly, with macabre pride – it was her passport into their world. They knew about lumps, her fellow patients. They were well informed and wise about the post-operative results of the top man's surgical procedures. They all spoke very highly of him. When Amy inquired hesitantly, and with a certain shrinking, about the site of their recent operations, she was told in every case that a colostomy had been performed upon them. The top man, they assured her, was brilliant when it came to the removal of colonic tumours.

In late afternoon Lali came to see her. She brought flowers and a Get Well card which she placed on the locker. Amy received the gifts with satisfaction – they added to her growing status as a proper patient. Lali was loving and solicitous. 'How nice you look,' she said, 'in the blue kimono. It really suits you. Pity about the amenity bed though. Do you mind very much?'

'If I'm going to be moaning and throwing-up I'd much rather do it privately,' said Amy. 'On the other hand, it's quite pleasant to talk to the other patients. They all seem to be old hands at this game.'

Lali's face had that blank expression which made Amy suspect her daughter had private knowledge which she was not about to share.

'Try to relax, Mum,' she said. 'You're much too tense. If you can't sleep tonight, ask sister to give you something –'

Amy reached out a hand and twisted a length of Lali's soft blonde hair around her finger, just as she had done when Lali was a little girl. Amy felt the old ache at the back of her throat which prevented her from speaking. She wanted to ask about Michael, if he knew what was happening to her. But the ache persisted, and she said nothing. Lali went away promising to return.

Afternoon tea was a cup of tea and two digestive biscuits. Supper was another inedible sandwich. The evening visitors began to arrive; husbands came carrying flowers wrapped in Cellophane, and grapes in brown paper bags. A nurse hung a card above the bed which bore the message 'NIL BY MOUTH'. Amy passed time in the bathroom trying out the perfumed products chosen by her daughter. She lay in the stained white bath among steamy clouds of something called Orchidée Sauvage. Hospital had changed in the years since the twins' birth. Patients were on first-name terms with house doctors. Baths were no longer scented with carbolic. Her bedspread was already badly creased by the numerous people who had that day sat upon it.

She went back to her corner and climbed in between the rumpled sheets. Across the end of the bed stood a table on wheels which held Lali's flowers, now arranged in a glass vase. With an effort of will she closed out every thought that touched tomorrow. When sleep finally came, it brought Michael to her.

The sign above the door read Sheldon Antiques. A smaller notice, printed unevenly on yellowed card read 'Removals. Distance no object'. I walked fast down Angel Row, my heels clicking on the cobbled surface, my heart thumping in my chest, my throat dry. The shop door stuck; I pushed hard against it. It gave way suddenly and I stumbled inwards, my face burning with embarrassment in case my ineptitude had been observed. I was seventeen years old and easily mortified.

No one had noticed my entrance. I was not about to be asked what I wished to buy. I began to walk between the shabby chairs and tables, the moth-eaten velvet drapes and musty-smelling sofas. I examined the shelves of peculiar and unsaleable objects. If my presence was challenged I would say that I sought a gift for my Aunt Mimi's birthday.

From a half-open door at the rear of the shop came the hiss

and smell of frying bacon. An open flight of scuffed wooden stairs led upwards into what must be Mr Sheldon's living quarters. Mr Sheldon and his nephew Michael.

Aunty Belle disapproved of the Sheldons. She referred to Michael's uncle as that 'reprobate gypsy'. He had recently appeared in court accused of receiving stolen goods, but nothing had been proven.

Her assessment of Michael was uncannily acute. Dangerous, she said. A dangerous young man. Predatory. You could see it, she said, in the very way he walked. Her hand shook slightly as she spoke, the teacup rattling back into its saucer; there was a dull flush on her cheeks. I wondered on what experience of men her reading of Michael could be based. Now if Mimi had used those same words about him I might even have listened; I studied her across the Royal Albert cake-stand, the cucumber sandwiches and the home-made greengage jam. I loved Mimi's shabby stylish gowns, the marcasite combs in her hennaed hair, the bright gash of lipstick across her wide and smiling mouth, her genuine crocodile-skin shoes with their four-inch heels. But if Mimi had described Michael Sheldon as predatory and rapacious it would, I felt sure, have been in tones of reluctant admiration. Or perhaps not all that reluctant? I knew things about my Aunt Mimi that were undreamed of by her sister Belle.

'And if you take my advice, Amy, you'll stop making that short cut through Angel Row.' I had suspected that Aunty Belle spied upon me when she could. What would she say now if she could see me, not only walking through Angel Row, but inside the shop of the notorious Sheldons?

He was a tiny man, Irish, soft-voiced and shy. He wore a brown coat-overall and a tweed cap. His eyes were blue, his cheeks as rosy and creased as a pippin apple. There was nothing the least gypsyish about him. He stood at my elbow and watched my hands as they lifted the bowl of deep pink glass.

I said, nervously, 'Good morning, Mr Sheldon.'

He smiled. 'Was it Michael you were after seeing?'

'No! No, of course not. I'm looking for a birthday present for my aunt.'

He nodded towards the glass bowl. 'You've got good taste, young lady. You've picked up the one fine piece in the whole shop. That's as nice a bit of cranberry glass as you'll ever see.'

'How much are you asking for it?'

'Probably twice as much as you can afford,' he said gently, 'but you don't have to buy, you know. There's no obligation.'

'I'll take it,' I said. 'It's exactly the sort of thing my aunt will love.'

He mentioned a sum of money which would empty my purse. He seemed to sense my consternation.

'If you were to come back next Saturday to collect the bowl, why then, our Michael will be minding the shop for me then, for I'll be away to the races. You can pay me when it's convenient to you. You look like a nice girl.'

'Well, thank you. It would be more convenient if I could leave it until next week. I didn't bring much money with me. I'll pay – your Michael – when I come. If that's all right?'

He escorted me to the shop door and bowed me through it, his manner so courtly that I saw nothing incongruous in his wearing of the coat-overall and the tweed cap. 'I'll be back,' I murmured, 'next Saturday morning.'

'Oh indeed you will,' he said. 'I'd put money on it.'

I was as innocent at seventeen as any other sheltered, well-brought up girl of my generation. Although I didn't know it then, we were of a type, the product of guardians or parents like Aunty Belle, on whom the dear dead hand of Queen Victoria still rested. We were, you might say, virgins by default, pathetically anxious for an opportunity to defend our honour. Especially from young men like Michael Sheldon, about whom the girls who worked in my office loved to whisper on a Monday morning.

There was something disreputable about him, a raffish quality which I found hard to pin down. His clothes came from Smith and Dacre, Bespoke Tailors. I had once seen him leaving the shop carrying their special bag. His shirts and shoes were hand-made. He wore a gold watch and tie-pin. In winter a long black trench coat hung from his shoulders and flapped about his ankles; on any other man this would have looked ridiculous, on Michael it was dashing and romantic. He had pale fair hair, and the gaunt and hollow looks that came from too many late nights or incipient tuberculosis. His smile, slow and lazy, was the sort for which girls waited. He was tall, too thin, and walked with a slight stoop. I indulged in fantasies in which he tore off all my clothes and did unmentionable things to me, quite against my will.

I had been convent-educated. I had no brothers. I could not remember having ever talked to a man who was not elderly or middle-aged. On Saturday morning I washed my hair and rinsed it in vinegar and water so that it would shine. I sat before my dressing-table mirror while Mimi persuaded the reluctant ends to curl under, so that it fell into a long bob on my shoulders. I was secretly convinced that this hairstyle made me resemble Lauren Bacall; but not always.

I had the sort of looks that changed from one day to the next. There were times when I was passable; on others I was positively plain. On this, the most important Saturday of my whole life, I prayed for beauty. The month was October. My summer tan had not yet faded. I leaned forward towards the mirror; my eyebrows were dark and heavy, but my attempts at plucking them had proved too painful. I borrowed one of Mimi's lipsticks and coloured my mouth a deep dark red. I rarely wore perfume, but today I dabbed Californian Poppy behind my ears and in the hollow of my throat. I put on my only nice dress, a blue tailored wool with white piqué collar and cuffs.

'Going somewhere special?' Mimi asked.

'It's a secret,' I said, and so it was, for I was about to collect her birthday present.

Aunty Belle said, 'Well it's nice to see you taking trouble with your appearance. But you're wearing far too much lipstick, Amy.' She gave me one of those up and down looks that miss nothing. 'And you're wearing your only unmended pair of silk stockings.'

'I'll be careful,' I said. 'I'll be very careful.'

He was wearing a pair of beautifully tailored tan-cord trousers and a beige lambswool sweater that had surely cost a fortune. He must have the use, I thought, of his uncle's clothing coupons as well as his own. His presence seemed to add a sheen to the chairs and tables, an elegance to the shabby sofas. The term 'junk shop' no longer applied to Sheldon Antiques when Michael was in charge. He sat at the rear of the shop, leaned back in a captain's chair, his feet in polished brogues supported on a desk edge. In the gap between his shoes and trouser-cuffs I could see that his socks were made of beige silk. He smiled up at me from beneath a swatch of thick pale hair. His eyes were blue, his brows and lashes an amazing black.

He said, 'Well – hello there. So you're the girl who spotted our only genuine bargain. My congratulations to you.'

It might have been his uncle speaking. Michael had the same soft and gentle voice, a little less Irish but with an undertone that was like an intimate caress. I couldn't stop looking at him.

He must have known the effect he was having on me. He swung his long legs down from the desk and came to stand beside me. He stood much closer than propriety allowed. He was taller than I was by about two inches. I could feel his breath on my forehead; the soft wool of his sweater brushed against the fingers of my clenched fists. He breathed in my perfume. 'Californian Poppy,' he said. 'It doesn't really suit you. I can get you a bottle of Evening in Paris if you'd like it.'

He glanced towards the open staircase and I wondered how

many girls he had entertained in the upper rooms when his uncle was absent at the races. If he had asked me, at that moment, to go with him up those stairs, I believe I would have gone. Instead, he asked me to go to the pictures with him. 'Gaumont,' he said. 'Monday night, first house, I'll be waiting for you in the foyer.'

I spoke to him then for the first time. 'Thank you,' I said. 'Thank you very much. I'll be there.'

I was all the way home and entering the front door when I realized that I had forgotten to collect the cranberry glass bowl.

They were short of anaesthetists, said the staff nurse, and so Amy's operation, scheduled for that morning, would have to be deferred for one week. So, would she please go home and come back again next Monday?

Amy said, 'If I go home now I shall never come back.'

The nurse went away and Amy dragged the holdall from its place between her locker and the wall. Rain poured down the windows; the ward was quiet. Many patients were already in the drowsy state induced by the pre-med pill.

Her mouth was dry, her stomach empty. At the top of the ward she could see Carmelita's broad, green-overalled rear, disappearing with the tea-trolley through the swing doors. Her West Indian voice had wakened Amy that morning. 'No tea for yo, darlin',' she had said. 'Operation for yo this mornin'.'

Amy began to pack, very neatly, her hands independent of her mind. She would never come back. The lump would be left to grow to pumpkin size. She would choke upon it. But she would not come back.

She began to check through the locker, making sure that it was empty, and there she was again, the staff nurse, breathless this time, a white cotton gown folded in her hand.

'You haven't eaten or drunk yet, have you?'

'No.'

'Oh – thank goodness for that! I had a word with the surgeon, I told him what you said. They've made a space for you, but you'll have to hurry. Get a quick bath and put this gown on. Then I'll bring you your pre-med.'

Amy never remembered bathing or putting on the white shift. She remembered the pre-med pill, the floating sensation, the slow dissipation of her terror. She was still in the world but not of it. When the trolley was wheeled alongside her bed, she giggled.

A red-faced man with a thick fringe of grey hair reassured her several times that she was perfectly safe in his hands. 'Our sole purpose is to make you well again,' he said.

She wanted to tell him that she did not feel ill, so not to bother. But the sky fell on her head, and all, as they say, went black.

She opened her eyes and sensed that her bed was no longer in the quiet corner of the ward. She tried to work out her new position, but concluded muzzily, that it didn't really matter. Her immediate concern was the feeling that the bed and she were rotating slowly in opposite directions. She closed her eyes but the giddiness persisted. She made some kind of sound, and felt the cool rim of a bowl touch her chin. She squinted briefly into the sweet concerned features of a little Asian nurse. 'You're feeling sick,' she stated. Amy tried to answer but no sound came. 'Don't worry,' said the nurse, 'I'm right here beside you. I won't leave you.' Amy felt a hand on her arm, and slipped back again into a world of nothing.

Her next return lasted longer. She looked up to find her Asian nurse and a young man in a white coat. The bag of a drip swung gently on the edge of her vision. 'I am just going to put this needle in your hand,' he said. She felt a short sharp sting, and the application of a bandage. She closed her eyes, and went back to the place where there was no pain.

The sound of Dom's voice brought her all the way back. 'Are you sure she's all right?' she heard him say. 'She looks awful.' Her eyelids felt heavy. She worked hard at lifting them open. The first faces she saw were those of her sons. They were talking to a senior nurse. Her mind felt oddly separated from her body. But not for long. Gradually she became aware of the bruised stiffness of her throat and neck, the ache of the needle inserted in her left hand. Her condition was one of acute discomfort rather than pain. It was unpleasant but bearable. She could now allow herself the forbidden thought: They've cut my throat and I have survived.

Her sons approached the bed, their lips smiling, horror in their eyes. She tried to speak, to reassure them. But no sound came.

Chris said, 'It's okay. Don't try to talk. The sister said your voice will come back in a few days.'

Dom said, 'How do you feel?'

The morning paper still lay on top of her locker. She gestured towards it, and he handed it to her. She mouthed 'pen' and he took a Biro from his pocket. In the margin of that day's *Guardian*, she spelled out very carefully the one word: KNACKERED. They looked at the paper and then at one another. Chris laughed uncertainly and Dom grinned. 'Didn't think you even knew words like that, Mother!'

'It's the pills they've given me,' she wrote. 'They release all my inhib – can't spell it – you know what I mean. You wouldn't believe the dreams I'm having –'

All at once she was very tired. Her eyelids drooped. They said they would leave now, would come back tomorrow. She did not see them go. At some point in the night two nurses stood beside her bed. The confident voice of one said, 'You're in a lot of pain, aren't you, Mrs Sheldon.'

Amy wanted to shake her head, to voice her denial, but neither option was hers. She felt the prick of a needle in her thigh, then slept again.

*

Amy awoke with a clear head and an instant realization of several facts. Carmelita was standing at her bedside, her black face smiling. 'Yo gets a cuppa tea this mornin',' she said, 'but don' yo drink him too hot. He hurt yo choat!'

Amy drank that tea as hot as she could bear it. It tasted wonderful, and instead of hurting her throat, it actually helped it. As she sipped, she acknowledged the disturbing fact that her bed was now as close as it could be to the nurses' station, and the swing-doors. She was also alarmed by the fact that her blood pressure was being checked about every twenty minutes.

She thought about Aunty Belle's prognosis on the possible survival of patients who found themselves close to the nurses' station. Her aunt had once said, after visiting a sick friend, 'They only put you near the doors for convenience sake when there is no hope left. It saves them trouble, you see, when you die; and it's less upsetting for the other patients.'

Carmelita took the empty cup away, and Amy began a tentative exploration of the appendages she had acquired. The drip in her hand was self-explanatory. More interesting were the two plastic tubes which began in the region of her neck and snaked away beneath the bed sheets. She followed the tubes with her unfettered hand, and found that they ended in a plastic flask which was wedged just underneath the mattress and clipped to the bedrail. Nobody had warned her about drips and drainage tubes, and she had no voice with which she might ask questions.

The soft-diet breakfast included lukewarm instant porridge and bread and marmalade. Swallowing was easier than she had expected it to be; only desperate hunger made the food palatable. She lay back on her pillows and observed her fellow patients closely for the first time. Their ages, at a guess, ranged from sixteen to ninety years. The greatest number of them came into the middle ranges, the period of life when a woman's body sometimes begins to break down. She watched the ambulatory ladies set off for the bathrooms; attractive in their frilly dressing-gowns and fluffy bedroom slippers, their left wrists attached to mobile drips, which they pushed before them, so that the drips looked rather like exotic standard-lamps. They waved as they passed her bed, and called, 'Good morning – feeling better, are you?' Amy waved with her right hand, in the only signal she was capable of making.

The ward was cleaned on Wednesdays. The young surgeon who had told her in the local hospital that an operation was necessary came picking his way across the ward between floor-polishing machines and plastic buckets. He looked down at his brown shoes and talked about the multi-nodular tumour which, until yesterday, was sitting on the right-hand lobe of Amy's thyroid gland. He had, he said, removed it, but could not yet tell her if the lump was malignant. She pictured him shaking it around in one of those dinky little kidney-shaped dishes, that one sees in medical documentaries on BBC 2. He would have poked it and probed it, then sent it off to some histology lab to be sliced like some rare and special salami.

Amy had feared the indignity of bed-pans, but mid-morning a wheelchair-cum-commode was brought to her bedside. The curtains were closed around the bed and a nurse helped her reach this very civilized convenience. Back in bed again she felt a sense of achievement, in more ways than the obvious one. Since recovering consciousness she had feared to make any energetic movement. The aching stiffness in her neck made her doubt the firm attachment of her head to the rest of her body. Offers of pain-killing tablets continued to be made by the staff nurse, but Amy did not need them. Blood-pressure checks were still being made at frequent intervals. When asked how she was feeling by medical persons, she invariably answered that she was hungry.

Lunch was a dab of mashed potato and a tiny cube of boiled cod, followed by the smallest *crème caramel* she had ever seen. She did not like to complain about her ravenous appetite and her rumbling stomach; to do so would have been unseemly in one who had, only yesterday, suffered a cut throat. She made a note in the margin of that day's *Guardian* to ask her visitors if they would in future bring food instead of flowers. Afternoon sunshine lay in swathes across the yellow floor. The telephones in the nurses' station were unusually silent. Amy closed her eyes, and slept.

The Gaumont cinema stood opposite the Angel Row Gardens. I sat on a bench beneath a sycamore tree and observed the slow fall of its leaves. I also watched for the arrival of Michael Sheldon. I truly did not believe that he would come. If he did not, my life would be over.

As far as looks were concerned it was one of my good days. An incipient cold sore on my top lip had subsided; my hair had curled under without trouble. Lack of sleep had put delicate violet shadows underneath my eyes. I wore a green skirt and a new fluffy yellow sweater. Mimi had loaned me her smart, three-quarter jacket of teddy-bear mock fur. My shoes were the flat, tan Oxfords I had worn at school, but the unladdered silk stockings boosted confidence. Aunty Belle believed that I was attending my shorthand-typing evening classes.

After all I had heard about Michael Sheldon I was still surprised that he had asked me, on such short acquaintance, to go with him to the pictures. Not that I was experienced in these matters; my informants were the telephonist and typist with whom I worked. These arrangements, they said, were generally approached more slowly. There was a certain protocol to be observed. Only after three, or at least two, 'chance' encounters in the street or at a dance, was the risky and serious step of a cinema visit to be even contemplated. It would entail sitting for three hours in almost total darkness with a strange man; and don't ever think, I was warned, that the proximity of a few hundred other people would cool the passions of a heated suitor. Hands, said my colleagues, would be everywhere. Tales were whispered of broken necklaces and loosened bra-straps, laddered stockings and, on shaming occasions, forcible eviction from the cinema by the manager himself. In cases of extreme indecency, faces were noted and names taken, and a total ban imposed on the offending couple. I found it reassuring that Michael Sheldon was clearly still *persona grata* with the manager and usherettes of the local Gaumont.

The cinema queue reached back into Vine Street; the film was *Brief Encounter*. I had seen it four times already, and could recite its more poignant lines verbatim. I had wept on each occasion; I wondered how Michael Sheldon would feel about tears shed by his companion of the evening. I thought he might be impatient with such silliness; on the other hand, he might be sympathetic. I imagined his comforting arm around my shoulders, his spotless handkerchief proffered gently for my use. Perhaps he would play Trevor Howard to my Celia Johnson? I saw his approach down Angel Row, that come-day-go-day saunter, the flap of fair hair on his brow, the black trench coat reaching almost to his ankles. He looked every bit as dangerous as Aunty Belle's predictions. I decided not to cry at the point in the film when Celia said goodbye to Trevor on the railway station.

I began to run. I arrived beside him out of breath and speechless. 'Good evening, Amy,' he said in that soft voice which melted my bones. He put a hand underneath my elbow and guided me towards the Gaumont steps.

'But,' I gasped, 'what about the queue?'

'I never queue,' he said. 'I have an arrangement.' He drew two green, balcony tickets from his breast pocket, and led me up red-carpeted stairs. A knowing usherette said, 'Hello, Michael, usual seats?' He nodded, and we followed her torch to the front row of the balcony. He took off his trench coat and folded it neatly across the brass guard-rail. He made to help me off with my coat but I hugged the teddy-bear around me. 'I'll keep it on for a bit,' I said. 'It's not very warm in here.' I felt safer in my outer garment; I half-regretted the coat's lack of buttonholes and buttons. The B picture had just started; I pretended an interest in an Indian massacre of a wagon train. For an hour I sat stiffly upright in the plush seat, my knees pressed tight together, my fingers knotted, and waited for him to make his move. When the interval lights went up I looked at him for the first time since sitting down. He held a cigarette in his right hand, a box of matches in his left. 'Smoke?' he asked.

'No – no thank you. I don't. I never have.'

He smiled. 'So what do you do, Amy,' he whispered, 'when you want a little fun?'

My face grew hot. 'I like to walk. I go to concerts, to the opera sometimes. I read a lot.'

'That doesn't sound much like fun to me. It sounds more like hard slog.' I looked for mockery in his tone, but heard only sympathy. He half-turned to face me. 'Mrs Cumberland keeps you on a tight rein, eh?'

I did not dare to meet his gaze. I said, eyes lowered, 'If Aunty Belle is strict – it's only for my own good.'

'And what about the other one? Mimi, isn't it? Now she looks like a lady who has really lived!'

I said, impulsively, 'Oh, Mimi's lovely.' I touched the mock fur coat. 'She lent me this to wear tonight. My navy-blue school serge didn't seem quite right for –'

'– for a first date?' and now both his face and voice were mocking.

I looked out across the balcony rail; blue smoke wreathed upwards from the cigarettes of smokers in the stalls. The ice-cream lady moved slowly up and down the aisles. An usherette pumped scented water from a metal spray in an attempt to clear the smoke.

I said, 'You think I'm pretty stupid, don't you? Not at all your sort of girl.'

'And what would you say my sort of girl is like?' His voice was serious now, the mockery all gone.

'Smart,' I said, 'pretty, well dressed. Able to dance. Somebody who is popular, has lots of friends. A girl who wears high-heeled shoes.'

The lights were dimming, the title of the A film was coming up on to the screen. Michael Sheldon said, 'You've got something that they don't have, Amy. You've got class.'

We left the cinema before the film was ended. It really wasn't his kind of thing, and I had seen it all before. We walked with a foot of space between us. His hands were pushed deep into the pockets of his trench coat. He turned, as if he already knew the route, into the part of town where Aunty Belle lived.

The streets looked different when I walked with Michael. The October moon had impaled itself on the spire of St Gilda's Roman Catholic church, leaking its light to make a path of silver for our feet. As we approached The Avenue he halted. He said, abruptly, 'I'll leave you here. It wouldn't do for your aunt to see us together.'

I stood, looking up into his face, willing him to kiss me, but he turned away without a word of farewell, and I watched him out of sight as he walked back towards the city. But for his supporting hand underneath my elbow, Michael Sheldon had not laid a finger on me.

As I let myself into the house and returned Mimi's coat to its peg on the hallstand, I was conscious of a growing sense of pleasurable unease. Michael Sheldon had known Mimi's name, Aunty Belle's reputation for strictness; the street where we lived. His possession of so much prior information about my family circumstances almost made up for the fact that he had never even tried to kiss me.

All the telephones were ringing in the nurses' station. Amy took some moments to identify the sound as she went through

45

the process of re-orientation which was necessary after only the shortest spell of sleep.

She was still in bed, in hospital, supported awkwardly on heaped-up pillows, her head and neck at an unnatural angle. Instinct warned her to avoid any sudden, unplanned movement. She still ached but was not in pain. She could never remember experiencing such a raging hunger. Her gaze moved from white walls and long windows, across the shining yellow floor to where her more mobile fellow patients sat talking and laughing together. She could not yet distinguish them by name, disease, or site of operation. She watched and wondered at their stoicism, at the camaraderie of women; sick sisters of misfortune with their hysterectomies, ileostomies, malfunctioning bladders and kidneys. All the accumulated damage caused by child-bearing and the stresses of life that are special to the female of the species.

The telephones stopped ringing. Ward sister and staff nurse emerged from their station and walked the few steps to her bedside. Her blood pressure and pulse were checked, the chart which hung at the end of the bed was studied.

'I think we can take your drip down now, Mrs Sheldon.' As she spoke the staff nurse was busy with the green clip which decorated Amy's left hand. Drip bag and stand were wheeled away just as Carmelita and her tea-wagon came squeaking through the swing-doors. The three o'clock cup of tea and biscuit were delivered with her usual warning about drinking hot liquids. No matter what their job, everyone who worked here was a medical expert.

It was not until she had drunk the tea and eaten the biscuit that Amy realized that, released from the drip, she now felt free to leave the bed. She followed the drainage tubes down to the small plastic flask which was tucked between the mattress and the bedrail. Other ladies in the ward, had, she noticed, been equipped with embroidered linen bags in which they carried their drainage flasks. Hers was too small to qualify for such a bag. She reached into her locker and pulled out kimono

46

and slippers. She put them on and slid her feet very slowly towards the floor. Before standing up she slipped the flask into the wide pocket of the blue kimono.

Her legs felt strong. She took several steps, keeping close to the bed. She felt quite normal, as if nothing had happened to her. She gathered her towel and sponge-bag; as she passed the nurse's station Amy pointed towards the bathroom door.

There were lavatories and bathrooms at either end of the long ward. She was surprised to find that she walked in a curious shuffling fashion, like a very old person, and her chin rested on her chest, limiting her vision. But she was up and moving, all by herself, and no medical expert had tried to stop her. Morning toilet had included the putting on of a clean nightdress, and a sketchy face wash in a bowl of warm water brought to her bedside by a young nurse. Her approach to the bathroom mirror was slow and cautious. She looked first at her hair which was smooth and neat. Her eyes were bright, her skin its usual sallow colour without make-up. From her chin down to where the frilled collar of her nightgown showed beneath the kimono, a thick wad of pale green paper, rather like kitchen roll and heavily bloodstained, encased her neck and throat. Even as she watched, the dressing loosened. Amy wondered what exactly lay beneath it, but lacked the courage to find out. She did her old lady's shuffle back into the ward and lay down on the rumpled bed.

The top man, on his daily round, had nodded briefly in her direction and passed her by. It was the young surgeon who arrived shortly before supper. He sat by her bed, his long white coat wrapped around his thin legs; he examined his fingernails. 'It looked quite good,' he said, 'but of course we won't be certain until the histology report comes in.'

Amy tried and failed to make sense of what he said.

'I think,' he continued, 'in any case, your surgery was worth doing. Although we may well find that we have performed an unnecessary operation.' She tried to speak, but no sound came. Before she could reach for pen and paper he had flapped away through the swing-doors.

Her head would hold only one thought at a time. She tried to work out why, after all the haste to get her on to the operating table, she was now being told that it was probably a big mistake. The surgeon had looked shifty, embarrassed. Had something gone wrong? Were there further revelations yet to come? Had her scan got mixed up with that of some other woman with a dodgy thyroid gland? Was she here under false pretences? Had her throat been cut for nothing? And then she remembered the lump; the pig-iron hardness of it. The conviction she had known every time she touched it that this was cancer.

The word, although still shocking, slid more easily into her mind since the operation. The gland with its attendant lump had been removed. Or so they said. She lifted a hand to the green paper dressing and knew that she would not sleep until she had seen what lay beneath it.

Amy went back to the bathroom and the square of mirror. The dressing now hung rakishly askew, attached only by the bloodstain. She turned on a tap and cupped her hand beneath it. She sloshed water on to the paper and waited for the bandage to come loose. Nothing happened. She shuffled back into the ward, her hand before her throat in case some nurse should see what she had done. As she bent forward to climb on to the bed, the wodge of soaked paper fell on to the bedspread; she pushed it underneath the pillow and glanced quickly at the nurses' station in case anyone had noticed. Without its covering her throat felt vulnerable. Keeping her shoulders stiff and her head unmoving, she climbed into bed and arranged herself against the pillows. Almost at once Carmelita brought her supper.

'Yo dressin' come off,' she said accusingly. Amy smiled. Carmelita looked closely at her neck. 'That lookin' awful. Better you leave him on.'

She handed Amy a plate which held mashed potato and a thin grey sausage. She said, 'I know you ordered macaroni cheese, darlin', but they ain't none left. Never mind, yo got orange jelly for yo afters.'

Amy ate the mashed potato with a teaspoon to make it last longer. She chewed lovingly on the gristly sausage. The jelly vanished in two mouthfuls.

The visitors started to arrive. She began to match husbands to wives, children to their mothers. A tall, thin, silver-haired man came pushing through the swing-doors and just for a moment she thought that he was Michael. The top man came into the nurses' station. Amy heard him say, 'Has she spoken yet?'

'No,' said the staff nurse. 'Not yet, sir.'

The curtains were drawn around three beds which stood directly opposite. She had watched the occupants return from theatre in late afternoon, saw them lifted, serenely unconscious, from trolley into bed. Tomorrow, they too would be propped up on pillows; Amy would see their faces, learn their names, their reason for being here. The bed next to hers remained empty.

The need to view her neck was becoming urgent, and yet she was reluctant to leave the ward. A trip to the bathroom mirror would bring her face to face with incoming visitors. Even Carmelita, who was used to such sights, had recoiled and used the word 'awful'. Amy remembered the mirror in her powder compact and was reaching for it when Chris and Dom walked through the door.

They kissed her and said that it was a relief to find her conscious and in her right mind. They had phoned the ward twice that day to inquire about her condition. They said that she was looking heaps better. As they spoke, her sons examined the pattern of the bedspread. One glance at her neck had been enough to make them lose their colour. Chris said, 'The staff-nurse says that you're doing very well; that you've been trotting around, got as far as the bathroom.'

Dom said, 'Be better when you can talk, eh? They say it will take a day or two. Don't worry about it. Lali came in twice today, but you were asleep. She'll come in again tomorrow.'

Amy had waited all day for them to come. Pen and paper were placed ready on the locker so that she might tell them about the iron rations and her hunger; about the contradictory information from the surgeon, about the constant care given by the nurses; their kindness and consideration. But even as Dom spoke she felt herself slipping down into sleep. She struggled with her eyelids, and then lost the battle.

Aunty Belle said, 'I've been told that you're seeing a young man.' She had known for some weeks that I was meeting Michael, but her approach was, as always, devious and complicated.

I said, 'I've been to the pictures with someone. We walk sometimes in St Gilda's Gardens.'

'Well I hope you know what you're doing, the kind of risks you're taking.'

I said, 'The young men who work in my office are all very decent and respectful.'

'That's not what I meant, and well you know it, Amy.' The set of her mouth, the intensity of her gaze caused my stomach muscles to contract. We had reached the point in the conversation when I was expected to make full and frank confession, for Aunty Belle could hardly admit that she had spied upon me, and I feared her too much to confront her with the fact that she had followed me on several evenings.

The Palm Court orchestra was playing the 'Skaters' Waltz'. The sound came from the brown Bakelite wireless set that stood on the sideboard. The music grew loud and then faded. The valves were unreliable. If they failed altogether I might be spared the Sunday evening boredom of broadcast hymn-singing from St Paul's Cathedral.

In the past month Aunty Belle had spoken to me only when absolutely necessary. I did not need or dare to ask the reason for her silence. I was being punished for a sin as yet unnamed.

The Palm Court orchestra faded into silence, but the valves

summoned up a final thrust of power. From the silk-covered fretwork speaker came a roaring rendition of 'Abide with Me'.

The risks hinted at by Aunty Belle had never been defined. I assumed they were of a sexual nature since on two occasions in recent days I had watched her through the half-closed bathroom door, examining minutely the underwear I had put into the soiled-linen basket. The few letters I received had been steamed open and carelessly resealed, as if she had wanted me to know that she was vigilant. Her lips moved silently, forming the words of 'Abide with Me'. The hot blood crept underneath my skin; I shook my head so that the heavy hair fell forward to obscure my blushing. She had always possessed the ability to make me feel dirty and ashamed.

Love had sharpened my awareness in other directions. I was learning the art of subterfuge from Mimi. She had a stock of varied and convincing reasons for being absent from the house. I sensed a change in her attitude towards me.

Whoever had first warned Aunty Belle that I was seeing Michael Sheldon, it had not been Mimi. Mimi had said that she was going out to post a letter, had carried a large white envelope as proof in her gloved hand. Now I heard her key in the front-door lock. I walked from the dining-room into the hall, even though the Evening Service was not ended.

'Nice walk?' I asked.

'Oh yes, dear. Very pleasant.'

She was wearing the teddy-bear mock fur jacket over a dusty, pencil-slim black skirt. Her stockings were black silk, their seams running ruler-straight down to high-heeled shoes of black suede. Her hair, richly hennaed, was upswept and secured on top of her head with marcasite combs. Her lipstick was smudged and she smelled of cigar smoke, and port and lemon.

On recent Sunday evenings I had noticed a sheen on Mimi. On Monday mornings, Mimi washed by hand her intimate laundry in the bathroom washbasin.

*

Night staff were coming on duty. Without opening her eyes, Amy recognized them by their brisk light footsteps and enthusiastic voices. While asleep, her neck had discovered for itself a more easeful position among the skimpy pillows. Fragmented conversations drifted from the nurses' station.

'. . . and I said to him, can't you see that I need my sleep? If you'd been on your feet all night you wouldn't exactly feel romantic.'

'So what did he say?'

'Same as he always says when we argue. You and your bloody job, it comes before everything and everybody. One of these days I'll have had enough. One of these mornings you'll come home and find me gone.'

'And will he, do you think? Go, I mean.'

'I don't know. Sometimes I wish he would. If I had the flat to myself I could just sleep and sleep for as long as I need to. But then . . .?'

Amy heard the doubt in the speaker's voice. It was, she thought, so often the man who chose to leave; who slammed the door, threw his suitcase into the car boot and drove off to an unknown destination. Women tended, on the whole, to stay, to rock the cradle, to keep the home fires burning and the wolf from the door.

No man leaves his wife, Aunty Belle had said, without a very good reason.

Amy lay still, her eyes closed against returning memory. She heard the metallic click as her chart was unhooked from the bedrail. Night staff asked day staff, 'Has she spoken yet?'

'Not a single peep. Himself is not too happy about her.'

They rustled away down the ward. Amy tried to think about her failure to utter; but for now it seemed quite unimportant. She could hear Michael's voice, soft and insistent down the years. 'Look at you! You're worn out. You and your bloody aunts! They come before everything and everybody. One of these nights you'll come back from that house in The Avenue to find me gone.'

And so she had. And so she had.

Day staff departed for the places they called home. For the first time since the operation Amy had no wish to sleep. She opened her eyes to find the ward in semi-darkness. Lamps above occupied beds had been switched off, a single overhead light burned at her end of the ward. Staff nurse and her assistant were moving silently from patient to patient, measuring temperatures and blood pressures, changing drainage bags and checking drips. Staff nurse was tall and slim, her golden hair rolled into a shining chignon at the nape of her neck. Surely, thought Amy, no man, however disgruntled, could ever bear to leave this lovely girl.

Amy reached for pad and pen. She wrote in ragged capitals, WHY CAN'T I SPEAK? When it was her turn again to be checked over, she handed up the pad. The nurses exchanged glances.

Staff nurse said, 'Haven't they explained it to you?'

Amy flapped a negative hand.

'Okay. Well, this is what has happened. The thyroid gland and the vocal cords are very close together. The greatest possible care is taken not to do damage when operating, but sometimes the vocal cords get a little bruised. Give it a day or two and you'll be fine.' She touched Amy's hand and smiled. 'Now don't worry about it. You're doing very well. Okay?' Amy smiled back and felt the ache of sudden tears. She could, it seemed, withstand anything but other people's kindness. She began to move, reluctantly, pulling herself upright against the pillows. She felt curiosity for the first time about her fellow patients, but to turn her head in their direction would involve a stiff and Frankenstein-type movement since her head and shoulders were no longer capable of independent action. Slowly and with infinite care she began to ease her body round until the rest of the ward came into view. There were others, she now saw, in trouble greater than her own, cases of recent surgery, bedfast and sedated. The dark-haired girl, who had

waved to Amy on several occasions, was herself awake and
propped up on pillows; she inquired in a stage whisper, 'How's
it going then?' Her bed was much closer than Amy had
imagined.

Amy smiled and held up her right hand, fingers crossed. The
girl left her bed and made her way painfully and slowly
towards Amy. She was very thin, in fact emaciated. As she
came closer Amy saw the yellow tinge of skin, the darkly
shadowed eyes.

'I'm Karen.' She sat down on the bed edge. Amy reached for
pad and pen.

'I'm Amy. Sorry I can't talk,' she wrote, 'they've cut my throat.
But they say it's getting better. How long have you been here?'

'Eight days,' said Karen. 'They call it observation. If you ask
me, they haven't a clue what's the matter with me.'

Amy wrote, 'You're very thin.'

'Not surprising, is it?' Karen said. 'I haven't eaten anything
solid for ten days. I've told them I'm going home tomorrow.
I'm fed up.'

Amy, conscious of her own empty house, wrote, 'Who will
look after you? You seem rather weak.'

'Oh, my husband's very good, and the girls are pretty
useful. I'll be all right.'

Amy recalled the grey-haired man and the two teenaged
girls seen at visiting time; the man with the grapes and flowers
whom she had at first though to be Michael.

'Are those pretty blonde girls your daughters?' she wrote.
'You don't look old enough to be their mother.'

'Oh, they're mine,' said Karen. 'My husband is quite a bit
older than I am. His first wife died of cancer. He'll be glad
when I'm home. He hates to visit this ward.' She smiled. 'I see
your sons come at visiting time. Dishy, aren't they?' Karen
wriggled her thin shoulders underneath the lace-trimmed wrap,
and fluttered her eyelashes, and just for a moment Amy saw
the coquettish girl she had once been.

The telephone rang and was answered. Staff nurse came out from the nurses' station. She said to Karen, 'Doctor's on his way to see you, dear. Let's get you back into bed, shall we.'

'I'm in trouble now,' Karen said to Amy. 'Threaten to go home and they all go bananas. Well, I'm going anyway. I told Greg to bring my clothes in.'

Amy watched her go, leaning heavily on the nurse's arm, saw her get into bed to make hardly a sign of occupation beneath the thin sheets.

To Amy, removed as she was from the familiar and safe, the ward at night had a dreamlike disconnected quality; the movements of the nurses seemed almost balletic. She thought of all the night hours of chemical sleep she had been granted since her admittance. Time in which she had not been allowed to suffer pain. Now she saw for the first time the ministrations to other patients of the night staff, their silent swoop from bed to bed, like white and slender birds of peace. They were distinguishable only in this dim light by a coloured waist-belt or shade of hair and skin. A special kind of female; unremittingly patient, thoughtful, observant of every smallest change in the condition of their charges.

Amy, whose purpose in living had also been the care of others, was beginning to find her role as patient both humbling and rather pleasant. She began to think about her life, the immediate problems, but her mind wandered off into dangerous channels. The doctors smiled in her direction but passed her by. They never actually looked at her. There was no believable good news, no talk about tomorrow or the next day. Even sneezing was a hazard. She had never imagined so simple a reflex involved the contraction of so many sore neck muscles. She looked across the ward at Karen who was already sleeping. From the nurses' station came the low rumble of a man's voice. 'She must be told now,' he said. 'We can't leave it any longer.' He left the nurses' station and walked towards Amy. He paused, studied her, and veered left to where Karen lay.

The chairs in the ward were metal-framed. Karen wakened abruptly when the chair legs scraped across the tiled floor. As the doctor sat down her voice came clearly through the silence. 'I'm going home tomorrow.'

He was young, very handsome, a Dr Kildare look-alike. Amy heard him say, 'I'm afraid that won't be possible. You need an operation.' Amy studied her wristwatch. It was ten minutes after midnight. She had no way of knowing if other patients were awake. Before sitting down, the doctor had switched on the lamp above Karen's bed. Amy had a sense of dread; she tried to think of other things, closed her eyes, but opened them again. Within that pool of light a drama was about to be enacted, and against her will she was compelled to watch and listen.

Karen said, 'What sort of operation?'

The doctor rubbed a hand across his face and sat up straighter in the chair. Amy wondered how many hours he had been on duty, and which senior surgeon had dumped this task upon him. He said, his voice impatient, 'The results of your tests are all in now, and we know what the problem is. A section of bowel will have to be removed. As soon as possible.'

'No,' said Karen. 'No way.' She gestured towards adjoining beds. 'Look at them. Drips and tubes and bags. That's not for me.'

He said, 'It's your life we're talking about.'

'Are you saying that I'll die if you don't operate on me?'

'Yes. That's what I'm saying.'

Karen reached out and gripped the white-sleeved arm. Her voice rose dangerously high. 'What's wrong with me then? What's bloody wrong? Come on, you've got to tell me!'

The doctor stared at the toecaps of his shoes. The observant staff nurse moved swiftly out from her station to stand by Karen's bed.

'We did a rather uncomfortable test on you yesterday. That test – unfortunately – showed a malignant condition in the lower bowel. I'm sorry.'

'You're sorry!' Karen's tone was shrill. 'I'm thirty-two years old. My girls are thirteen and fourteen. Who's going to tell them I've got cancer? I'm going to die, I can see it in your face. What right have you to tell me such a thing. I hate you, you bastard. Get away from me. Get away!'

Karen threw herself back against the pillows, and Amy heard the crack as Karen's head hit the metal bedrails. The doctor stood up, and walked quickly from the ward. Two student nurses came running and together with the staff nurse they held and tried to control the hysterical patient. At some point it finally occurred to a nurse to draw the curtains around the bed. Above the screaming Amy heard the staff nurse say, 'I'm going to phone her husband. He really should be here.' Twenty minutes later the man called Greg came hurrying through the swing-doors. He no longer reminded Amy of Michael; deep grooves were etched from nose to mouth, his eyelids were already pink and swollen. Amy imagined him weeping as he had driven at speed through the summer night. 'His first wife died of cancer,' Karen had said. 'He hates to visit this ward.'

Aids to sleep were being handed out to patients who were wakeful. Amy swallowed her tablet, grateful for the oblivion it promised.

She awoke to Carmelita's smiling face, the cup of hot sweet tea, the usual admonition. Her gaze went at once to Karen's bed; it was empty, the covers thrown back. Amy sipped her tea; she attempted to utter, to bid herself good morning, but no sound came. The ward was quiet, muted conversations came from the nurses' station. The swing-doors came open and Karen, carrying sponge-bag and towel, made her slow way to Amy's bedside. She sat down on the bedside chair and said calmly, 'They're going to operate. I've had my bath. I'm first on this morning's list.' She opened her wrap to reveal the white shift. She smiled. 'Not much style about it, is there?'

Amy reached out a hand to touch Karen's arm. The

compulsion to speak had never been so powerful. The sound that came from Amy's throat surprised them both.

'It's not so bad,' she croaked. 'You'll be all right. I know you will.'

The recovery of speech had changed her mood. From one moment to the next Amy moved from resigned acceptance of her state to a questioning aggression, which propelled her from the bed and towards the bathroom mirror. She halted by the swing-doors to allow the passage to the theatre of sedated Karen. The same kindly porter who had promised safety to Amy, now held Karen's hand.

The bathroom mirror was large and square and bolted to the wall. Its position, above the washbasin and facing the door, made confrontation with her image as unavoidable as sunrise. She stood for a moment, chin on chest, and then she raised her head, very slowly, willing her gaze towards her neck.

What she saw made her reach for the basin's rim. Amy held on with both hands. Now she knew why her sons had stared at the bedspread rather than at her, why patients and visitors at sight of her looked quickly away. The surgeons had fastened her together, not with stitches but with staples. Set in raw and lumpy flesh were twelve wicked-looking barbs, a tortuous necklace, the kind of hooks used by carpet fitters, and put in place by a gadget called a punch. The wound was broad; she could not imagine it healed. She leaned in towards the mirror. She had always been a woman of little vanity, and her neck, to be truthful, was already wrinkled. It was, she thought, a part of her anatomy which could in the future easily be hidden. She had no plans to wear low-necked evening gowns, or swimsuits. Even so, she could wish at this moment for an operation site that was decently concealed beneath her nightgown. Since the wad of green kitchen towels had fallen from her throat, no one had offered to apply a dressing.

There were croissants on that morning's breakfast menu. Faintly warm and served with a plastic-packed spoonful of marmalade, they made a pleasant change from instant porridge.

When her cup of tea arrived Amy growled, 'Thank you.'

Carmelita smiled, then she made a crowing sound of pure delight. 'Yo talkin' again! Well, halleluja! Yo sounds jes' like Louis Armstrong. Yo feel better, eh? Now yo can speak yo mind.'

The ward was filled with noise and movement. Trolleys, pushed by green-suited men, rattled through the swing-doors taking patients to theatre. Carmelita collected breakfast dishes. The house doctor named Joanna, pale from lack of sleep, walked swiftly to some emergency at the far end of the ward.

Karen's locker was wheeled to stand beside a freshly made-up bed that stood directly opposite the nurses' station. A student nurse placed on top of the locker the pink carnations which Greg had brought; she positioned the vase with care, rearranged the flowers and smoothed the white bedspread like a housewife preparing a guest room.

Amy counted the days since her operation. How long did it take to pop a specimen of tumour beneath a microscopic lens? And when they had come to a decision, which doctor would be unfortunate enough to draw the short straw? Who among the callow youths in white coats would be the bearer of bad tidings?

The physiotherapist came striding through the swing-doors. Slim and straight in her navy-blue trousers and crisp white jacket, she sought victims among the bed-bound. Amy, slumped sideways on the pillows, in the only position which eased the discomfort of her neck, was a likely target. The navy-blue-clad thighs came into her line of vision; she heard the rustle of charts as the physiotherapist consulted her clipboard. The girl began to read aloud. 'Mrs Amy Sheldon. Fifty-eight years old. Admitted on August 10th for –' The young voice faltered then ceased. The pause that followed was a long one. When she spoke again, the voice was falsely bright. 'Now, now, Mrs Sheldon – we can't have this, can we? You really must sit upright and lift your chin as high as you possibly can. There are little exercises you can do –'

Amy ceased to listen; her eyelids drooped, she feigned sleep. The bossy voice still reached her from the far end of the ward, upbraiding sick and bedridden ladies to 'pull in your tummy, dear, take deep breaths, and don't let your shoulders droop like that!'

The television set, the telephone and armchairs were in the dayroom. To reach these amenities would mean traversing the whole length of the ward. Amy felt unsure of her ability to make the journey, the weariness seeming like a failure on her part to utilize the nurses' care.

She pulled on the blue kimono, tucked the drainage flask into her pocket, together with her coin purse, thrust her feet into slippers, and began her shuffling, head-bent progress through the ward. Still unable to turn her gaze in any direction but forward, she spoke only to those who stood immediately within her view.

The dayroom stank of old cigarette smoke. A notice on the door said in large red letters, PLEASE KEEP THIS DOOR CLOSED. In a corner stood a large television set; grouped around it was a half-circle of armchairs upholstered in mustard-yellow vinyl. The room was used by both male and female patients; its single occupant was a pale young man who wore blue pyjamas and a towelling robe. He waved his half-smoked cigarette at Amy, and continued to watch the television programme. The portable telephone was on a trolley in the furthest corner of the room. She sat on the upright chair beside the trolley, pushed a coin into a slot, and punched the buttons for a familiar number. As the distant ringing began to peal out she grew nervous and began to replace the handset. But before the connection could be broken her husband's quiet voice said, 'Sheldon Antiques. Mike Sheldon speaking.'

For how long, she wondered, had he identified himself as 'Mike'? In all their years together he had been known only as Michael. She answered in her unrecognizable growl, 'So sorry. I seem to have dialled the wrong number.'

'Not at all,' he said. 'No trouble,' and then he was gone.

She put down the handset with great care and moved slowly from the upright chair to an armchair. She had heard Michael's voice for the first time in four years and the sound had achieved what major surgery had not. Amy felt hot and then cold; great waves of weakness swept through her body. She leaned back into the softness of the padded vinyl and thought that she might faint. The young man stubbed out his cigarette in a metal ashtray and switched off the television. He stood up and turned towards Amy and this time he looked directly at her neck. 'My God!' he said. 'You made a rotten job of that! Bread knife needed sharpening, eh? Better luck next time.'

Amy, who had never liked black humour, felt laughter welling up into her damaged throat. Her stomach muscles tensed, her shoulders shook with silent mirth; the sensation of weakness passed. How right he was, she thought, to see her wound as being self-inflicted. Smoking was not, perhaps, the only indulgence which caused cancer. In her head she still heard Michael's voice, soft-spoken, polite. 'Not at all. No trouble,' he had said.

'Not at all,' he had said, 'no trouble,' when I asked whether he would mind if we got married. Relieved as I was at his polite acquiescence, I would have preferred a more positive reaction. The prospect of impending fatherhood might have been expected to provoke in most men exclamations of delight or horror. But not from Michael Sheldon. Although I did not know it then he was one of life's gamblers: philosophical when the dice did not roll in his favour, blasé when they did.

'So when will you tell Aunty?' he inquired.

'I'll tell Mimi first.'

'Good idea,' he said thoughtfully. 'Mimi will need to take care to keep it in the family.' He smiled, and I knew then that he was capable of moral blackmail if he thought it necessary. Oh, but I was no better. I would have lied to a benchful of judges, perjured my immortal soul, if only to escape the wrath of Aunty Belle.

All her predictions had come true, leaving me defenceless. I had done those things that no nice girl ever did. I had forfeited the right to wear white at my wedding. There would, in seven months' time, be talk by her of a premature baby. But no one would believe her.

The serious lying had begun two weeks ago. The onset of morning sickness had obliged me to leave the house very early in the day. I told a tale of the increased workload in my office, and my need to put in extra hours. I hid in St Gilda's Gardens on those cool May mornings, shivering and being sick among the forsythia bushes. From the bench where I sat I could see the upper windows of Sheldon Antiques. I remembered those Saturday afternoons when old Mr Sheldon was absent from the business and at Newmarket races; the winter days when Michael closed the shop much earlier than usual, and I had followed him for the first time up the scuffed wooden stairs.

I had expected the Sheldons' living quarters to be an extension of the shop below; a collection of shabby, damaged objects, even more unsaleable than their priced stock. I could not have been more mistaken. The floor space was vast and without division, except for a tiny bathroom and kitchenette at the far end. Heavy rugs lay haphazardly on black unpolished boards. Thick blue velvet drapes, pelmeted and swagged, almost covered the windows, shutting out daylight. Several cabinets, sideboards and occasional tables were ranged along the walls. Against the opposite end-wall stood two long blue velvet-covered sofas, deeply cushioned and as broad as single beds. Pictures and mirrors covered every wall; lamps, which I learned later had been made by Tiffany, cast pools of coloured light into the gloom. Every cabinet was filled with porcelain and coloured glass. Each sideboard held displays of carved ivory and silver. Michael and his uncle lived on familiar terms with the best of their stock. Items from the upper floor were sold only, so Michael told me, when a bill needed to be paid or the profit on the sale was too high to be passed up.

We had never repeated the cinema visit; all our subsequent meetings took place in what I was always to think of as The Room. On this first occasion Michael entertained me to after-noon tea. A table which he said was Sheraton was set with Limoges china and heavy cutlery on an embroidered linen cloth with matching napkins. We ate hot buttered muffins from a silver muffin-dish so highly polished it showed me my reflected face. I tried not to think about the vulnerable, eager-to-please expression which was mirrored by the silver. I said nervously, because I had never been quite so alone with any man, 'You must have spent hours polishing and cleaning. You really shouldn't have gone to all this trouble on my account.'

He gave me a long cool look. 'Nothing was done on your account, Amy. This is the way I like to live. Beautiful objects deserve to be cherished.'

In the silence that followed I sensed his deep displeasure. I dropped my napkin; melted butter from the muffin dripped on to my skirt. I studied the pattern on my valuable plate. 'I'm sorry –' I began.

'Don't be,' he interrupted, 'it's just that I'm over-sensitive when people make assumptions about Uncle Fin and me.'

I remembered the dismissive words used by Aunty Belle about the Sheldons and knew how wrong had been her judge-ment of them. Michael and his Uncle Finbar were exceptional men, unselfconsciously stylish, believing themselves to be worthy of the finer things life had to offer.

The curfew imposed by Aunty Belle was set at ten. I had begged for an extension, pointing out that the Saturday evening cinema programme ended at eleven. Aunty Belle, who never visited the pictures and was innocent therefore of what went on there, decided that, even when accompanied by Michael Sheldon, I could come to no harm in so public a building.

The conspiracy was compounded by Mimi who, to my knowledge, was never in town on Saturday evenings. Her bridge club, she said, also closed down at eleven, and if Aunty Belle so wished, Mimi herself would see me safely home, thereby making it unnecessary for Belle to wait up.

In that winter of my eighteenth year I grew from a child into a woman without the intervening time of adolescence. While my office colleagues whispered together about dates and crushes, and their favourite film stars, I planned the entrapment of Michael Sheldon. I had read enough romantic novels to be aware that muffins for tea, taken tête-à-tête in a young man's living quarters, was a possible if unusual prelude to seduction.

The decision to lose my virginity was made on a rainy afternoon in February. I remember the low skies, the greyness, the feeling of hopelessness that no matter how circumspect my behaviour, how innocent my actions, Aunty Belle had me marked down as a 'bad girl'. In which case, I told myself, I might as well fulfil all her expectations.

'So there you are, Mrs Sheldon! You've missed your elevenses but you were sleeping so soundly we didn't like to wake you.'

Amy opened her eyes to the concerned face of the Asian nurse. 'We need you back on the ward. It's time to take your clips out.'

Amy raised her head and shoulders from the yellow vinyl; she smiled, recalling the humour of the young man in the towelling robe. 'Are you sure I'm ready to have them removed? It's only three days since the operation. I have this nightmare, you see, that without the staples my head will fall off and go rolling down the ward.'

The nurse smiled back, unsure if this was meant to be a joke. 'Oh no,' she said, 'I'm quite sure that won't happen.

Your clips can't be left in any longer; as your wound heals the skin grows around them, you see, making them awkward to remove.'

The nurse in the bright green uniform was unknown to Amy. 'I'll do my very best not to hurt you,' she said.

Amy, lying as flat as her condition would permit, studied the profile of the new nurse. Michael and I, she thought, once bid at auction for a Meissen figurine that looked exactly like this girl. She watched the unwrapping of the sterilized instruments, the pulling on of the rubber gloves, and willed herself to recall the Meissen. A ballerina, it had been. Pink porcelain tutu, white arms upraised. The face and hands as delicate as those of angels. The drainage tube pulled free without any trouble.

The removal of the staples was indescribably painful. The Meissen ballerina, poised gracefully over Amy's throat, plucked delicately at each metal barb until it came loose from the healing skin. Amy felt the trickle of blood, saw the agonized features of the young nurse as the tears rolled down her patient's face.

'I can't bear to hurt you like this,' she muttered. 'I am so very sorry. Would you rather I stopped for a while?'

'Not your fault,' Amy growled, 'job has to be done.' She paused. 'How many clips have you taken out?'

'Only three, I'm afraid.'

'Do three more, and I'll have a little rest.'

As the sixth staple clattered into the metal dish the nurse said, 'That's it. No more. We'll do the rest tomorrow.' She patted Amy's hand. 'If I can't bear to do it, then you can't bear to have it done. I'll see you in the morning.' She laid a loose dressing across Amy's neck. 'I'll ask someone to bring you a cup of tea.'

Carmelita held the cup while Amy drank. 'Shook yo up proper, don' it,' she stated. 'I don' know why they can't use stitches. Nasty old things, them clips.' She hitched the dressing higher across Amy's throat. 'Yo gettin' blood all down the front of yo nice nightie.'

The bed next to Amy's had stood unoccupied since her admission. She awoke from an uneasy doze to see the unconscious form of a young woman being transferred from a trolley and into the bed. Amy eased her body into a bearable position against the pillows. Carmelita brought the three o'clock cup of tea and digestive biscuit. The ward was quiet; several beds were unoccupied, many patients had gone down for surgery that morning. Amy thought about the early morning hours in Ward Forty-Seven. Women waking up to a fear which they concealed behind a shaky smile, a nodded good morning passed from bed to bed. We are all afraid, thought Amy, and the fear has a label. Its name is CANCER. Allusions were made; women mentioned casually, as if it hardly mattered, their reason for being in this ward. They referred to a small growth, a possible tumour, a slight blockage, a lump, a cyst. They never actually said THE WORD.

Amy said the word. In a voice that was Louis Armstrong-going-on-Eartha Kitt, she spoke aloud the name of CANCER. She said it several times, so that its hard edges softened into something she could contemplate with less than utter terror. She glanced up to find Lali standing by the nurses' station. She could not be sure that her daughter had not heard her chanting. Lali said, in a high unnatural tone, 'Well, isn't that wonderful – you've got your voice back.'

They smiled at one another. Amy unpacked the cool-bag Lali had brought; it was filled with cartons of yoghurt, and mousse in pretty colours and tempting flavours. The tears, embarrassingly on tap, filled Amy's eyes. 'Oh, how thoughtful of you, darling. You can't imagine how I've longed for – I'm not usually so fussy – but the food here is so –'

'I know, Mum. I know. They do their best.'

'I'm sure they do. I'm not complaining. The nurses here are incredible. I never knew that one human creature could tend another with such patience. I thought – well, you know – only one's nearest and dearest – it's a kind of loving, I suppose. I lie here and watch them. After this experience I shall believe in angels.'

Lali said, 'I've been talking to Sister. They plan to take the rest of your clips out tomorrow. She says that if you feel up to it you can go home on Sunday.' Lali paused. 'I wanted to look after you, but Dom insists on moving in until you feel strong enough to cope. I agreed in the end. Well, he was in a bit of a state about certain matters. It seems things are going badly wrong between him and Chantal. A short separation might be very helpful to them.'

The sunshine of late afternoon lay gold upon gold across the yellow floor. Amy walked, for the first time since entering the ward, to the long uncurtained window which looked out across the hospital complex. She looked down upon red-brick and tiled roofs; patchy grass burned by the summer heat, a few limp trees. Cars moved on a distant road which led back into the city. Nothing, she thought, will ever be the same. She had touched a different stratum of being. That ride with Dom last Tuesday, stopping for coffee in the red-clothed café; the paralysis of fear. Walking into the surgical ward, taking possession of the space between armchair, bed and locker, all of which had become uniquely hers. Well, that was in another life, when she had been a different person. She had gone down into the darkness of the anaesthetic knowing she was Amy. Now she was certain only of her lost identity, and the terrible anger which was growing in her soul.

The adjoining bed was finally occupied.

'She an emergency,' Carmelita informed Amy. 'Collapse in Debenhams, she did. They bring her in, shopping an' all.'

Nurses spoke at intervals to the new arrival. 'Are you going to wake up for me, Dawn?' they said. But Dawn slept on. A glass jar, two-thirds full of greenish-yellow pebbles, was placed on the patient's locker. A Debenhams carrier bag was put in her cupboard. The girl's face was flushed; damp blonde hair clung wispily around her head and temples. Other patients were brought back from theatre and tucked up safely in their beds.

Amy walked to the bathroom. She ran water into the bath and flung an extravagant amount of Orchidée Sauvage upon the rising steam. Getting into and out of the bath required the utmost concentration. She was, she discovered, still unsteady. She clung to taps and rail, for fear of slipping and falling. The green stain on the bath was the exact shape of her lawn. She wondered if Chris had mowed the grass, watered the flower-beds. It might have rained on Wednesday; she remembered vaguely dull skies seen from the ward's windows. 'If you feel up to it, you can go home on Sunday,' Lali had said. Amy lay in the cooling water and tried to think about home. How it would be. How she would manage. How long Dom would stay with her; and if she really needed him to do so. But her thoughts turned irresistibly back towards the ward. Karen had not yet returned from theatre. She had been absent for so many hours. Amy towelled her body dry, put on a clean nightdress and the blue kimono. She combed her hair and fastened it back with a blue clip. The activity had loosened the temporary dressing on her throat. Even as she stood before the mirror, the gauze fell into the washbasin. She made no attempt to replace it, but put it in the bin.

Back in the ward her gaze went at once to Karen's bed. In addition to the usual drip and tubes an oxygen cylinder had been wheeled into position. Karen lay, as unobtrusive as a paper bookmark between white sheets. She looked like a small frail child, her eyelids closed and purple-coloured in the ivory of her face, the oxygen mask placed across her mouth. Greg sat beside her, his body hunched uncomfortably on the upright chair. He twisted the gold ring on his wedding finger. His hand strayed at intervals towards his jacket pocket in search of the cigarette he was not allowed to smoke. Amy turned her chair around so as not to see his tears.

Turning the chair brought her neighbour of the next bed into direct vision. Amy looked into open but unfocused eyes. She said quietly, 'Hello, Dawn. How are you feeling now?'

'Wonderful! Absolutely bloody wonderful!' The voice was weak, the words slurred, but there was no mistaking the girl's jubilation. Her gaze turned towards the glass jar almost full of pebbles, and all at once her eyes were focused, her voice strong.

'Gallstones. That's what the trouble was! I was so sure that I had cancer. I was too terrified to see a doctor. Rolled on the floor in agony sometimes. I keeled over in Debenhams. I don't remember much about it.'

'Yes,' said Amy, 'your shopping is in your locker. But why did you think that you had cancer? You can't be more than twenty –?'

'Five. Twenty-five last April. My mother died of cancer. A year ago. I nursed her until the end.' Dawn's mouth twisted in a near-smile. 'They were pretty annoyed with me in Emergency. Said I should have known better. I'm a nurse, you see.' Her lids drooped across eyes still fixed upon the glass jar. 'Gonna have a necklace made of them,' she muttered, and then she slept.

Chris and Dom came in, hell-bent on reassurance. 'You're looking much better. Lali says you'll be coming home on Sunday. We'll have a trip up to the coast when you're feeling up to it. Your voice is almost back to normal.'

The visitors left. Only Greg maintained his vigil. He studied a copy of that evening's paper, but never turned a page. Staff nurse supplied him with cups of tea he failed to drink. At nine o'clock he rose from the chair and walked away.

From the island of her bed Amy watched the ward. Day staff were replaced by night staff, rounds were made, lights were lowered. Except for the one above Karen's bed, where a nurse or two was in almost constant attendance.

Chris had brought roses, cut from the bushes which grew in Amy's garden. Other flowers had arrived from friends and neighbours, and her many clients. There were cards and letters, more than she had expected. Only Michael had failed to acknowledge the fact that she was ill. Michael, and Aunty Belle and Mimi. Amy thought about cousin Rose, who was now responsible for the safety and well-being of Belle and Mimi. She reviewed the many tasks and errands which she herself had performed for so many years. Gladly, of course. Willingly. But of course, willingly and gladly. Hadn't she owed it to them? Hadn't they deserved the very best that Amy had to offer? They would expect that Amy, after a period of convalescence, would resume her duties. Cousin Rose must almost certainly assume that her own shouldering of the burden would be only a temporary nuisance. Across the ward three nurses and a doctor now worked at Karen's bedside. Cancer. It stole away time and life. Amy thought about her own time, her own life. So much that she had meant to do; so many places that she had longed to visit. There were dawns and sunsets still to be seen; grandchildren as yet unborn. Love to be received and given.

But her life, her time, had always belonged to Aunty Belle and Mimi. Even here, in a hospital bed, she could feel the tug of the bond which bound her to them. Her gaze was drawn back again to Karen, who might or might not survive this night. Cancer, Amy thought, pays all other debts. Cancels all responsibilities. Sets the prisoner free.

'But what will happen to us?' Aunty Belle had said, when told of Amy's impending operation. 'Who will see to paying the bills, collecting our pensions, keeping the house clean?'

Amy had said, very gently, for she feared her aunt, 'Just at this moment I'm feeling pretty upset myself. I'm sorry, but your pensions and shopping are not my first consideration.'

'Well, they are mine! Somebody has to think about these things, even if you don't!'

There had been not one word of sympathy, of kindness.

Mimi had sat absolutely still in her chair, fearing to speak. When the telephone had rung later that evening, Amy's anger had spilled over to include Mimi, who did not deserve it.

Amy moved uneasily against her pillows. She closed her eyes and then opened them. Staff nurse said, 'A tablet for you tonight, Mrs Sheldon?' Amy thought about the long hours stretching out into early morning, when one memory would inevitably stir up others. And then where would she be?

She accepted the tablet, and within minutes had fallen headlong into uneasy dreamless sleep.

She awoke to the clatter of a fresh oxygen cylinder being wheeled into position beside Karen's bed. The night staff, after long hours of duty, were unflagging in their attention to very sick patients. Up and down the ward they went; blood pressures, pulses, temperatures; adjustments to the machinery without which those patients might lose the battle back to life.

They spoke to Karen even though she showed no sign of hearing what they said. Three nurses in attendance, bowl of warm water, washcloth, towel: 'We're going to make you a bit more comfortable, dear. Your husband brought in such a pretty nightie for you. We'll take off this old operation gown; you'll feel better for a little wash. Perhaps a sip of tea later on, eh?' Their voices were gentle, their hands busy.

The nightgown was a soft shade of eau-de-Nil, smocked and beribboned. Amy gave the garment a professional scrutiny. Top of the range, exclusive, expensive; she imagined Karen's daughters searching through lingerie boutiques in their lunch break, obeying their father's instructions: 'Only the prettiest, only the best.'

Two nurses held Karen in a sitting position, while a third nurse slipped the nightgown over her head and eased her arms into the sleeves. The garment gave fullness to her emaciated body; she looked like a pale and pretty child dressed up for a party, except that her eyes remained closed.

The top man made his visit soon after breakfast. He sent the faintest of nods in Amy's direction, but did not speak. He halted at the foot of Karen's bed; at the end of a murmured consultation with the staff nurse, he raised his voice and spoke to Karen, who opened her eyes for the first time.

'You'll feel better tomorrow.' His tone lacked conviction. He turned back to the staff nurse. 'She will have to fight now,' he said. 'It's all up to her.'

Just for a moment the top man's voice faltered and Amy saw the humanity she had believed he lacked.

The removal of the last six staples from her throat was made easier by the knowledge that this was the final pain she would have to suffer. Amy stood once again before the bathroom mirror and studied the thick scarlet rope of unhealed flesh which reached almost from one earlobe to the other. Her chin still gravitated downwards to her chest, but she could now turn her head from side to side without pain. Just remember, she told herself, never attempt to look upwards.

She had planned that today she would walk about the ward, get her sea legs, test her strength. But she climbed instead into her bed, lay back upon the pillows, and let the tears come. There was no shame in weeping here. Among the women of the ward each one had her turn, while the others feigned ignorance, were careful not to look towards the bed of the one who had, temporarily, broken down. Yesterday it had been the elderly, irascible lady who demanded more than her fair share of the nurses' attention. She had been shaken with a storm of weeping which she covered with anger. When the ward assistant had brought round the luncheon menus, the old lady had said 'no' to every item.

Amy woke from a light doze to find two white-coated girls seated at her bedside. Pretty as starlets, she could not at first imagine who they could be.

'We saw you on your first day here,' said the dark-haired one.

'We observed your operation,' said the blonde girl.

'Oh,' said Amy. 'You must be the medical students who were with the surgeon –?'

'Your operation was quite fascinating. Enormously interesting. We're so glad not to have missed it.'

Amy said, 'So do I get the Oscar for best performance?'

They smiled, wished her well, and went away.

Lali came that evening. Amy wanted to say, 'I phoned the shop one morning, while my throat was still croaky. Your father answered. The sound of his voice turned my bones to water.' The words ran around in her head but she could not speak them. She said instead, 'Karen's daughters were here all afternoon. I felt so sorry for them, they're hardly more than children. They sat side by side in those upright chairs. They never spoke to one another. They didn't look at Karen.'

Lali said, 'The clothes you came in must be awfully creased. I've brought a leisure suit in for you. I know it's not your usual style. I hope it fits.'

The leisure suit was an attractive shade of apricot; packed with it were matching socks, and a pair of white trainers with apricot laces. The labels on every item were well known and expensive. The incongruity of such an outfit embarrassed Amy; it made her look like a health fanatic, a jogger, a woman who might live for several years.

Now that the day had come she had mixed feelings about leaving. Her mind began to turn tentatively outwards; she gathered up the get-well cards, packed the kimono, slippers and nightgowns. Wearing the leisure suit she began to feel fraudulent but comfortable.

The staff nurse brought a sheaf of forms. A clinic appointment had been made with Amy's surgeon; she would receive a letter from her local hospital giving date and time. There was a letter to be given to Amy's GP. Another letter was for the district nurse who would call to check on Amy's progress.

Nobody talked about the waiting. The waiting for the verdict. The verdict which would set a limit on her life.

She said goodbye to Dawn who was contentedly convalescent. She stood at Karen's bedside, touched her hand, and muttered words of hope. As Amy was about to move away, Karen's eyelids lifted. She smiled, said, 'Thanks,' and slept again.

In a way that Amy had never imagined or expected it was hard to leave Ward Forty-Seven. She said goodbye to the nurses and to Carmelita, and followed Dom's thin shadow through the swing-doors, down the stairs, and out into the hot sunshine of the Sunday morning.

Aunty Belle was as angry as I had expected her to be when I confessed that I was pregnant. There were no scenes, no shouting. She said that she would take care of me, no matter what happened. Michael Sheldon would not marry me; of course he wouldn't! And even if he did, what kind of life could I expect to live, wedded to a rag-and-bone man? Underlying her words was a corrosive, tight-lipped rage which terrified me.

Mimi, who felt guilty at having abetted me in deception and sin, was concerned only with the possibility that Michael and I might not love one another.

'Are you really sure about this?' she asked. 'Do you really want to marry him?'

'I've never been so sure,' I said, 'of anything in all my life.' Since I had come to live in Aunty Belle's house, uncertainty had been my normal state of mind.

'You'll need to have Belle's signed permission to get married.'

'Oh, she'll sign fast enough. She could never live with the shame of an unmarried mother in the family.'

'Don't be too hard on her, Amy. She has your best interests at heart.'

'I know,' I said, 'it's just – I always feel that she's punishing me for something. Half the time I don't even know what sin I'm supposed to have committed.'

We were married in a registry office. Uncle Finbar was Michael's witness, Mimi was mine. Seeing the two of them together, behaving like strangers towards one another, caused Michael and me a great deal of secret amusement. On that night when Michael made love to me for the first time, I had found, wedged between the velvet cushions of the sofa, a marcasite comb of unique and splendid design; a comb which could only have belonged to Mimi.

Chris had mowed the lawn, watered the flower-beds, set out the garden furniture underneath the pear tree. Amy stood in the middle of the kitchen, which now seemed smaller and a place of no importance. She wondered how, in the days to come, she would pass her time. She moved to the tap, filled the kettle, plugged it into the socket, assembled teapot and cups, milk and sugar, tea-bags and biscuits. She moved slowly and without purpose. The kettle boiled and Amy poured water into the pot. She seemed to be functioning, but as if from inside a bell-jar; could observe herself living her life, but could not seem to feel it. Reality was back there, in Ward Forty-Seven where Carmelita brewed tea by the gallon in a huge enamel pot, and brought it to the bedside in a thick white cup and saucer.

Chris carried the tea-tray into the garden. He adjusted the sunbed so that her feet were slightly raised, her head and shoulders supported. He smiled at her across his teacup. 'I restocked your fridge and freezer. You won't need to go shopping for at least a month. I'll be bringing in some fruit and salad.'

'Thank you,' she said, 'that was very thoughtful of you.'

He began to talk about the Roman coins he had recently acquired, their provenance, the velvet-lined case he would make, in which they could be shown to best advantage. Amy watched his face, the high bright colour of the skin across his cheekbones, the deep blue of his eyes, the chestnut glint of his thick hair. His lips were moving, but she did not hear his words.

Survival. The will of the mind above the cowardice of the body. But what is there still to fight for? Why is it necessary for me to see another sunrise, another midday? Another dark night?

But here I am, eating and drinking because instinct tells me so to do. But there is, at the very edge of being, a sweet lethargy, a slow slide down towards oblivion, a temptation to say — to think — so what! I've had my sad times, my little triumphs. So why linger?

Chris said, 'I'll go now. You're looking tired. Dom will be back very soon. Perhaps you should sleep for a while. Are you sure you'll be all right?'

She smiled at him. 'Of course I'll be all right. I'm not an invalid, you know. I was trotting around in the hospital as if nothing had happened to me.' She heard the slam of his car door, the start of the engine. She waited for a full ten minutes before rising from the sunbed and making her slow way through the garden and back into the house.

The rooms looked strange as they never did after she had been absent on holiday or business trips. The sitting-room had the unnatural appearance of a stage set. Amy wondered why she had never noticed this before. The woman who walked towards her in the long hall mirror was equally a stranger. She had put on the leisure suit that morning because it was easy. It would be some time before she opened her wardrobe doors on the good tailored suits and blouses, the garden-party dresses, the high-heeled shoes. She went back to the sunbed, making efforts to lift her feet when she walked, to raise her chin to a more normal position; to hint to any interested observer that here was a woman who might at any minute break into a jogging pace.

*

The district nurse was not deceived. She examined Amy's neck. She said, 'H'mm. That looks really nasty. Sore, I'll be bound.'

'Yes. It's also very lumpy. I went into hospital with one lump in my neck. I've come out with seven or eight.'

'It's early days yet,' said the nurse. 'It will all settle down in time. Just try to relax. Don't worry about it.'

Amy said, 'They didn't tell me anything in the hospital.'

'The tests take time,' said the nurse. 'When do you go back for your first check-up?'

'Not for six weeks.'

'I'll have a word with your doctor, ask him to come out and see you. He can tell you more than I can.'

Dom brought in Chinese take-away food on that first evening; lemon chicken and egg foo yung, and other dishes to which Amy could not put a name. She spread a cloth across the coffee table and on it Dom set out the many pots and cartons. They sat side by side on the green brocade sofa, and Amy failed to worry about the food smells which must be permeating her upholstery and curtains, and the many grains of rice which she dropped on the carpet.

'I'm hopeless with chopsticks,' she said. 'I hardly ever get any practice with them.'

Dom fetched her a fork and spoon; he recommended those dishes which were easier to swallow. When the meal was finished he made coffee. Amy felt uniquely safe and almost happy. She surveyed the debris of silver foil and empty cartons, which reminded her of picnics taken with her children. She tried to remember the picnics of her own early childhood, but could not. To do so would involve herself in attempted recollections of her own parents. The parents of whom she had no memory at all.

Her body had become accustomed to the thin hard hospital mattress and lumpy pillows. By comparison her own good bed was too accommodating, the room itself too quiet. She lay, half-propped, her neck and shoulders rigid and prepared for pain or at least discomfort. The bedroom seemed fussy and over-furnished. The white and gold wardrobe units had a threatening aspect as if they might step forward and advance upon her. The dressing-table was overloaded with bits of old silver and empty perfume bottles, which she saved only for their pretty shapes. She pushed back the duvet and slid her legs towards the floor. The carpet felt hot underneath her bare feet. She walked to the window, parted the nets and opened the casement.

Down in the garden Dom smoked the last cigarette of the day. She watched his long thin shadow cross the moonlit lawn, heard him come into the house, heard the click of locks as he made the doors secure. She looked out across the roof-tops to where Aunty Belle and Mimi were sleeping – or not sleeping. She wondered if they thought of her.

The sky was a deep unbroken blue; the sun shone. The sunbed, which she had rarely used, was turning out to be a wise investment. She had persuaded Dom that it was safe for him to leave her; which was not altogether untrue so long as she moved slowly and not too often. But she had been quite unprepared for the dizziness and nausea which affected her on waking and persisted well into mid-morning. She had felt fitter in the hospital. Safer.

Lali came at lunchtime, bringing salad and minced chicken, and a carton of gooseberry yoghurt, her mother's favourite sweet. Lali fetched the little aids to comfort which only women think of: a box of tissues, an extra pillow, a jug of iced water and a glass from which to drink it.

When Amy asked about Dom and his problem with Chantal, Lali was dismissive. 'Nothing you should be worrying about, Mum. It will probably blow over. You know how he is: mad as hell one minute – laughing the next. They've been together for seven years – that has to count for something.'

Amy said quietly, 'Your father and I had spent thirty-six years together. And we were married. It didn't stop him leaving, did it?'

Lali looked uneasy. She adjusted the parasol, piled cutlery and plates together. She said, abruptly, 'You really ought to go away; have a month in Spain. There are bits of the Majorcan coast that are beautiful in autumn. Or there's Ireland. One of those luxurious hotels beside a lough, where the cooking is cordon bleu and every guest room has a four-poster bed.' She gazed assessingly at Amy. 'You should at least get out of the house. Convalescence is always more effective in unfamiliar surroundings.'

Amy had not thought of herself as being convalescent. It was an old-fashioned word which called to mind hot milk and egg custards, and old gentlemen in wheelchairs being pushed along the seafront at Bognor Regis. She said as much to Lali who gave her that look of faint exasperation that had been learned long ago from Michael, her father.

Amy said, 'I'll think about it. In any case it will be weeks before I feel up to coping with luggage and airports.'

'I could come with you,' Lali said. 'Dad says he'll –'

'I don't want to hear about what your father says. Please don't ever mention his name again in my presence.' She saw, with regret, the closed expression that crept across her daughter's features, shutting Amy out, dispelling the little, warm closeness which had lately grown up between them. But there was nothing to be done about it.

Michael must have known that she was ill. He had not phoned or sent a card, not even a flower. His indifference was a wound that would never heal. But what else had she expected?

Clients, who had also become friends, came to sit with her underneath the pear tree. They brought magazines and books; they also brought packed lunches so that they might stay until mid-afternoon, leaving Amy with only an hour or two of uncertain isolation until Dom's return.

*

They came, her very dear friends, bearing gifts and flowers. They offered her their time, their company, their conversation; and she was grateful for it. But there was a time when she needed to be alone. It was then that she thought about Karen. 'You'll feel better tomorrow,' the surgeon had told her. What else could he say? Oh, how arrogant she had been, believing that the ills of the body could be subdued if she paid them no attention. Well, that game was all over now. CANCER. Today she could say it without flinching. Every day she grew more easy with the thought. It was a disease like any other.

It was as curable or incurable as any other illness.

She had no more right to go on living than any other person.

She would be grateful for any extension that surgery allowed her. After all, she never thought she was immortal.

The doctor came on yet another day of endless sunshine. Amy hardly knew him; she had never been one of his regular patients, taking up space on the surgery chairs. He greeted her cheerfully, and then told her that he himself had undergone a thyrectomy five years ago. He understood, he told her, how it felt to await a histology result. His own thyroid tumour had turned out to be benign.

Amy thought about the word 'benign'. It called to mind a smiling Buddha, a sunlit landscape. An unreal situation. But the doctor was demonstrably alive, going about his daily stressful business. He was himself benign, and more sympathetic than he might have been had the site of her affliction occurred in some other area of the body.

'It will quite possibly turn out,' he told her, 'that you have had an unnecessary operation.' He paused. 'But you shouldn't have to wait for the histology results until your check-up. I'll phone the hospital. I'll come to see you as soon as I have definite news.'

*

'Stillborn,' said the doctor. 'There was nothing we could do.'

'Stillborn?' I echoed. 'What exactly does that mean?'

'She was dead at birth. Perfectly formed, no blemish or deformity. But she never breathed.'

I began to laugh. 'You've got the word wrong,' I told him. 'You mean "still life". Like paintings of apples and grapes on a dish. Is that what you did? Put my baby on a dish and called it "still life"?' I went on laughing; I thought that I might never stop. He was old and grey and weary-looking. He had seen it all before. Many times. He called a nurse. 'Sedative,' he said, and walked away.

They asked, much later, if I would like to see her. I said yes, although I didn't really want to; I needed to know for myself that what they said was true.

They brought her to me wrapped in a little pink blanket, as if she was a real child. Some nurse had brushed her fair curling hair into a quiff as if she might have her photograph taken. Stillborn babies, explained the nurse, could not be baptised or registered, since they had never lived.

They left me alone with her for about three minutes. I wet my finger and made the sign of the cross on her forehead. I said out loud, 'I name thee Annis,' which had been my grandmother's name. I asked the nurse if Michael had seen the baby.

'No,' she answered. 'He said he'd rather not.'

'I want you to go home,' she said to Dom. 'You've been with me for over a week and I'm feeling so much stronger. I appreciate all you've done, but it's time you were going back to Chantal.' She laughed. 'And anyway, if you stay here much longer I shall get to like it. I shall be thinking up reasons why you shouldn't go.'

'As a matter of fact,' he said slowly, 'there are a few things I haven't told you. The situation is pretty bad between Chantal and me. About as bad as it can be.'

Even though she had been forewarned by Lali, Amy could

not control the involuntary stiffening of her facial muscles. Dom said, 'I know what you're thinking. You believe, in the circumstances, that I ought to cool it – don't you?'

She was not sure to which particular set of circumstances he referred. There was the fact of her own almost certain state of terminal illness. There was his father's desertion of his mother, for reasons still unstated; a desertion of which Dom himself had deeply disapproved, and which he must surely have no wish to copy.

'You're talking about leaving her, aren't you?'

'Yes,' he said. 'To be honest, I can't see any other solution.'

He stared down at his clenched fists. 'Tell me,' he said, 'what you think I ought to do.'

She thought about his mercurial temperament, the many previous crises which he and Chantal had managed to survive. She thought about her own present inability to deal with any problem but her own. She knew that at the moment all he really sought was to escape from an intolerable situation. Amy knew what Dom wanted her to say; what he expected of her. She studied the face which was so like that of Michael; the dark colouring, which had been her own contribution. Dom had inherited equally from both parents certain characteristics; no wonder, she thought, that he was confused. She had always loved him in a way which made refusal difficult if not imposs-ible, and yet this time she knew she would deny him. Her need to be quite alone grew more urgent every day. For the first time in her life an overpowering self-interest caused her to turn away from her beloved son. The decision had already been made in the part of her mind that dispensed with reason.

'I want you to go back to Chantal,' she said. 'I want you to cool it.'

Dom had not been easily persuaded to depart; she had watched him toss socks and shirts into a holdall. Time was when she would, before he left, have washed and ironed his soiled clothing, but now she had neither the energy nor the inclination. He promised to phone her at breakfast and lunch times. Chris was to visit every evening. Lali would come on her off-duty days. She wondered if they knew something which she did not.

Warm sunshine slanted down across the sunbed. The clematis which she had thought lost to winter frost was putting forth late, but large dark-purple blooms. The old brick walls which gave shelter on three sides of the garden were almost hidden at this time of year by the climbers which Michael and she had planted in the first years of their marriage. Honeysuckle, jasmine, roses that were budding for a second flowering; a fan-shaped cotoneaster, heavy with red berries. She observed the industry of bees, the varieties of butterflies, the fledgeling birds. She imagined her workroom, the tidiness of it, the shrouded bales of coloured silks; and tears, the old repressed kind, rose in her throat, causing it to ache.

'Do you smoke, Mrs Sheldon?' they had asked her.

'No,' she said. 'I do not. I never did.'

The young men in their white unbuttoned coats beamed their approval. 'Good,' they said, 'very good indeed.' They entered her reply in the appropriate box on the long questionnaire. SMOKING CAUSES CANCER was their collective opinion.

So what about the thing lodged in her throat? What about that, eh? How did they explain it?

'Let me tell you something, doctor. But come closer if you want to hear me, since your scalpel has quietened my voice. Had I but known, dear doctor, that this disease was waiting for me, I would have chain-smoked; puffed away my tensions, learned from Mimi how to blow the perfect smoke-ring (Mimi, who at the age of eighty-seven shows no sign of cancer).

'I would have smoked foul-smelling, black cigarillos, Camels and Woodbines; deposited ash in a million ashtrays. Ground butts beneath my heel. Oh yes, doctor, had I but known, there are many things I would have done. Or not done. When Michael asked me to accompany him on buying trips in Europe I would not have made excuses. Would not have said, "but what about my aunts? They need me, Michael."' That's what she should have replied.

The people in the streets moved quickly in the early mornings. They were young, on their way to offices and schools. Amy strolled, because she was obliged to; she dawdled in St Gilda's Gardens where only the gardeners were to be seen at this early hour, mowing and watering.

The weather continued to be fine and hot. Her belief in the restorative powers of the leisure suit was such that she washed it every evening and wore it every day. In the shopping mall, boutiques were opening their doors. Amy wandered into one which had a SALE notice on its window. The clothes were of the casual kind favoured by Lali. She found a rack of trousers made of pastel-coloured cotton. CAPRI PANTS said the label. HALF PRICE. On another rack hung matching T-shirts and loose cotton jackets. She began to collect sets of these garments in lemon, coral, mint green, white and deep blue.

'Going on holiday, madam?'

'Well, no – not exactly. I want something cool and comfort-able –' Amy leaned against the counter. 'Do you have a chair? I need to sit down. The heat –'

A chair was brought, a glass of water. The girl who had seemed so self-assured looked frightened.

'I hope it's not your heart. A lady of your age died in here last week. I phoned the ambulance, but it was too late.' She saw Amy's scarred throat. 'Oh! Your poor neck. You didn't – ?' The girl was embarrassed. 'But no. Of course you wouldn't?'

'No.' Amy smiled. 'It's not self-inflicted. I had an operation, that's all. I'm getting better every day.'

'You shouldn't go shopping on your own. You're not up to it, anyone can see that. I'm going to phone a taxi for you.'

Amy rose from the chair, walked to the pay desk and offered her cheque card. 'I'm feeling fine now,' she said, 'it was just the heat.' She picked up the processed card and the oversized carrier bag. 'Thank you for being so kind.'

'You shouldn't be out on your own,' the girl repeated, 'really you shouldn't!'

Normality was what she wanted; just to turn the clock back, to be as she had been, feel as she had felt, a year ago, a month ago. Before the first hospital appointment, the scan, the operation.

The concern of strangers touched and unnerved her, robbed her of control, placed her among the needy, the disadvantaged. She upended the carrier bag on to the bedspread. Away from the boutique, the inexpensive cotton garments no longer pleased her, and there were so many of them. She stuffed them back into the carrier bag and thrust the whole mistaken purchase into the guest-room wardrobe.

She was in the kitchen when he came. She stood at the counter chopping lettuce and cucumber, beetroot and tomato. She wiped her fingers on a paper towel, opened the door and let the doctor in.

He sat on the chesterfield, and she faced him from the wing chair. He was not smiling this time.

'Good news and bad news,' he said. He had phoned the histology department as promised. The good news was that the hospital doctors said that she was not to worry. 'But,' he went on, 'they found some cancerous cells.'

'What now?' she asked him.

'A hospital appointment to discuss what further treatment you may need.'

'And what might that be?'

He could not tell her. He offered her any help that it was in his capacity to give, but she could think of nothing useful he might do.

'What were you doing when I came?' he asked.

'Making a salad for my lunch.'

'What will you do for the rest of the day?'

'Lie on the sunbed, I expect.'

'You will want to think about this.'

'Yes.' She could see that she was not supposed to take this news so calmly.

He repeated, in case she had not understood, 'It was not benign.'

She longed to reassure him, to say, 'Don't worry, doctor. I won't cut my throat because you brought me bad news. It's been done already; and by experts.' But black humour belonged back in Ward Forty-Seven. And perhaps, so did she.

The half-prepared salad no longer looked appetizing. Amy made a mug of strong sweet tea and carried it into the garden. The branches of the pear tree cast shade across the sunbed; she sipped the tea very slowly and examined the blank spaces of her mind.

'You will want to think about this,' the doctor had said. But there was, in fact, hardly anything to think about. She had done all that before the operation. If they had told her that the tumour was benign, she would never have believed them.

For reasons she did not understand, it was easier to tell bad news to Dom than to her other children. At five o'clock she dialled his number. She said, 'The doctor came today. He told me it was cancer.'

Dom did not answer straight away. When he spoke his tone was quiet. 'I'll be over in an hour.'

'No,' she said. 'That's not why I called you. There's no need for you to come. I'm perfectly all right – it just seemed that I ought to tell somebody –'

'I'm coming,' he said.

Dom sat beside her on the sofa. He held her hand. He said that the worst was surely over, the tumour surgically removed; that all she needed now was rest, good food and fresh air. He left her feeling reassured and calm. She made her usual supper of a sandwich and hot chocolate, watched an hour of television, and then slept to dream that Aunty Belle and Mimi had both remarried.

Finbar Sheldon was a sweet man, soft-voiced and shy. As I began to know him better he took the place in my life of the father I did not remember, and of Uncle Ken who had left Aunty Belle one April evening and not returned.

Nobody talked about the baby who had never lived; my still life. Even Mimi and Fin could only, between them, manage a quick hug, a warm pressure of hand on my shoulder. On my return from the hospital Fin led me to the rear of the shop and revealed the warren of storerooms which he had cleared and painted to make a separate home for himself.

'You'll be needing the upstairs to yourselves, you and Michael. No doubt you'll be wanting to make changes. Sure an' it needs a woman's touch up there.'

'How long has Michael lived with you?' I asked him.

'Has he never told you?'

'No.'

Fin sighed as if at the memory of old sorrow. 'He was but a baby when I brought him over. I had no knowledge of caring for small children. Fell down those stairs a dozen times, he did, before I had sense enough to put a gate up.' He smiled. 'But the boy had a hard head.'

'Hard heart, too,' I murmured.

'Ah no! Never that, girl. Soft he is, on the inside. You must remember he was not reared by women. Females make him nervous.'

We were standing in the space which only a month ago had

housed damaged chairs and tables, empty picture frames and boxes filled with antique tools which, one day, might just come in handy for something. The transformation had required more determination and skill than was possessed by either Fin or Michael. I could see Mimi's touch in the draping of a silken Spanish shawl across a sofa, an arrangement of gardenias floating in a black bowl; the long-fringed lampshades and bowls of pot-pourri, the well-brushed velvet of comfortable chairs.

'You've worked a miracle,' I told Fin.

He smiled the deprecating smile that reminded me of Michael. 'Your aunty took a hand in things.'

'I guessed as much.'

It was, I thought, a natural progression of the understanding which had grown up between us, that Fin had not found it necessary to define which one of my aunts was his special friend; and I had not needed to ask.

I had lived the first months of my marriage in Aunty Belle's house. Michael stayed with me at weekends, a barely tolerated house guest. Oh, she was polite, even pleasant to him; but it was clearly understood that this was a temporary arrangement, permissible only because of my unfortunate condition. I felt even more than usually guilty and beholden to her; and yet I still craved her approval, was grateful for her grudging kindness. I needed both her love and that of Mimi, for I was quite sure that Michael Sheldon did not care about me.

The time spent in Aunty Belle's house had been an uneasy occupation, but now it was over. I felt the first stirring of excitement at the thought of my impending freedom, for I knew that my aunt would never set foot across the Sheldon threshold.

The hospital check-up was ordered for the first week of September. Amy laid out the smart green suit and matching strappy sandals; the outfit she had worn when life was normal;

correct wear for a visit to a surgical consultant. She stood for a long time looking at the clothes and remembering the feelings she had experienced when she had last worn them. She reached out a hand, curled a finger around a sandal strap and allowed it to swing in a wide arc. A slow destructive anger began to build somewhere deep inside her. She longed to rip the suit seams, tear out linings, burn every garment and then trample on the ashes. But to do so would be foolish, wasteful; she was not that kind of woman. But what kind of woman was she now? The anger seeped away leaving her weak, unsteady. She sat on the edge of the bed and considered her helplessness. It's quite possible, they had said, that you have had a totally unnecessary operation. The lie had been cruel and superfluous.

She collected the cheap cotton garments from the floor of the spare room wardrobe; she selected the lemon-yellow trousers and top, and the matching yellow jacket. The clothes sat light and easy on her body; she twisted her hair into a coil and fastened it high on her head with a yellow clip.

Dom worked hard at looking unsurprised.

'Laugh if you want to,' she told him, 'all I need now is a lampshade on my head and I'm dressed for working in the paddy-fields of China.'

'You certainly look – well, different. Is this going to be your new style? I thought you were wearing that leisure suit just to humour Lali.'

'I was,' she said, 'in the beginning.'

They sat once again in the red vinyl chairs beside the tea- and coffee-bar. Amy tried to relax, crossed and uncrossed her yellow-trousered legs, pulled the collar of her jacket across the sore and lumpy horror of her neck, and then in a fit of irritation pushed the collar far back to reveal her scar. This was a hospital, wasn't it? All around her people coughed and gasped, limped and passed her by in wheelchairs. To have credibility in this place one needed to be damaged. She remembered the respect gained among fellow patients by the lump before its removal.

The top man was not alone in his consulting room. The junior surgeon was seated side-on to the desk; two other men who were strangers to Amy sat on the far side of the room. The top man beamed on Amy. 'Please sit down,' he said, and then in congratulatory tones, 'you have – or rather, you had, something very rare!'

She waited for him to name her treasure, but he looked down at the records in the file and shuffled them together. 'I'll write it down for you,' he said at last. 'No doubt you will want to read it up.' He pushed a scrap of paper towards her. She read his spiky doctor's script: PAPILLARY CARCIN-OMA OF THE THYROID GLAND. She wondered if he knew that her GP had already passed on the bad news. Once again she felt the anger rise; she wanted to scream, 'Why couldn't you just say it to me? Words got stuck in your throat, did they? Just like the bloody carcinoma was stuck in mine?'

He was speaking again in the self-assured manner she was learning not to trust. 'One-half of your thyroid gland has been removed together with the tumour. You will be given thyroid hormone in tablet form to replace the lack of natural hormone caused by the operation. Radiotherapy is not indicated. I do not, at present, intend to remove the rest of your thyroid gland. But I must warn you that the trouble could recur. Because of this I propose to keep a careful watch on your condition. I shall want to see you again in six weeks.' He leaned back in his chair. 'I have seen,' he said, 'only one other case of thyroid cancer in my surgical experience. Because of this I have taken advice from a surgeon who has himself seen only five previous cases.' Amy picked up the prescription form and the scrap of paper on which were written the words that had changed her life.

'Thank you,' she said. What else was there to say?

To Dom she said, 'Another appointment in six weeks. No further treatment, only tablets.'

She saw the tension leave his face. 'That's great,' he said. 'Nothing much to worry about, is there?'

'No,' she said. 'They're not proposing to operate again, and that was what I feared most of all.'

'I think we ought to celebrate, don't you? Chantal suggested that we might go out for dinner. There's a new place just outside of town. It's quiet and secluded, and they start serving early in the evening. Would you like that?'

'Oh yes,' she said. 'I would love it.'

'Right then! I'll pick you up at seven tomorrow evening.'

Chantal wore designer clothes and narrow shoes of fine Italian leather; much of her time was spent in health clubs where she lay on a sunbed in order to preserve an all-year tan, and performed aerobics to perfect her figure. Her hair was cut and styled by experts; her diet was severe. She submitted regularly to massage, manicures and facials.

Amy, awed by the sophistication of Chantal, put on a skirt of pleated silk and matching jacket, tights and shoes with slender heels. She washed her hair and applied make-up for the first time since the operation. Her body, in the tights and silk suit, felt hot and constricted. When she walked, her shoes pinched.

The restaurant was the kind of new place favoured by Chantal. The tables and chairs were made of wrought-iron, the lighting was dim, the clientele pseudo-smart and loud-voiced. The menu was written in Gothic script on imitation parchment. Amy, to be on the side of safety, chose the poached salmon. Conversation was made difficult by the rowdy six-deep crowd standing at the bar. Chantal spoke exclusively to Amy, said how nice Amy looked, and hadn't she done well! After giving his order to the waiter, Dom made no attempt to join in the conversation. Chantal talked about her friends, all of whom were successful career women referred to respectfully as 'role models' by Dom's partner. Amy's husky, whispered replies were lost in the surrounding din. When the meal was finished it was easy to plead tiredness, to say thank you for the pleasant evening, and ask to be taken home.

She lay awake that night for a long time, and thought about Chantal, who had changed in so many ways since their last meeting. She thought about Dom who had been uncharacteristically silent.

There had been a brittle hardness in Chantal's face, a bitterness that Amy had never previously seen. Did Chantal know that Dom had recently sought sanctuary in his mother's house, and been refused? It was a question which, in times past, would have caused her to pass a sleepless night. Amy switched off the lamp, arranged her head and shoulders carefully upon the pillows; reminded herself that any unwise movement made in sleep would wake her. The troubles of Chantal and Dom were not her business; she had problems of her own. It was almost impossible for her to feel sympathy for them.

She awoke to early morning sunshine, birdsong, and the first thoughts of the day. She had, indisputably, grown without her knowledge a papillary carcinoma of the thyroid, which had been removed but might have already spread to other tissues. The concept of this interloper, this uninvited succubus, made her feel unclean; filled her with such loathing of herself, her body, that she feared she might vomit. She sat on the edge of the bed, dug her fingernails into the mattress, and felt the aching stiffness in her neck. For the first time since the finding of the lump, Amy asked the question: Why? She had never smoked, disliked alcoholic drinks, lived a quiet, uneventful life. There had been no contact with harmful substances, no treatments by X-ray; no bloody reason! She had done nothing in her life which merited such retribution. The surgeon had offered no prognosis, had not promised her a month, six months, a year. The trouble could recur, he had said, I shall keep a careful eye on your condition.

The early-morning café opened at six-thirty. Amy had need to be among the healthy, the whole, the normal people of the world. She sat among commuters, lorry drivers, men who had just finished the night shift in the textile factories. She ate two poached eggs on toast and drank two mugs of milky coffee. From the table by the window she could see the traffic, the street-cleaners, postmen on their rounds. A longing for well-being overwhelmed her; she loathed her convalescent self, the slit and lumpy neck, the way she needed to sit down after only minutes spent in walking, the trembling in her stomach which was fear.

There had always been too much preoccupation with the future, counting down to some self-imposed target. From the café radio Abba sang the line, 'I believe in angels'. Amy recalled Karen of whom the top man had said, 'It will be up to her to fight now.'

How did one fight?

She would really like to know.

'I'll write it down for you,' the top man had said. 'No doubt you will want to read it up.'

Amy went to the city reference library, travelling on a bus because she did not yet trust her ability to drive the car. The study tables were occupied by students; young men and women who wore multicoloured clothes and chewed Mars bars as they filled the pages of their notebooks. Amy, in her turquoise cotton coolie's outfit, did not feel as out of place as she might have in her former tailored glory. She found a vacant seat and sat down for several minutes before approaching the Medical–Surgical shelves.

Information on the subject of thyroid carcinoma was almost as rare as the disease; she had trawled through many volumes of learned works by eminent men before dredging up the kind of information she really did not want to know. She wrote in her notebook:

The condition is a rare one, which occurs annually in thirty persons per million of the population. Of those thirty, six people per million die annually of the disease. Little or nothing is known about the causes of thyroid cancer, although, after the dropping of the atom bomb on Hiroshima and Nagasaki, many hundreds of Japanese died of this disease. Papillary carcinoma is slow growing and may metastasize to bones and lungs. Survival rate among eighty per cent of sufferers can be as long as ten years.

In the days that followed her library visit, Amy tried to estimate her chances of survival. Since she was not Japanese, the cause of her affliction must remain unknown. When in hopeful mood she expected to be among the twenty-four patients per million of the population who survived yearly, rather than the unfortunate six who did not.

As for the eighty per cent who lived on for as long as ten years, where did the counting start? Since her cancer was said to be slow growing, how long before diagnosis had it been with her? Let's say, she reasoned, for argument's sake, that it had been present for four years. Assuming that she was among the lucky ones, that estimate would give her a possible further six years of life. It was not enough. It was never, however long the prognosis, going to be enough. That was the trouble with setting limits; if they had quoted a survival rate of fifteen years she would have wanted twenty.

She began to think about survival, of being single-minded, battening down hatches; about wanting desperately to hold on to a life which, until threatened with its loss, had held little value for her. She had tried not to think about Aunty Belle and Mimi, who failed to phone or visit since learning of her illness. Amy thought about them now, about their long lives and invariable good health. They would, she was sure, live to be a hundred, receive telegrams from the Queen and be interviewed upon their birthdays by local newspaper reporters.

'And to what do you attribute your great age?' they would be asked.

Aunty Belle would speak smugly of early bedtimes and regular bowel movements. Mimi would smile, blow a smoke ring and say that she had never denied herself anything that she really fancied.

When Lali asked, 'Have you heard yet from the aunties?' Amy had lied. 'Oh yes – they call up regularly.' She felt shamed by their neglect of her, and yet she understood it. She remembered other times when her troubles threatened to disturb their uneventful days; the way they would close ranks against her, deny all knowledge of her anguish. Protect themselves: be selfish. Amy felt uneasy at this new insight of them, and yet it could not be denied. It was the selfish people of the world who were the great survivors, the ones who said, 'Don't cry. You know it only upsets *me*.'

In mid-September a letter arrived from the top man. After further consultation with a colleague he had decided that Amy should have an ultrasound scan and an isotope test performed upon her neck. These tests were to be carried out some time in October.

The autumn days were mild and windless. Amy walked in the early mornings in St Gilda's Gardens; she sat in a white chair on the café patio, drank lemon tea, and watched the imprisoned aviary birds. She thought about Aunty Belle and Mimi, both of whom had abandoned her; about her children who showed her undeserved devotion. About Michael, who remained characteristically silent. Depression hovered, in a small grey cloud just above her head; when she moved it stayed with her, there was no way to outrun it, to escape back into a normal world, to the time before cancer. Her physical condition improved daily: her voice was stronger, she swallowed without pain, her legs no longer ached after ten minutes' walking, her appetite returned. Even Lali was bound to admit that, six weeks after surgery, her mother was no longer convalescent. So why did she leave her house in the very early morning, to return only when forced to by exhaustion? Why did her moods swing so violently between inertia and anger? There would be precious little to be gained in beating cancer if she should end up in a psychiatric ward, having lost her mind. But there was, of course, no way of beating cancer. Amy had read magazine articles, newspaper reports, heard friends and relatives talk about the subject. No matter what you did, it got you in the end. And what could anybody do? Even the experts could only lop off some bits, irradiate others, or stuff patients full of drugs which eventually killed them.

She could do something about the garden. The thought surprised her; she retreated at once into convalescent mode. Supposing she felt ill while working? But how would she know what could happen if she never tried? That evening she telephoned the garden centre, and asked them to deliver compost and an assortment of spring-flowering bulbs. On the first day of October Amy, wearing old clothes and gardening gloves, washed her garden furniture and stored it in the garage. She cut down overhanging creepers, pruned the roses, filled the tubs and borders with fresh compost. The packets of assorted bulbs contained highly coloured pictures of their contents when in full flower. For the first time since August she permitted expectations, allowed her mind to envisage Russian Snowdrops, Giant Crocus, Chinese Daffodils, Chinodoxa, Dwarf Tulips striped in red and yellow. She planted the bulbs and then fetched water and a stiff broom. It was not until she had scrubbed down the terrace paving that exhaustion overcame her. A hot bath, supper on a tray in bed, and she slept for a full eleven hours.

Chris came to see her on Monday evenings, Lali dropped by on a Wednesday. Dom was liable to arrive on either Saturday or Sunday, at times when he might reasonably have been expected to be with Chantal. With Chris, Amy talked on many subjects; they sat quietly together and his presence soothed her. He never spoke about Camella, and Amy asked no questions. With Lali she went shopping; they had tea in a café, but never, she noted, in the Copper Kettle, which was obviously still the special meeting place of Lali and Michael.

The ultrasound scan was performed in the City hospital. The remaining half of her thyroid gland was monitored by a silent young woman who wrote up her findings in red ink. The isotope test involved an iodine-laced drink, and a lengthy session before a porthole-shaped machine. Amy had not told her children of either appointment. It was time to stand on her own feet; keep her own counsel. She walked away from the hospital, her mind as deliberately blank as she had planned it would be. When she reached St Gilda's Gardens her energy failed. The day was mild and still, the skies overcast yet with a hint of sunlight about to break through. The white chairs and tables stood on the café patio. Amy ordered lemon tea and honey-and-oatmeal biscuits. She thought about the people who were no longer in her life; about Michael and Aunty Belle and Mimi. For a few insane seconds her mind tipped and lurched. Could it be, she wondered, that they are all dead and nobody has told me? Or is it I who am dead and have not yet realized it? She sipped the tea and broke the biscuits into tiny pieces. Her careful calm was shattered. She saw again the operator of the ultrasound machine, her empty face turned deliberately away from Amy, her stubby fingers writing up results. In red ink.

Amy felt the terror in her stomach muscles. Back in the house, she telephoned her GP. 'I want to see a specialist who knows about thyroid cancer,' she told him. 'I need a second opinion, and I need it very quickly.'

'I'll contact your surgeon,' he said. 'I'm sure he'll be perfectly happy for you to see another consultant. I'll phone him today.'

Days passed, became weeks – three weeks to be exact – and

no word had come from the top man. Amy phoned his secretary who denied all knowledge of her request for a further consultation. The top man, she said, was away on holiday but would return to his office on the following Monday. Amy's request would be mentioned to him.

Amy cradled the receiver, leaned back in her chair, and was conscious of the first flicker of a really consuming rage. She recalled the days before the operation; the almost frenetic keenness of doctors to get her on to the operating table.

'Get that lump removed from your neck,' one had said, 'before it kills you.' There had been urgent appointments, strong persuasion towards surgery. Having stapled her together, the medical profession appeared to have lost interest.

Her increasing capacity for anger surprised and alarmed her.

'You're not settled here, are you?' It was Fin's way of asking me if I was happy. He did not, I thought, really need an answer. 'You could,' he went on, 'come downstairs and talk to me. Michael is away on a house-clearance job. He'll be back late.'

'He's always back late,' I muttered, but I went with him down into the shop. I made coffee for the two of us. I prowled the dusty aisles between piled-up furniture, cup in hand.

'There are some really nice pieces here,' I told him, 'if you only took the trouble to display them.'

'We keep the good stuff upstairs, Amy. We've always done it that way.'

Because I was myself in pain, I wanted to hurt him. 'That's just because you and Michael are lazy,' I said. 'My Aunty Belle calls this a junk shop. She says that you're gypsies.'

Fin smiled his sweet smile, and I was instantly ashamed. 'Ah now, she's the smart one, is Belle. Sure, and I reckon we've a few pints of tinker blood between us, me and Michael.'

I said, more to make amends than because I really meant it, 'I could sort things out for you down here.'

'You could? Well, I'd be obliged to you, Amy. But call me when you want things moved. You don't look too strong since – since you came to live here.'

I had moved into Angel Row rather like an excited child who goes to spend a holiday away from parents. But I was soon to discover that my presence in Sheldon Antiques had a feel of impermanence; even the furniture could not be depended upon to remain in place from one day to another. As for Michael, he never talked about feelings, he never spoke about my loss. If he had any thoughts about the haste with which we had married, the subsequent pointlessness of it, he kept them to himself.

I began by taking down the fly-blown notice which offered house clearance and removals. 'I'll get a new one printed,' I promised Fin. I cleaned the glass panes in the wide bow-window. An absorbing hour spent among the stock revealed a seven-piece Victorian sitting-room set; two carved-back sofas, two armchairs, an occasional table, a chiffonier and a foot-stool. I wiped away the dust of years to find glowing mahogany and blue silk brocade.

'Look,' I told Fin. 'It's really beautiful. How could you have left it to get so filthy?'

'Victorian,' he said dismissively, 'nobody will give it a second look.' He sighed. 'People are throwing stuff like this on the town tip.'

In a shed behind the shop I found a square of blue and gold Brussels carpet. Fin helped me to lay it in the cleared area of floor beneath the bow window. We carried the Victorian furniture piece by piece and arranged it tastefully upon the carpet. I hunted for and found several ornaments in shades of blue. 'Tell me, which of these are Victorian?' I asked Fin.

His hand went out to a tall piece of glass in a greenish holder. 'And if you look in the trunk in the storeroom you'll find some bits of Sowerby pressed-glass.'

The Sowerby glass was a collection of little baskets, jugs,

and ornamental dishes. Their colour, when held against sunlight, was the same as wild cornflowers. The greenish holder which held the tall glass appeared, when cleaned, to be hallmarked silver. The glass itself was turquoise shading into palest lemon at its edges. It was, said Fin, called an epergne; a trumpet of flared glass, frilled around its edges, which had been a centrepiece that held flowers on Victorian dinner tables.

Just looking at the epergne gave me pleasure; when I touched it something deep inside me seemed to lift and soar, a physical sensation that I recognized as pure joy. I felt the first stirring of interest in this business of buying and selling which went on around me. Fin said, 'There's some books about glass in the upstairs' bookcase.'

Michael and Fin had imposed a kind of scrubbed, squared-away order on their surroundings. The Room, furnished as it was with beautiful if transient objects, had a bleak aspect.

'It needs a woman's touch,' Fin had said, but I lacked the will to make changes.

I learned many things in those empty months, I became skilled in the concealment of my misery, practised at dissembling when in the company of my aunts. I would have suffered defenestration rather than have them know of Michael's offhand treatment of me. His awful silences. The absences from home when he attended auctions and roamed the country on buying trips, without once inviting me to go with him.

The wide velvet sofas which were also beds stood one at each end of the long room. I collected my pillows and quilt each evening from an oak chest. I had chosen on that night when I returned from hospital to sleep in the bed which had been occupied by Fin. Michael, without comment, had gone to the sofa which had always been his. I waited each night for him to make the move which would prove he loved me, but he did not. There were times when I was tempted to tell Fin, but embarrassment prevented me from speaking on so intimate a subject; especially since he and Mimi, to judge from the sounds which came from Fin's bedroom, had no problem when it came to making love.

The letter from the top man began with an assurance that he had not forgotten about her. An appointment, he said, could be made, if she so wished, with a consultant thyroid surgeon who practised in the North. In the interests of speed, he advised that the consultation should be private.

Amy drove the four miles to the top man's house. On the envelope which held her reply and yet another plea for swift action, she had written in large red letters BY HAND, URGENT. She had only recently and by chance learned the address of the top man. Had she known sooner that he was so accessible, she would have battered down his front door.

She was standing at the exit counter in the library when the words CANCER SELF-HELP GROUP caught her attention. The poster was small, almost indistinguishable among fifty others. Beneath the logo of a yellow sun ringed by orange flames she found two handwritten names and telephone numbers. Later that evening she punched out the number which belonged to someone called Jan. Amy heard her own voice, nervous and staccato, admitting the fact of her cancer as if it were a crime which needed absolution. The answering voice was warm and sympathetic. 'We feel that we have a lot to offer,' Jan said. 'But it would be up to you to take from us what you think you need. We meet on Monday evenings in the James Johnson Community Centre. Why don't you come along next Monday? We'd be so pleased to see you.'

Amy told Chris about the Cancer Self-Help Group. He became enthusiastic in the manner of one who clutches at straws, which astonished Amy since she was sure that her depressed state was well concealed from all with whom she came in contact. Especially her children.

The Johnson Community Centre lay on the far side of St Gilda's Gardens. 'Get your coat,' said Chris. 'I'll walk there with you.'

'No,' she said. 'I've changed my mind. I've been thinking it over. I can't imagine anything more awful than to be suffering oneself from cancer, and to sit in a roomful of people who are similarly afflicted.'

The early November day was mild and golden. Her second appointment with the top man was for late afternoon. She put on the black, tapered slacks and the scarlet duffle coat, recent purchases which made her feel good for the short time that she wore them. She retained the coat in the top man's overheated office, hugging the bright wool around her body against the horror of his message.

'Your isotope test was clear,' he said, 'so that's good news for you, isn't it?'

She waited for the second half of the results, but he stayed silent.

'So what,' she asked, 'about the ultrasound?'

The top man looked nonplussed, although he surely must have known that she would ask. He raised both hands, palms upward, and then lowered them back on to the desktop. It was a gesture which told her everything, without his need to say a single word.

'I want that second opinion,' she said, 'as soon as you can arrange it.'

'You should hear something,' he said, 'within the next week.'

She drove through the dusk of the late afternoon until she found a garden centre. Amy bought several trays of winter-flowering pansies, and four bushes of pink heather; in the morning she planted them in tubs close to the house, in positions where they would be easily visible from her windows when they bloomed.

*

The room in which the Cancer Self-Help Group held their meetings was large and warm. Chairs were arranged in a circle on a plain brown carpet; in the middle of the circle stood a tall, unlit red candle. People stood around in little groups talking and laughing; men and women whose faces were familiar to Amy, people she had seen in cafés and supermarkets, or seated on benches in St Gilda's Gardens. For a moment she thought that, in this building where meetings of all kinds were regularly held, she must have wandered into the wrong room. This surely could not be a gathering of the terminally ill? These jolly people were probably members of the Bridge Club, or the Photographic Society. The candle was probably symbolic of something. She hesitated beside the table which stood just inside the door; on it lay books and cassettes set out in neat rows. She began to study the titles: *A New Approach to Cancer, Love, Peace and Healing, You Can Fight for Your Life*. There were also several books on diet. She peered into one or two, and quickly closed them. Whatever her expectations had been she had not envisaged the quackery of false hope; nor was she prepared for the kind of cynicism which offered nut cutlets and faith healing to cancer victims. She looked again at the books and then at the laughing chattering groups and wondered at their ability for self-delusion. Perhaps, she thought, they were members of some obscure and way-out religious cult; or more simply, patients like herself, no-hopers who were near the end of the line, clutching at any fad which promised cure.

She was almost through the door and out, when a voice said, 'Are you the lady who telephoned me?' Jan's smile was welcoming. She looked quite normal in a leisure suit which, but for its colour blue, was the twin of the one that Amy wore. 'I'm so glad you found us. Did you have very far to come?'

'Well – no. I live just across the Gardens. My son walked here with me. He pushed me through the doors and the main entrance, and then kept watch from the street in case I changed my mind.'

Jan said, 'Why don't you just sit in with us this evening?'

'I don't think so. It's not really my sort of thing. I'm not much of a joiner.' The words trailed behind her as she edged again towards the door.

It was the entry of a tall, very thin man, which prevented her from leaving.

'Ah – Nick!' said Jan. 'This is Amy, the lady who telephoned. Perhaps you could have a word?'

Politeness demanded her acquiescence; Amy walked with Nick to the ring of chairs. He sat down beside her. 'Jan tells me,' he said, 'that you've had thyroid cancer.'

'*Have*,' she corrected him. 'I still *have* thyroid cancer. They were supposed to have removed it all when they operated, but they didn't. I shall have to go through that bloody awful operation yet again, and it could have been avoided.'

It was the first time she had voiced her actual situation; even in her head she had not allowed the words to form. Her anger spilled over on to the man who had forced her into speech. 'I don't know why I'm here,' she said. 'Talking about cancer isn't going to cure it.'

'I'm one of the founder members of this group,' Nick told her. 'We've been meeting for several years; so long, in fact, that some of us have become ex-patients.'

Amy stared down at the brown carpet, at the unlit red candle on its tin tray.

Nick said, so quietly that she barely heard him, 'You don't *have* to die, you know.'

'Oh, but I do.' She spoke between clenched teeth, her fingers interlocked and twisting. 'Everybody dies from this one, some of us sooner rather than later.' She turned upon him the full force of her rage. 'They got it all wrong when they operated on me, and then talked to me as if I was too stupid to work out what they had done. You wouldn't believe the rubbish I've listened to from doctors. One half of my thyroid gland was left in position, and I know there's still more cancer present in it, but nobody is willing to admit it. I get so angry, I want to smash things. And yet at the same time I feel helpless.'

Nick said, 'It's very good that you feel angry.'

'Is it?'

'Why, yes. It means that you haven't lost your ability to fight. As for feeling helpless, there are lots of things that you can do.'

'I can't imagine what.' She paused. 'All I've managed so far is to ask for a second opinion from another surgeon.'

'We believe,' said Nick, 'that cancer appears only when your immune system is weakened. Everything we do in this group is aimed at strengthening that system. We offer healing, relaxation exercises, meditation, advice on diet and vitamin supplements – oh, I know it sounds a lot all at once, but you can take it gradually. Sit in with us this evening, and perhaps we can offer something that you feel will suit you.'

'Thank you,' said Amy. There was nothing else that she could say. They were all so nice to her, so concerned; to leave now would have looked churlish, but her feeling of unease increased.

Nick moved away, and as if this were a signal, voices were stilled, people sat quietly in their chairs. Amy gazed around the circle which contained at least fifty people. A woman moved forward, matches in hand, and bent to light the candle. Her actions were those of one who performed a regular ritual. Amy heard her say, 'This candle, when lit, represents the healing light which will help us all.'

The overhead lights were dimmed and another woman spoke; she asked the assembled group to watch the flame and take it into their hearts; they should then close their eyes and visualize the light growing wider and higher until it filled the whole room. This candle glow, she said, represented the healing power that is within every person's power to summon.

Amy looked at the flame and then closed her eyes. Nothing happened; if there was magic to be felt it had eluded her entirely. The next instruction was that she should grasp the hand held out to her by the stranger on either side, and then experience the flow of healing goodwill which would flow between them. Feeling foolish but compliant she obeyed.

What happened next was so unexpected that she almost cried aloud her shock. Her whole body was suddenly suffused by a charge of energy and heat which made her tremble. Hands were slowly lowered and unclasped; Amy was held and hugged by her immediate neighbours. There followed an exercise in relaxation, and then came a meditation, spoken by the lady who had lit the candle. Amy closed her eyes and attempted to visualize the seashore, the cliffs and sky suggested by the speaker, but she was conscious only of sudden weariness, a longing to be home and solitary.

She left the Group carrying a relaxation tape in one hand and a book entitled *Getting Well Again* in the other.

The seven-piece Victorian sitting-room furniture sold within a week to an American dealer. It was a sale of almost total profit; Fin insisted that one-quarter of the cash belonged to me. He also gave me the Sowerby blue glass and the epergne, which I set out on an ebonized table in The Room. I waited for some sign from Michael that I had done well, but he said nothing.

'Not getting on too well, are you?' Mimi said. 'Fin and I are worried about you.'

'He's hardly ever at home. I cook meals for him that dry up in the oven. When I wake in the morning he's already gone.'

'You have to find ways to please him, Amy. You must have loved each other once.' She believed in love in the way that Aunty Belle believed in camphorated oil for chest colds, and Epsom salts for constipation. I studied Mimi. She sat on my blue sofa, one slim, silk-stockinged leg crossed above the other, her narrow skirt hitched back just that extra inch that made it daring. Everything about her – the tilt of her head, the way she held her coffee cup – exuded what was known in film-stars' terms as sex appeal. Mimi had been born knowing how to please men. There had been many other lovers before Fin.

'Why have you never married?' I asked her.

She shrugged. 'I like variety,' she said. 'I get bored with just the one man.'

'I could never get bored with Michael. Just to look at him still turns my heart over.'

'Then why are the two of you living as if you have not yet been introduced?'

'Because,' I burst out, 'I lost the baby, didn't I? He would never have married me but for the fact that I was pregnant. Now he regrets the whole thing. He's the kind of man who prefers to be single.'

'But he isn't single any more; and even though you lost the baby, Michael *is* still here with you.'

'Oh, that doesn't mean a thing. He lacks the initiative to leave Fin and the safe little life they've made together. Haven't you noticed, Mimi, the way they talk and talk but never actually *do* anything? It's all dreams, and what's going to win the 2.30 race at Epsom. They only stir themselves to make a sale when they're desperate for cash.'

Mimi looked amused. 'Why, Amy,' she said, 'I had no idea there was so much passion in you. You've always been such a quiet little girl. Although Fin did say that you'd bullied him about that Victorian furniture set –'

'And he sold it, didn't he? But for me it would still be mouldering away in a back room.'

An edgy silence fell between us. Mimi said at last, 'It doesn't always do to try to change people, Amy. Fin and Michael are easy-going men, they enjoy life; they don't respond to being organized. They go at their own pace. If you're wise you'll love Michael for the man he is, not the smart alec you would have him be.' She hesitated, recrossed her legs, and regarded me with something close to irritation.

'It's like this,' she said. 'Men are creatures of habit. If Michael isn't sleeping with you, he'll be warming some other girl's bed. He's an attractive fellow. So you'd better make an effort, Amy.'

I had believed that I was making all the effort which was needed to please Michael. I vacuumed and polished, cooked his favourite meals, washed and ironed his exclusive clothing. I was always present when he decided to come home. If few words and no loving passed between us, it was hardly my fault. As Mimi would say, it takes two to tango. I opened the cupboard which held the layette I had made for Annis. There was a hand-knitted shawl delicate as cobwebs, white woollen garments, six of every kind; bootees and mittens, embroidered pillowcases; an ivory and silver teething-ring and rattle, given me by Fin. I found a cardboard carton in a kitchen cupboard and lined it with tissue paper; into it I packed the layette and pushed the box towards Mimi.

'Hand this into the Salvation Army on your way home,' I said.

'But won't you need –?'

'No,' I told her. 'These clothes were made for a particular baby. I shall keep only the rattle and teething-ring.'

'Well, I should hope you would,' said Mimi. 'Those things were bought for him by Michael's parents.'

I sometimes thought that my life was like a book from which many of the more interesting early pages had been torn. It occurred to me now that Michael and I were similarly disadvantaged. Although he, at least, had once been sufficiently loved to have been bought a teething-ring and rattle. On my sixteenth birthday, Aunty Belle had handed me some photograph albums, which, she said, contained photos of my mother and father, and myself as a small child. At the time, I had put the albums away unopened into a bureau drawer. When I moved into Angel Row I brought the albums with me. If Annis had lived I would perhaps have been sufficiently curious about the past to look at those ghosts from my other life. As it was, I regarded those albums with a degree of fear I did not wish to think about.

Mimi said, 'It's Michael's birthday next week. Why don't you do something special for him?'

She had gathered around her a barricade of small and pleasurable indulgences against depression. To the sporty duffle coat she now added red leather boots; she breakfasted late in the Patio Café, took long walks through unfamiliar areas of the city, and rarely visited Belle and Mimi.

The depression was deepest in the early morning. It was as though during sleep her mind disowned all memory of cancer, and each awakening required of her a brand-new acceptance of her situation. She would think about her workroom, the bales of silk and lace, the spools of pastel-shaded thread; but the door which led up to the attic room remained closed, leaving her in a limbo of idle days, and nights in which she slept only lightly, and to dream of Michael.

Lali questioned her about the Cancer Self-Help Group. Amy said, 'It wasn't a bit as I expected it would be. I thought, well, it seemed likely that people would sit around and bemoan their fate – you know, commiserate with one another, compare symptoms and treatments, tell horror stories about their operations, but they didn't.' She paused. 'Have you heard of something called holistic medicine?'

Lali nodded.

'Well, it seems that this is what they're about. They teach relaxation and meditation, and healthy diet. They offered me healing, but I didn't fancy it.'

'That sounds harmless enough, but why didn't you accept the healing?'

'Well, for one thing, I'm not religious. I don't believe in that sort of thing. They sort of hover and move their hands. I felt uncomfortable just watching.'

Amy pushed away her cooling coffee. She stood up and began to roam about the kitchen. She adjusted the window blind and refilled the kettle. She said, 'There's something else. They call it visualization. It involves imagining one's cancer, picturing it in one's mind and then, by an effort of will, sort of magicking it away.'

Amy cleared the drainer of clean dishes, slamming cup and plates into a cupboard, crashing cutlery into drawer. 'I might as well join a coven. Take up witchcraft. You must admit, Lal, the whole thing sounds absolutely crackpot.'

The letter arrived on a Thursday morning. The appointment was for the following Thursday at a private clinic, which was situated on the outskirts of Sheffield. The consultant surgeon was Mr D.A. Rhys-Jones. Dom had said that he would drive her up there.

'You must be relieved,' he said, 'now that things are moving?'

'Oh, I am. I'll be glad to know – one way or the other.'

Dom stood in the middle of the room; she saw a tiny muscle move above his jaw. 'I want – we want – Chris and Lal and me – we want you to know that whatever happens we'll look after you. You know that, don't you?'

'Yes,' she said. 'I know that.' But she had not known it; would never have presumed to lay her illness on them. Suddenly she needed urgently to talk to someone who was not a son or daughter; some disinterested party to whom she could voice the unspeakable thoughts that were in her head.

On Monday evening Amy walked again the short distance to the James Johnson Community Centre. She sought out Jan. 'My consultant's appointment is for Thursday. In Sheffield.'

Jan held both of Amy's cold hands. 'That's good,' she said. 'You need to get things sorted out.'

'I know. But I'm terrified of what he'll say. I don't think I can bear another operation. I know there's more cancer in my neck. I can sense it; I don't need to go to Sheffield and pay for the consultant's verdict.'

'But you will, won't you?' Jan said quietly. 'Because if you don't there'll be no peace of mind. Unless you know the truth you can't face up to cancer. And unless you face it – you can't fight it.' She smiled. 'We're here to help you. But you have to want our help.' She paused. 'Would you like to have a healing this time?' Amy raised both her hands in refusal as if fending off a blow. 'No,' she said awkwardly. 'No. Thank you.'

They set out for Sheffield in cold and cloudy weather. The motorway drive was swift and boring. Dom chose to leave the car in a city-centre multi-storey car park; he then collected maps from a Tourist Information Centre. They lunched on giant Yorkshire puddings filled with hot-pot, a speciality of this northern city. Amy studied the street map. She said, 'I have this feeling that I'll be seeing quite a lot of Sheffield in the future.'

The clinic was so exclusive that, in spite of the map, they could not find it. After driving twice down the same road, Dom finally saw a small discreet board almost hidden by laurel bushes and set high among trees. The approach was along a narrow winding driveway at the end of which stood a large old stone-built house to which modern wings had recently been added.

The décor was all blues and greys with a touch of pink. The carpets were thick, the lighting discreet; the atmosphere of hushed luxuriance was a long way from the shabby reds and greens of her local Outpatients Department. Even so, the overheated waiting room was full of people. Amy still waited thirty minutes longer than her scheduled appointment. She rifled through the glossy magazines, memorized the colours of dried-flower arrangements on the waiting-room window sills; made a covert study of the other patients. Like her, the women were dressed in their Sunday-best, tastefully smart, visiting-the-consultant's-office outfits. Amy's hand had hesitated over the scarlet duffle coat and matching boots, but she had chosen in the end a tailored skirt and jacket of navy blue, and a high-necked scar-concealing cream blouse. When her name was called she stood up on legs so weak and trembling that she doubted her ability to walk.

The consultant was tall and thin, dark-haired and hand-some. Just old enough to know what he was doing, but not so old that he would be out of touch with modern medical procedures. He was pleasant, friendly; very concerned. He told her at once that a second operation would have to be performed and the remaining half of her thyroid gland re-moved. She could tell by the repressed anger in his voice that he believed the whole gland should have been excised last August. He had requested her histology reports from the southern hospital, but had not yet received them. From the notes which had arrived, he suspected that her pathology results were incorrect and not in her favour. He would not be making any final decision about her future treatment until after conferring with an histology professor. Amy's name was to be placed on the 'soon' list of a Sheffield city hospital. He said that time would now be a vital factor in the eventual outcome of her illness. Her present dosage of thyroid replace-ment was too low, and he increased it. He invited Amy to ask him any question she so wished. There seemed to be nothing useful that she could ask.

They drove back down the narrow driveway through heavy rain and fading light. She reported the surgeon's words to Dom, rephrasing and diluting so as to minimize their dramatic impact. Even so, Dom swore softly and then struck hard at the steering-wheel with his clenched fist. They travelled in silence for a long time; he pulled into a motorway services' restaurant and they sat over tea, and coffee gateau, and tried to gather their separate thoughts. Dom gripped her hand across the table; there was nothing to say.

*

Visits to Aunty Belle and Mimi needed, since the illness, to be impromptu; if Amy had given thought to what might happen on these occasions she would have driven at speed in the opposite direction, away from The Avenue and the net-shrouded windows of their house. She rang the doorbell, hammered on the iron knocker, but no one answered. As she began to walk away, the front door opened and Mimi said, 'Oh, it's you. You'd better come in.' She preceded Amy down the tiled hall, shuffling in blue-plush slippers, white hair now showing through the henna. 'We're in the kitchen,' Mimi said. 'It's warmer in there. Something's gone wrong with the central heating.'

Aunty Belle sat in a small low armchair beside the boiler. One yellow knitted shawl was draped around her shoulders, another in pink was swathed about her right hand and forearm. She stared accusingly at Amy. 'Well, you can see the state I'm in, can't you! I don't know what I have done to deserve this.' She unwrapped the hand, carefully and slowly to reveal a swollen wrist and puffy fingers.

'It's your arthritis, surely,' Amy said.

'And how do you know that? You're not a doctor. It could be something else.'

Amy said, 'Are you taking your tablets?'

Mimi said, 'She doesn't always take them. She tries to make the prescription last as long as possible these days.'

'You do know,' said Amy, 'that you can have help in the house? The Social Services will arrange it for you. They will also do your shopping.'

'I've told you before,' said Aunty Belle, 'I won't have stran-gers in my home. And anyway, they are very expensive and do next to nothing.'

Amy said, 'I need another operation. As soon as possible. I shall have to go to Sheffield this time.'

Aunty Belle reached for her handbag. She opened her purse with the good left hand, fumbled for and found the television rental card, and placed both card and money on the table. 'You can pay this bill for me on your way home.'

The room was lit only by the amber glow of street lamps. Against the indigo sky of late November a pair of rockets, left over from some child's bonfire party, arced high above trees and then fell to earth in a cascade of golden stars. Amy felt the pressure of Jan's hands upon her shoulders and she tried to relax the stiffness in her neck and limbs. Too much tension, they said, would negate the healing power, deflect its purpose. Amy willed her body to be receptive, to accept whatever it was the healer had to offer. Or perhaps there were no miracles, but only the comfort experienced when the sick are tended lovingly by the healthy?

The pressure lifted from her shoulders; she felt a light touch on the crown of her head. Amy closed her eyes and the lowered lids caused unshed tears to roll slowly down her cheeks. A warmth which increased to a great heat began in the middle of her chest and spread slowly through her body. In her mind she saw again the rockets as they burst against the night sky. It seemed to Amy that the shower of golden stars now fell directly from Jan's fingers on to the cancer which was growing in her neck. And this was faith, which could, she tried to believe, if total, cause the growth to shrink and eventually depart.

The phone rang very early in the morning. Dom said, 'Hope I didn't wake you?'

'No,' she said, 'I was in the kitchen waiting for the kettle to boil.'

'I was wondering,' he said, 'if you would like a drive out into the country. We could have a pub lunch.' He paused. 'I need to talk to you.'

'Yes,' she said. 'That would be nice.'

She heard the relieved note in his voice. 'Good,' he said, 'I'll pick you up at nine.'

The woodlands had been crowded in summer with school parties which followed nature trails and picnickers who played transistor radios beneath the trees. In December only dedicated walkers trod the fallen leaves of autumn. The air was cold; rags and tatters of grey cloud hung just above the hilltops.

On the drive from town she and Dom had avoided the direct look; their speech had been inconsequential. As they began to walk Amy pulled up the duffle-coat hood and bent her cowled head into the wind. Dom lagged a step or two behind her; now that the moment had come she sensed his reluctance to begin.

She said, 'I can guess what you have to tell me.'

'I'm sorry,' he said. 'Sorry as hell. I tried to do what you asked, to cool it, I really did, but there's no hope left. I've reached my limits, and beyond.'

The agony in his voice alarmed her. She halted on the path, caught at his arm and turned him around to face her. She saw the drawn greyness of his features, his defeated aspect, and could not believe that this was Dom, who had never in his life allowed anything or anyone to down him.

She whispered, 'It's that bad, is it?'

'If I don't get away from her something terrible is going to happen. We're destroying one another. I can't bear to be near her any more – not that it's a problem these days – she hardly ever comes home.'

They began to walk again. Dom said, 'I know this isn't fair of me, dumping my troubles on to you. But there's nobody else that I can talk to.'

'Don't apologize. You were there for me when I needed you. In fact, I couldn't have got through these past few months without you.' She turned again to face him. 'Are you sure it's as hopeless as you say? Have you tried talking to her?'

'Look – a lot has happened in the past few years between Chantal and me. Those holidays: Tenerife, the Algarve, the walking holiday in Wales – they were all meant to heal the rift. We came home each time resolved to make a fresh start. But the underlying problems were never solved. I've accepted now that they never will be.'

'You didn't tell me any of this. When I saw you together you seemed to be content. If I had known that you were so very unhappy –'

'What could you have done?'

'Well, to begin with, I would never have refused to help you last August. I thought it was just another bad spell; the kind that occurs in every relationship.' She smiled, and there was an edge of bitterness in her voice. 'I still have this totally unsupported theory that full and frank discussion can mend the most hopeless situation.'

'But only for other people. Never in your own case.'

'The trouble between your father and me is altogether different.'

They walked in silence to the wood's edge. Dom took the path which led down towards the restaurant. He reached back and grasped Amy's hand and the gesture warmed away the small coldness that his words had caused. Men did not really suffer heartbreak. She had always believed that. Especially young, good-looking men like Dom. They might feel the sting of damaged pride, the fleeting sorrow of a parting. He could soon find another partner; make a new life for himself. He was a man, and men were different.

The restaurant was cosy; a log fire burned in an open grate, pink-shaded lamps cast a glow that encouraged confidences and confessions. They sat in a high-backed settle close to the fire; Amy sipped pineapple juice, Dom drank Bacardi. The warmth of the room had failed to take the greyness from his skin, the heavy sweater could not conceal the thinness of his body.

'For a long time,' he said, 'I believed that all our problems were my fault. Chantal said so, and she can be very convincing when she tries. I couldn't tell you at the time what was happening with us in case you thought badly of me.'

Amy had believed that she knew Dom, could have predicted his reaction to any given situation. She had lived with his explosive rages, his touchy pride, his loyalty to those he cared about, the unexpected sweetness of his smiles. So how could she not have known that he was also vulnerable, so capable of self-doubt, so needy.

'But you no longer believe that all the problems were down to you?'

'No,' he said.

'What changed your mind?'

He looked carefully beyond her, through the window and into the leafless trees. 'I talked to someone. A person whose experience was similar to mine.'

There was a strangeness in his tone and words which brought the coldness back to lie between them. A suspicion she could not bear to contemplate was seeded in her mind.

She said, fear sharpening her words, 'I'm listening now, Dom.'

In times of stress she abandoned the principles of healthy eating advised by the Group. Dom ordered fillet steak, mushrooms, and french fries.

'I'll have the same,' she told the barman.

They cut up meat, speared mushrooms, and then laid down the knives and forks and gazed at one another.

'The first few years were wonderful. Oh, we fought at times, but then who doesn't? She had this way of making me feel good, as if I was the best thing that had ever happened to her. Before I knew what she was up to – she had sort of zoomed in on me. She wanted every minute of my time. She wanted to change me, to make me realize what she called my full potential. She kept asking me how anybody who had spent three years at University could be willing to work as a furniture restorer.'

Amy chewed on a piece of steak but found it difficult to

swallow. Dom pushed the cooling food around the plate but did not eat. We should have ordered sandwiches, thought Amy, and, oh God, I don't want to hear this, but how can I stop him.

'I still can't believe that I was so naive for so long. I really thought she loved me, that all her efforts at improvement were for my sake. I know now that I was just another of her projects. As long as I allowed her to manipulate me she was happy. I tried to explain about Chris and me, and you and Uncle Fin and Dad. I told her how the three of you had built up Sheldon Antiques from a grotty little junk shop to a high-class international business. I described the way it was when Chris and I were little kids, always wanting to be with Dad and Fin among the varnish and the sawdust. She never seemed to hear what I was saying. Over the years I began to recognize the danger signals, and take evading action. A certain set of her mouth, a tone of voice, had me running for cover. It can't possibly go on. If we are to continue living together it has to be on her terms. I feel now as if I'm teetering on the rim of a volcano; one more step and I'll fall into the crater.' He pushed away the plate of cold food. 'I'm also angry. Mad as hell when I think back on all the wasted years. What have I achieved? Nothing that *I* want, that's for sure! A house that's too large and too expensive. A lifestyle that bores me to distraction. Just lately she's begun to lecture me on the delights of Culture – me, with dirty fingernails and varnish stains ingrained into my fingers.' He paused. 'She spends too much time with her parents. It's like she never left them.'

Amy said, 'Would you like to come and stay with me? Just to give yourself a breathing space. Think things over.'

'Yes,' he said. 'I'd like to do that. I won't be any trouble – won't bring any trouble with me – I won't even let her ring your number.' He touched her hand across the table and she was almost reassured. 'It'll take about ten days for me to sort things out, and then I'll be over.' He attempted a smile. 'It'll be like old times. Me and my dirty laundry. Overflowing ashtrays.'

'This person,' said Amy, 'the one you talked to about your problems, the one who had been through a similar experience. What did he advise?'

'He said if I valued my sanity I would leave Chantal. Get out – and stay out. A manipulative woman, he said, especially one who has interfering parents, will destroy a man – if he gives her the opportunity to do so.'

Do something special, Mimi had said. You'd better make an effort, Amy. If he isn't sleeping with you he'll be warming some other girl's bed.

The woman in the travel agent's office found the transaction intriguing and romantic. 'My husband doesn't know about it. It's to be a birthday surprise. A second honeymoon,' I told her. With my share of the profit from the furniture sale I bought two airline tickets and accommodation for five nights in a small and respectable hotel on the edge of dangerous Montmartre. I drew on my Post Office savings to buy two fashionable dresses, one in pink and one in cream, with nipped-in waistlines and full, flowing skirts. I made an appointment to have my hair washed and cut by a proper hairdresser, and bought two expensive lipsticks and three pairs of nylon stockings.

I confided my plans for pleasing Michael to Fin and Mimi, who would, quite predictably, tell him about my wish for a reconciliation. I had no doubt that they would make it clear to him, however obliquely, that he would be wise to accept my offer.

If only Michael could be persuaded to come with me, I was quite sure I would conceive in Paris.

I went down to the workroom on a Wednesday morning at a time when I knew that Fin would be absent for at least two hours, visiting first of all the bookmaker's shop in Vine Street, and then the saloon bar of the Prince of Wales. I walked down the stairs and through the shop as nervously as if I had no right to be there. Now that the time had come I was full of dread, fearing that Michael might reject both my plans and me. I stood in the doorway breathing in the smells of old wood and varnish. He sat on a high stool, the swatch of fair hair flopped across his forehead, his thin shoulders hunched across the workbench, his head bent close to a small carved box. He had not heard me enter. I moved to stand beside him. I looked down at the box which was made of fruitwood and intricately carved.

I said, 'Hello. That's nice,' as if I was a customer and not a person with whom he had once made love. He looked up, taking his time to focus upon me. He said, 'Amy' as if he could barely remember my name.

I spoke very fast. I said, 'I've bought airline tickets to Paris. I've booked a room in an hotel. If you like, you could come with me.'

He said, 'If I refuse, will you go alone? Or perhaps you would rather take Aunty Belle or Mimi with you?'

'I will go with you, or not at all.'

He tapped the box with his index finger. 'In that case,' he said, 'I'm surprised that you haven't booked us into separate rooms.'

I walked away between the rickety three-legged tables and the seatless chairs. I trailed my fingers over their dusty surfaces, and my tears were of chagrin as well as bitter disappointment. He was so sure of himself, so certain that I loved him. I thought about leaving, going back to Aunty Belle, but knew that I could never do that.

I was through the shop and on to the first treads of the stairs when he came up behind me. As I turned towards him he slapped me hard across the face, then he put his arms around me. His hands were gentle now; he touched me in all the places that he knew would make me weak. He swung me up into a clumsy fireman's lift, carried me upstairs and dropped me on to the sofa that was his. He sat down beside me. We faced each other, out of breath and speechless; shocked by the uncharacteristic violence of his behaviour. But when he spoke it was not to apologize. He said, 'I don't know what made me hit you. Yes, I do know. You've been asking for it.' I could hear Mimi's voice inside my head. 'You've almost lost him, Amy.'

I moved closer to him; my hands were gentle, I touched him in all the places that I knew would make him weak. I said, 'Come to Paris with me.'

'I don't know. I'll have to think about it.'

'Come to Paris with me. You owe me that much, Michael.'

April in Paris. Sunshine and showers. Lilac and mimosa. In Montmartre the owners of the glass-fronted cafés were folding back their doors and setting out striped umbrellas, chairs and tables on the pavement. The air was softer, warmer than in London. I wore my pink, full-skirted dress on that first morning. Michael said that I was beautiful, and I believed him. We walked hand-in-hand through narrow winding streets and under trees which were already green. We climbed the steep hill called the Butte and saw the white façade and domes of Sacré Coeur shining against the blue sky. From the basilica steps we took in the floating, misty view of the city.

There were flowers everywhere, and singing birds. The enchantment was subtle but very strong. It affected us both in the same way, at the same time. We were no longer Amy and Michael, but lovers stepped down from a Renoir painting, our inhibitions loosened, our defences vanished.

We were drinking coffee, seated underneath a red umbrella in the Place du Tertre when Michael said, 'What happened to your mother and father?'

It was a question I had learned to sidestep, both at school and in my mind. 'They died,' I said, 'when I was a baby. In an accident. Death was instantaneous. They never suffered.' As I spoke I could see the child that I had been, pale-faced, unsmiling, two thick dark plaits bracketing my face.

'*So why don't I have a mother and a father? Everybody else does.*'

'*Your parents,*' Aunty Belle had said, '*died in an accident when you were a baby. Death was instantaneous. They never suffered.*' *There came a time, when I was older and more persistent, and inclined to demand details, when she grew angry with me. 'Don't be so tiresome, Amy. I've told you all I can. The subject is closed. Do you understand?*'

I said to Michael, 'What happened to your parents?'

'My mother was a harlot. She ran off with a fella who worked on the Dublin ferry. When he found that she'd gone, my father parked my pram outside a pub in Cork Street, and then threw himself off the O'Connell Bridge into the River Liffey. A policeman handed me over to Fin. He brought me to England. We've been together ever since.'

I said, 'At least you know you've got a mother – somewhere.'

His face, warmed by the pink glow from the red umbrella, had, until now, been unusually serene. Now his expression changed; the tense and edgy look that I had seen just before he hit me came back and this time my fear was all for him. When he spoke his voice was quiet, dreamy. 'If she ever came back,' he said, 'if she ever tried to find me, why then, one of us would have to die.'

The hotel on the Rue Blanche was respectable and clean, its interior gloomy with brown varnish and fringed chenille curtains. The room smelled of paraffin from the stoves which provided occasional warmth. There were aspidistras on the window sills, and in the dining-room there was a caged bird which never sang.

The bed had brass rails and a wire-mesh base which sagged

in the middle; the resulting dip in the mattress brought us together more surely than any deliberate word or touch. I found myself thinking about Mimi, who never made plans and was therefore seldom disappointed.

I was happier in Paris than I had any right to be. I discovered that it was possible to admit things in the darkness that would have been unutterable in daylight.

'What were your best things when you were little?' Michael asked.

I stirred in his arms, and opened my eyes to the soft pink glow which reflected from the street. 'The best times,' I said, 'were when I stayed with Archie and Mimi; school holidays mostly, and always at Christmas. Mimi did things that Aunty Belle would never do. She smoked cigarettes in a long jade holder and drank port and lemon. Sometimes she drank Guinness. We never had proper mealtimes in Mimi's house. We ate when we felt hungry; I remember one night when we cooked sausages at midnight. They never made me go to bed. I would fall asleep on the sofa and Archie would carry me upstairs.'

'Was Archie her husband?'

'No. She was never married. She had gentleman friends. Archie was the one who lasted longest. She lived with him until he died.' I paused, remembering Archie. 'He was big and bearlike; very slow and deliberate in all he did and said. He was the most uncomplicated man I ever knew, and he worshipped Mimi. He never said so, but I knew he loved me. We would go shopping on Saturday afternoons, he and I. Aunty Belle said Woolworth's was cheap and nasty, but Archie took me there. He bought me necklaces and bracelets. Mimi found an old jewel box covered in green velvet, which had belonged to my grandmother. I kept my Woolworth's treasures in it. In the evenings we would dance to records on the wind-up gramophone. I knew all the words of those old songs. "Daisy, Daisy, give me your answer do", and "Joshua, Joshua, sweeter than lemon squash, you are".' I laughed at the memory of those days. 'On Sunday evenings Archie read the *News of the World*, aloud. He wasn't a very good reader; sometimes he mispronounced the long words. Mimi loved to hear the bits about divorces, all the scandal. They played a game. They pretended that I was their little girl, and just for the time that I was with them, I pretended too.'

'What happened to him?'

'He owned a haulage business. He was unloading timber when a heavy beam fell across his legs. He was taken into hospital, but there were complications. He died within the week.'

'How did Mimi take it?'

'She behaved as if nothing had happened. After the funeral she came to stay with Aunty Belle and me. I was told that I must never mention Archie's name to Mimi, in case it upset her. So I also behaved as if nothing had happened.'

Michael sat up in bed and reached for his cigarettes and matches. In the blue light of the flame, the angles of his face were pale and sharp. As he moved away from me I felt again that old loss and bewilderment, the swallowed tears. I reached for the burning cigarette and stubbed it in the ashtray. I pulled him down to lie beside me. I put my arms around him.

'Whatever else you do,' I said, 'don't ever leave me.'

We found the figurine on the morning of our last day in Paris. We had not failed to enter and explore every junk shop in Montmartre; Michael had bargained for a few small items, but this piece was different. I could tell by the way he held it, the reverence of his expression. 'What is it?' I asked. He hunched his shoulders in that way he has when holding something precious. He turned the glass over so that I could read the signature etched on its base. *Réné Lalique.*

'Is that good?'

He nodded. He said, 'We have to buy this, Amy. This is our good-luck charm, our new beginning.'

We pooled most of our remaining francs, and Michael bartered and argued with the shopkeeper, speaking his Irish-flavoured French, and using all his charm. When the purchase was made we walked to a café. Sitting in the sunshine, at an outside table, Michael laid aside the sheets of tissue paper to reveal the slender figure of a young girl, one arm slightly raised, her hair flowing loose to touch her waist. I would not have believed that so much beauty could be achieved in the medium of glass. She emerged now from the swathes of tissue, a pale, opalescent beauty, faintly blue in the April sunshine, while in the dimness of the shop she had gleamed a frosty white.

I found it difficult to speak. I touched her with one finger but did not dare to hold her.

Michael said, 'You have a feel for the glass?'

I nodded. I said, 'But this isn't old glass. Not like Fin's Victorian pieces.'

'No. This is art deco. Made in the Lalique factory, maybe thirty years ago. It's going to be worth a lot of money one day.' He paused. 'But that's not why I wanted it so badly.' He picked up the figurine and gently touched her face. 'When we have a daughter, she'll look exactly like this girl. We'll call her Lalique.'

He began to rewrap her, his fingers as gentle as a father who folds a shawl around his child.

I spoke the words I had vowed never to utter. 'You never saw our baby, did you? The nurse said that you didn't want to.'

The glass girl disappeared into a cocoon of tissue paper.

'Let's hope she doesn't break,' he said, 'before we get her back to England.'

'Give me ten days,' Dom had said, 'to put things in order, and then I'll be over.' Three days later, when she came back from a walk during which she had bought stamps and posted a letter, returned her library books and discovered two pink, late-blooming roses in St Gilda's Gardens, she found him sitting in the dining-room, his bags and cases covering the carpet. He had a cold, pinched look although the house was warm. She switched on the gas fire, filled the kettle for tea.

He said, 'I rang but you weren't here. Hope you don't mind my coming early but I couldn't stand another day.'

'It's all right,' she reassured him. 'I'm glad you've come. When you make up your mind to do a difficult thing, it's better not to linger.'

He had stayed with her in the first days of her convalescence, but this time it was different. His fishing-rods and basket now stood in a corner of the garage. He had brought his books and a treasured chess-set carved for him long ago by Fin. The foods preferred by Dom took up separate shelves in her fridge and freezer. The washing machine rumbled throughout one whole day while she caught up with the grubby state of his shirts and jeans. There was little else that she could do to help him.

All he really wanted was to talk, and once begun there seemed no limit to the revelation of his private feelings. Amy had not known that men were capable of so much hurt.

Days would pass during which they spoke only on subjects unconnected with his troubles, and then the pretence that all was now well would see him so finely strung-out that she feared he still might snap. At such times she tried to convince him that it did her positive good to think about his problems rather than her own. She reflected briefly that lack of communication had been one among many of the causes of her unhappy years with Michael. It occurred to her now, seeing Dom's pain, that her husband, before leaving her and after, might have felt similarly distraught.

Lali and Tim were to spend Christmas as usual with Tim's parents. Chris was to fly to Rome to be with Camella. Dom suggested that he and Amy might eat lunch at a restaurant.

They dressed up for the occasion. Amy wore one of her silk dresses. Dom put on a suit which required the wearing of a tie. All around them happy families pulled crackers and wore funny hats.

Dom said, 'I sometimes wonder if things went wrong between Chantal and me because we weren't married. Because we never had children. Chantal said as much in the days before I left her.'

Amy said, 'Marriage lines and babies don't necessarily mean that you'll live happily ever after.'

Dom thought about it. He said, 'I tried at first to do all the things that Chantal wanted. To live up to her expectations. Without saying a single word, she had this knack of making me feel guilty. And then, one day, it came to me that it's really not my function to make the whole world right for other people.'

It poured with rain on the day that we left Paris. The warm damp air enhanced the scents of mimosa and lilac. Michael held my hand at take-off and landing. In this week, every hour of which had been lived exclusively in one another's company, Michael's curious containment had been breached. His heart and mind were opened to me; his body became sweetly and achingly familiar. Our Lalique girl was packed safely between his pyjamas, socks and shirts.

The rain travelled with us into London, but the primrose glow persisted. We climbed the stairs up to The Room, still talking and laughing, still touching. We unpacked our cases. I laid the gifts we had bought for Aunty Belle, Fin and Mimi on the sofa which had once been my bed. Michael unwrapped the Lalique figurine. He cleared the top shelf of a glass-fronted cabinet and set her gently inside. I said, 'Won't she be lonely in there, all by herself?'

He looked surprised. 'No,' he said. 'How could she be lonely when she has us to love her?'

I paused before a mirror, saw my face, and thought how easily happiness had transformed me. Michael came and stood behind me, he pulled me close against him; he nuzzled my ear. He said, 'Come to bed, Amy.'

I became very still. 'What – right now?'

'Why not?'

'It's the middle of the afternoon.'

'It didn't bother you in Paris.'

I looked at our reflected faces; his fair head bent above my dark one, the tenderness of his expression, the panic of my own. I knew that I was going to fail him, but there was nothing to be done about it. I could not possibly please everybody. I moved out of his embrace. I said, 'I promised to go round to Aunty Belle and Mimi. I said I'd go the very minute we got back. Well, you know how they are. They believe that flying is dangerous. They'll be worrying about us.'

He turned away. He stood before the cabinet and gazed at the Lalique girl. He said, '*I'm* worried about us, Amy.'

'There's no need. It's just, well, I hate to disappoint them. They'll have worked out the time our flight got in and how long it takes for us to drive home.'

What I could not admit was my longing for Mimi to see me now, still looking pretty in the pink dress. I had been such a plain little girl, and Mimi was always so attractive, so chic. I had also not bent easily to the will of Aunty Belle; but that was before I learned that disobedience was followed, inevitably, by guilt. I once dreamed of achieving the single admirable feat that would have deserved their unqualified approval. But my baby had been stillborn.

Two days into the new year and the telephone rang. The caller identified himself as the consultant she had visited in Sheffield. He said, 'I now have all the information from your previous doctor.' He paused. 'I must impress upon you that what we are dealing with is not a life or death situation. But your histology tests show a tumour which tends to be at the aggressive end of the spectrum.'

'Yes,' she said. 'I understand. I'll come into hospital as soon as you can give me a date.'

The letter from the Sheffield hospital arrived on the first of February. Her date of admittance was to be the twelfth. She drove out to the village pub and sat in the high-backed settle beside the log fire. Today the bar was busy; the jodhpur crowd were in. She had noted their Land Rovers and horseboxes in the car park. The laughter at the bar was loud.

A white mist shrouded the vista of trees seen from the pub window; it leached colour from the day, making the familiar view seem strange and eerily romantic. Amy tried to visualize her cancer, to summon up the power of her will which could perhaps make the tumour shrink and go away. She had, until now, imagined the rogue cells as being unwelcome, sinister; but not immediately fatal. Since the phone call from her new consultant she had been obliged to revise her estimation of the danger. 'Aggressive' was the word he used, and Amy thought how strange it was that her personal invaders should possess so strongly the very characteristic which she herself had always lacked.

A mild and rainy morning; February weather. Dom's car, vacuumed and polished, stood before the front door, her holdall already in the boot. The tension she experienced was slight, but still it betrayed her through small repetitive actions. Twice she adjusted the thermostat on the central heating unit. Three times she checked the contents of the freezer. She reviewed the neat stacks of pressed shirts in the airing cupboard, the folded sweaters and rolled socks. She counted the spare toilet rolls in the bathroom cupboard, tested the locks on the windows of the house. She had not this time reassessed the carefully packed holdall, or visited her redundant workroom. Those had been her last year's rituals before departure for the hospital. To repeat them now would bring bad luck. She wore a new cream leisure suit. A filmy scarf of brilliant colours concealed the thick scar on her neck. Her hair had been shorn, cut short at back and sides, left longer and curling on the top. Lali liked the new style. Amy said that shorter hair would be easier to manage, cooler in the overheated ward.

Twenty minutes down the motorway which led to Sheffield the front right tyre blew. For a second or two the car slewed dangerously sideways, and then they were safely on to the hard shoulder. Dom changed the wheel, working calmly and swiftly, remembering at intervals to give her a reassuring smile. They called at the next service station. She ordered coffee and doughnuts, while he washed his oily hands. She remembered last summer, her delaying tactic on that other journey; the coffee they had drunk from flower-painted mugs. Back on the motorway they travelled for miles in companionable silence, and then Dom said, 'How was last night's meeting?'

'Good. Very good.' She glanced sideways, studied his firm chin and broad forehead, the pronounced nose that was a legacy from his Irish forebears, the deepset eyes. She could never tell him how it had really been. How to explain the inexplicable to someone who was young and strong, and quite untouched by fear of illness and of dying.

She recalled last evening's walk through the rainy street, entering the foyer of the James Johnson building, passing through the room where the Bridge Club sat in groups of four at little tables. Their faces were deadpan or frowning, their concentration total, the silence awesome. The world could end, she thought, at this precise moment, and this group would perish thinking only of their next bid.

She walked up the stairs and paused in the familiar doorway. The meeting this evening was a large one. Diana had just lit the candle which represented healing light. As Amy entered and took her place among them, she stood for a moment, and a great wave of warmth, of concerned love, rolled towards her. They were sending her their courage; which then became her courage. Without their support she might not even have dared to contemplate a second operation; and ten weeks ago they had all been strangers.

Their little ceremony began. They were bidden by Joyce to link hands and concentrate all their attention on the candle flame. 'Imagine it grown tall and wide,' she said, 'until it fills the room; and then take that warmth and light into your hearts, that healing warmth and light which is there for all of us if we care to take it. Close your eyes. Feel the love and strength of the Group all around you. We are here to help one another.'

Amy closed her eyes. She saw the candle glow grow huge and bright behind her eyelids. She felt a surge of energy and power pass through her body. Intellect informed her that this could not possibly be so. But what had intellect to do with healing? She had come here as a sceptic, and had stayed just long enough to become a believer, forever grateful to Chris who had pushed her through the entrance door on that first evening.

Joyce said, 'When you feel ready, give the hands you are holding a little squeeze. Then open your eyes slowly and give the person on either side of you a big hug.'

The hugging had not come easily to Amy, who was not, nor ever had been, enthusiastic when it came to cuddling anyone older than nine or ten years. Her initial embraces of her neighbours had been tentative, unwilling. She had learned at successive meetings that some unique and quite distinctive emanations came from different members of the Group. She loosened her hands' grip and turned towards Kathleen whose touch conveyed, bewilderingly, a steely strength overlaid with comfort. Gill's thin body, on the other hand, communicated a powerful sense of purpose, a terrifying will towards survival.

Amy thought about Gill in the night hours when she could

not sleep. She wondered how it must feel to be fighting cancer for a fourth time; and this one was pretty bad; the chemotherapy was already causing hair loss, which would soon be total. But Gill, the lecturer, had so far missed only one attendance at her college. Her voice, when she told them about her treatment, still held its delicious underlying chuckle; for Gill even horror had its humour.

She told the Group about last weekend's surprise party planned for her husband's birthday. How she had driven after dark to a secret hiding-place, the back seat of her car packed with trays of food. She had come up to a set of recently installed traffic lights, and was forced to brake hard at an unexpected red. Salmon mayonnaise had slithered over trifle and vol-au-vents. The party, said Gill, had been a great success, the surprise as complete as she had intended. 'Bill has had so much to cope with,' Gill said. 'He's done so much for me. I just wanted to do something in return.'

Amy said to Dom, 'Does your father know that I'm going into hospital again?'

'Lali might have told him.'

There was a note in his voice, a hesitancy she had never heard before. She said, 'You and Chris – you're on good terms with him, aren't you?'

'It's difficult for us. We're in the furniture-restoring business. Dad is an antiques dealer. He puts a lot of work our way. It doesn't mean that –'

'I'm very glad,' she interrupted. 'I never wanted you and Chris to be involved in my trouble with your father. It's right that you should see him, talk to him.'

Dom said, 'I wish that you and –'

'Don't! Don't wish anything for me at this particular moment. Life itself will do me very nicely, to be going on with!'

The hospital stood on a hill. From the approach road she could see the façade of the great grey building. Tier upon tier of elliptically shaped windows faced directly eastward to give an uninterrupted view of the high moors and heathland of this part of Yorkshire.

Dom drove slowly, his head inclined forward to read the blue and white signposts. The car parks were full. He drove into an area that was clearly designated for doctors and consultants. He left the car beneath a sign which promised, in foot-high yellow letters, that all illegally parked vehicles would be immediately clamped.

Ward J was on the tenth floor. They walked through a carpeted hotel-like foyer which contained a newsagent and a flower-shop. Amy gave her name and that of her consultant to the lady in Reception. A lift carried them upwards; in the corridor that led towards Ward J, Amy saw a door which bore the words THYROID CLINIC.

The wards were small and open-plan; four beds to each bay, a semi-circle of comfortable armchairs, a table and chairs at which meals could be eaten; and flowers, beautiful arrangements in vases and in baskets. Her bed was positioned beside the window. Seen from the inside of the building the vast expanse of glass took up the space of one whole wall. She turned her gaze deliberately from it, and back into the ward. Dom set her holdall down beside the bed. His departure was abrupt: a quick pressure of the hand, 'I'll phone tomorrow,' and he was gone. She watched him walk away, his head thrust forward, his back held very straight. All of this, she thought, is becoming too much for one pair of shoulders.

The other admissions were young women. Maureen had fair, curling hair and a pale skin; the two visible lumps in her neck, she told Amy, were thyroid-related. Sylvia was tall and very thin; she talked compulsively about her two small children. A colostomy, performed upon her six months ago, would, she hoped, be reversed tomorrow.

In the occupied bed a grey-haired lady slept the deep sleep of the recently anaesthetized. All the flowers were hers. As they started to unpack, a nurse came in holding three keys.

'Your wardrobes,' she said, 'are on the right-hand wall just beyond the bay.'

The wardrobes had shelves and coat hangers. The pleasure Amy took in hanging up her clothes was, she knew, disproportionate, and would in no way increase her chances of survival. And yet such provision seemed to her significant, an unexpected sign of caring on the part of an impersonal administration.

Maureen changed into a matching set of nightdress and housecoat in a pretty, flower-sprigged cotton. Sylvia wore a white terry-towelling robe; her slippers and her hair were coloured gold. Amy had brought the cotton nightgowns she had worn to hospital last summer, but the dressing-gown of crimson nylon velvet was brand new. Lunch was substantial; light diet here included cottage pie, followed by ice-cream. The food was hot and appetizing. They sat at the melamine-topped table, Amy taking the chair that faced away from the window. The young women talked about their children; their husbands; the lives which they had temporarily abandoned but would soon resume. Amy had no such conversation. No one waited urgently for her return. She had been vehement in her refusal to allow family visits. Don't even think of coming, she had said. I shall only worry, thinking of you making the journey in this winter weather.

Sylvia asked, 'Was that your son who brought you in?'

'Yes. Yes, it was.' The next words were so easy, she almost believed them to be true. 'My husband,' said Amy, 'is in Italy on business. He tried to get back in time, but his flight was cancelled.'

The afternoon began with blood tests. She was taken in a wheelchair pushed by a hospital porter to the rooms where X-rays were taken and electrocardiographs performed. Her vocal cords were examined and approved of. Back in the ward, the doctors and students came with their clipboards and ballpoints;

like market researchers on street corners they gathered the minute details of her life and condition. She thought it was fair exchange for her to tell them things they really did not wish to know. She proselytized without shame, informing them of the benefits of alternative medicine, visualization, meditation. She pointed out the bottles of vitamins standing on the bedside locker; the tall white drum which contained the magic crystals of Vitamin C. She said, aggressively, that she intended to take the medicines she had brought with her, throughout her stay in their hospital. They agreed, surprisingly, politely, that they saw no reason why she should not do so.

The thin dark medical student lingered at her bedside. She felt undermined by his solicitousness. He said, hesitantly, 'How much do you know about your previous operation?'

'Everything,' she said. 'I had told them it was cancer before they operated.'

Relief flickered in his eyes. His curiosity, until now suppressed, got the better of him. He sat down again. He said, 'Do you fear the future?'

She thought about it. 'No,' she said. 'Oh no! After all, I don't know how much future I've got left. Why should I waste time feeling frightened of it?'

She had imagined last year's slimy salad sandwich to be the required food for a pre-operative patient, and today's tasty lunch a rare aberration. But supper again exceeded expectations. Cod in mushroom sauce and lemon meringue pie was the Sheffield hospital's interpretation of 'light diet'. She ate slowly and with enjoyment; she took her vitamin pills, and mixed five grammes of Vitamin C in an inch of mineral water and drank it. The laughter around the melamine table was a little too high-pitched. Sylvia worried about her youngest child who was difficult at bedtime. Maureen had the beginnings of a headache. Amy tried to recall how she had felt on her previous eve-of-operation, and found that she had no clear memory of it. They agreed together that their problems were simply the result of a natural tension.

The visitors came: husbands, sons and brothers; daughters and sisters. Amy felt bruised by their sympathetic glances; she tried harder to believe in the travelling husband, unavoidably detained in Rome. She read the expensive magazines which Chris had given her. At last, she turned her armchair towards the window, and confronted the view that she had reserved for this precise moment and situation.

A full moon was rising in the black sky, lifting itself slowly and inevitably above a rim of distant moorland. In between, the streets of Sheffield were delineated in orange and yellow coloured lights. An eagle, poised on the crag of a bare mountain must feel as she did; the unreality of it made her dizzy. The beauty cancelled out the sounds of voices in the ward behind her. She was more alone than she had ever been.

The renewed desire to live entered her mind slowly. For all her defiant words to doctors, her head had privately, and without permission, accommodated the certainty of death by cancer. Possibly in this hospital? Possibly while she was deep beneath the anaesthetic? The doubt had slipped in while she was busy concentrating elsewhere.

The nurse had crisp brown curls and blue eyes. Her figure in the dark blue uniform was neat, compact. Her words were clipped, but the blue eyes softer. 'I'm your theatre sister, Mrs Sheldon. Your op is scheduled for ten-thirty in the morning. You should be back here on the ward by half past twelve.' A pause. 'You may find that you're on oxygen when you wake up. Don't worry about it.'

Amy had never considered how it would feel to be put in prison. If she piled up the full soft pillows and lay on her left side she could still see the midnight city, the dark moorlands. The moon was high now, small and orange. And yet there was a feeling of incarceration, although she had walked into this place voluntarily, willingly.

The price of freedom was a stretch of days, a week of close

confinement during which she would be subjected to the will of others. Well-intentioned others, capped and gowned, scalpel in hand, wielding the instrument that might secure her freedom.

She could leave if she so wished; get out of this bed, take her clothes from the wardrobe so kindly allotted to her. She could ride the down lift, walk out through the four-star foyer into the black night. A taxi would take her to the Sheffield railway station. She could board the warm, clean, hourly Intercity which would rush her down the line to London. She could watch the orange moon from the train window. She still had choices, didn't she?

She slept, finally, as the first pale light streaked the sky. She awoke, thirsty, the dryness of her mouth accentuated by the NIL BY MOUTH sign clipped above her bed. Maureen was the first to go; she waved to Amy from the theatre trolley, and Amy waved back.

The pre-med tablets were as big as horse pills, one white and two green. The operation gown was made of pale blue crinkly paper, and came with a pair of matching and ridiculous paper knickers and long white woollen socks.

She signed the consent form, which meant that from that moment anything could happen. She thought about Michael, invoking his face as though it was a charm, but unable to recall a single feature of it. In the London hospital they had insisted that she remove her wedding ring before surgery, even though she said how much she hated to be parted from it. Here the nurse had smiled and covered the ring and Amy's finger with a piece of sticking plaster.

Her eyes came open to the dazzle of overhead lights. There was a tightness across her nose and mouth. Her body was on fire, the flames leaping high about her neck and head. The hands on her shoulders were gentle; the voice was soft, motherly.

'We're just going to take off this damp nightie, dear. We'll give you a little sponge-down, you won't feel so hot then.'

She felt the wetness of the washcloth, the roughness of terry towelling; and then the fresh cool cotton slid down over her head and the plumped pillows pulled her inwards. She closed her eyes against the unkind lights, and slept.

Grey-trousered knees, creased white coat, the ends of a stetho-scope dangling from a pocket. When he spoke she could just see the wagging point of a thin black beard. His accent was one she could not place. Possibly Oriental.

He held her hand briefly, the way they do; at least some of them do. 'You're doing very well,' he said. 'Your surgery did not give us the problems we expected. Your tests had indicated serious trouble.'

He probably, she thought, said that to all his patients.

There was still a tightness across her mouth and nose. A voice, very close to her ear said, 'Your husband phoned early this morning to inquire about you.'

She opened her eyes, pulled at the plastic gadget on her mouth, tried to speak and could not.

The oxygen mask was replaced, gently but firmly. 'Just for a little longer, dear. We'll take it off quite soon now.'

Tea, fragrant and steaming, came in a big white cup. The porridge, in a blue bowl, was thick and creamy. But this was the north country, where they really knew how oats should be cooked. Somebody had said that Michael called, but she did not believe it.

She pulled herself up, very carefully, on to the pillows. The clip which secured the drip in her left hand was a brilliant emerald green. It looked like a sinister insect, perched just below her knuckles. She located the flask and its attached tubes; the apparatus which would drain her throat wound.

Familiarity blunted horror. The post-surgical gadgets seemed as ordinary this time as the cheese-grater in her kitchen, the whisk, the apple-corer.

She sipped the hot tea and remembered Carmelita. She wondered, incuriously, why porridge should be on the supper menu. Perhaps it was a Yorkshire custom? She had read somewhere that the pudding they invented in this county had been served in harder times immediately before the main course, in order to blunt the voracious hunger of the poor. She ate cautiously and with enormous pleasure. Using the all-in-one movement she had learned last year, Amy turned towards the window. The heavens were dark and wild, a Wuthering Heights sky. Great columns of grey-black clouds towered over Sheffield and the distant heathland. A few white flakes drifted past the window. Snow.

Maureen said, 'It looks as if you enjoyed your breakfast. You've scraped the bowl clean.' She sat down in the chair beside Amy's bed, looking fresh and rested in her flower-sprigged white nightdress, her fair curling hair brushed back from her pale face, a broad band of transparent plastic covering her neck wound. Maureen's voice was faint and husky.

Amy also tried to utter. Her words came out fainter and huskier than Maureen's, but she achieved speech. 'Breakfast? This must be supper. I had my op this morning.'

'We had our operations yesterday. Today is Thursday. You've been right out since they brought you back on to the ward. You were on oxygen all day and all night. I was getting worried about you.'

'I couldn't speak for three days last time.' Amy touched her throat and found her own thick plastic dressing. 'They also used carpet staples on me.'

Maureen said, 'That sounds awful. They make one long running-stitch here, with a little white bead fastened at each end.'

They smiled at one another, like prisoners who, although still on the rack, had been excused the thumbscrews.

Maureen said, 'Your husband phoned. All the way from Rome. He was very anxious about you.'

Tell a lie, thought Amy, and see how it expands. Because she had said that Michael was in Rome, his presence there would from now on be assumed. She found herself longing to elaborate, to tell a romantic tale. Oh yes, she might say; he didn't want to go to Italy but business here hasn't been too good just lately. He's promised to take me to Paris when I'm feeling stronger. We had our honeymoon there.'

She said instead, 'He should be back in England any time now.' It could not, of course, have been Michael who phoned. It would have been Dom or Chris, both of whom had promised to inquire.

She was detached from the drip mid-morning. The unexpected freedom made her incautious. She launched herself confidently from the bed and into slippers and dressing-gown; there would be no need this time to request the wheelchair-cum-commode. It was on her way back from the bathroom that dizziness struck. She clung to the washbasin, sloshed cold water on to her face, careless of the dressing on her neck. The bed was achieved by taking small slow footsteps; she was consumed by heat, her head felt muzzy. For an hour she lay very still, practised relaxation and prayed that no medical person would come with thermometer and blood-pressure cuff.

Lunch was a pleasant fish dish followed by ice-cream, and a cup of tea. Amy swallowed her Vitamin C; a house doctor took a blood sample from her. The terrifying heat had subsided to a faint warmth, her head was clear; she was as tired as if she had unloaded, single-handed, a wagonful of coal.

There must have been a time when I lived permanently with Mimi and Archie, but whenever I sought my infant self there was nothing to be found. I seemed to have erupted into life fully equipped and functioning at about the age of five years.

Any effort to recall before that time has always brought on an ache, deep in my throat.

'Don't cry,' Aunty Belle had said. 'You know it only upsets *me*.'

Mimi and Archie lived in an ugly house built of yellow brick. The bay windows and the front door were painted spinach-green. There were rooms in the house where bad things had happened, places where I feared to be left alone. Mimi and Aunty Belle talked about old ghosts as if I was deaf or not bright enough to understand. The stairs were very steep, unlit, and covered with brown linoleum which was held in position by thick brass stair-rods. My grandmother had once fallen down those stairs, top to bottom. To this fall was attributed her cancer and subsequent death. I would tell any lie which would excuse me from climbing those haunted stairs alone.

The master bedroom reached across the full width of the house. It had two long sash-windows, a string-coloured carpet, and mahogany furniture which would, in these times, fetch thousands at auction. Two paintings by Simeon Solomon, a Pre-Raphaelite artist, hung on the walls. Mimi and Archie disliked these pictures, but kept them in place to cover damp patches caused when the roof had leaked. The dressing-table had triple mirrors and many little drawers which were faced with brass handles and beading. I was allowed to investigate these drawers, to push Mimi's marcasite combs into my dark plaited hair, to clip on her dramatic rhinestone earrings, hang her necklaces around my neck. Her perfume was Attar of Roses; her face powder spilled from a bowl of yellow glass, her powder puff was stitched to a many-coloured chiffon hanky. Her lipsticks were always left carelessly uncapped, from their gilt and silver holders.

The room was lit by gaslight which burned with a bluish flame and hissed like a snake. The bed was wide and high; the headboard of carved mahogany was inlaid with a broad band of quilted blue silk. The silk was torn, the padding hanging loose on the side of the bed where my grandmother had lain in the last days of her illness.

'Poor mother,' Mimi would say. 'The pain was so bad in the end that she often clutched at and ripped the quilting.' No attempt was ever made to repair the damage; it stayed as a dramatic reminder of my grandmother's suffering, a keepsake at which I could hardly bear to look.

I had not needed to ask why I could no longer live with Mimi and Archie. The matter was discussed in my presence as openly and brutally as if I was an unpaid bill, a charge of bankruptcy. It all had to do with what Aunty Belle called Mimi's irregular domestic arrangements; her unsuitability to have the charge of an impressionable child. Although his name was never mentioned by either aunt, I knew that the term 'irregular domestic arrangement' meant the presence in the house of Archie, who was not Mimi's husband, but whom Mimi and I loved.

There was also the fact of Uncle Ken, who was Aunty Belle's proper husband, lately returned from the War, and willing to bring me up as if I was his own.

'Ken would love to bring her up as if she was his own. Well, we shall never have a child now. Not after the injuries he got in France.'

We were sitting in the only room of the house which held no terrors for me. We made toast at the open fire. Mimi allowed me to hold the long-handled wire fork to the glowing coals, and to judge the exact moment when the thick slice of bread should be withdrawn. The walls in this room were panelled in dark oak, there was a circular mahogany table, the pedestal of which was carved in the style of lions' paws. The white damask tablecloth was clean and starched and riddled with moth-holes, so that in places it resembled uneven lace. The pictures were gilt-framed and what Mimi described as 'sweetly romantic'. Two children done in oils, who picked bluebells in an impossibly green Victorian meadow; fluffy kittens whose water-coloured periwinkle eyes crossed alarmingly as they pursued balls of pink wool. The wind-up gramophone stood in a corner; the threadbare tapestry-covered armchairs were of no particular colour, but comfortable. If I stood close to the velvet window-curtains I could smell the stale smoke of Mimi's Turkish cigarettes.

'It won't be so bad, chick,' Mimi had said. 'We'll come up and see you on your birthday. We'll go out, have tea in a Corner Lyons, go to the pictures. You'll still be able to come back to us in the school holidays. Belle can put you on the train at Waterloo, and I'll be waiting for you at this end.'

I said, 'I'd rather stay with you and Archie.'

'Belle's had a bedroom redecorated for you, and Uncle Ken has painted the furniture white and stencilled a pattern of flowers on it. You won't remember Uncle Ken. You were just a baby when he went off to the War.'

The population of Ward J was as fluid as water. Maureen, while Amy slept, had been floated off into an adjoining bay. The owner of the spectacular flower arrangements had also disappeared. Sylvia had been sent home, her colostomy still intact. For some reason which, although explained to Amy, she could not altogether comprehend, the proposed reversal had proved impossible to perform. Sylvia would have to return to the hospital at some future date; even as the clean topsheet was smoothed across the empty bed, the space was claimed by a young Asian woman who was suffering extreme pain.

Her name was Jacinta, and she was clearly well known to all the nurses; there was at one time ten family members allowed at the bedside, which proved that the patient must be a hospital employee, possibly a nurse. Late that afternoon two heavily sedated ladies were wheeled in to occupy the other vacant beds. The dramas of the bay became totally absorbing. Once again, Amy felt like a voyeur made captive by a head and eyes which could not easily be turned away. The occupant of the bed which stood directly opposite to hers was receiving almost constant attention from the nurses. She wore an oxygen mask. A weeping husband sat beside her and held her hand. The tears rolled endlessly down his face as if a tap had been turned on behind his eyes and he lacked the will to check the flow. Amy also wept because she had no husband to weep for her.

The high-backed armchair supported her head and shoulders, easing the ache in her throat and neck. She turned the chair around to face the window and watched the snow clouds building, pillowy and black, edged with dirty-yellow light. Her head was cool now, her thoughts coherent. She tried to recall how she had felt during this same previous stage of her convalescence, but could not remember.

The staff nurse studied Amy's chart. She said, 'Your family rang again.'

'Which particular ones?'

'Your husband. Two sons. One daughter.' She hooked the chart back on to the bedrail. 'I told them you were doing very well.'

The tale of the travelling husband, trapped by snow in Italy, must by now, have spread all around the ward. The invented Michael, whom Amy herself now hardly recognized, this anxious regularly inquiring man, was slowly taking on a terrifying reality. She could actually see him, trapped as she was trapped, seated at a lofty window, watching snow clouds build, phoning the Sheffield hospital, spending millions of lire in the easement of his mind and conscience in faraway Rome. Maureen and she held husky, croaking conversations on the subject. Maureen, whose tall, good-looking husband never missed the chance to visit, said, 'Oh! The poor man. He must be so worried about you.'

My babies were almost three days old when their father saw them for the first time. He was not the sort who would ever be present at the birth, and I did not expect it. But some sins of omission are unforgivable. Most men would wade through floods, brave fire, to see their firstborn in the first few hours of life. But Michael had longed for a daughter. The arrival of twin boys must have seemed to him like a double error on my part. I have never forgotten his tardiness, his lack of natural feeling. Nor have I ever permitted Michael to forget it. On my return home I pushed the Lalique girl to the back of the cabinet, and arranged my very finest Victorian cranberry-glass in such a way that she was almost totally concealed. Ten years we had waited, latterly without hope. When our duplicated miracle finally happened, Michael had a prior appointment. (I now know that I am capable of deep depression – not the sort that shows . . . I tend to smile a lot when all I really want to do is hide beneath the duvet. But as Aunty Belle always says, breeding tells. I have been bred to stoicism, to hide the bruises, never to bleed on other people.)

Aunty Belle and Mimi were seated at my bedside when the twins were only two hours old. They charmed the Ward Sister, who was not easily enchanted, into letting them hold the babies for a minute or two. The aunts wore their best navy-blue suits and their good pearls, looking for the first time since childhood like the twins they really are. The hectic red on Mimi's cheek bones was for once entirely from excitement. Aunty Belle was very pale; she smiled so much I hardly recognized her. They spoke like a pair of radio entertainers, each one delivering only half a sentence.

Mimi began, 'Oh Amy, sweetheart, I can't take it in –'

'– we can't believe it, Amy. Two of them –'

'– and both so big and strong. This one looks –'

'– like you. And this one is the image of Michael –'

'– we saw him as we were coming into the hospital –'

'– not to speak to. He seemed to be in a hurry –'

'– he rushed past us without a word. He'll be just as excited as we are –'

'– now what about names?'

For the first time in their lives Belle and Mimi were in harmony. I had given each of them a child to hold, to cherish. And you can't, no matter how hard you try, be fairer than that, can you?

By the time he at last showed up, Michael's sons were already second-third-fourth-hand. They had been kissed and cuddled by a succession of visitors. Fin had come bearing rare gifts; he was a three-in-one Magi, already a worshipper, a slave. But it was Belle and Mimi who had known my babies when they were still brand new, before even I had been allowed to hold them.

Before the night nurse went off duty Amy checked with her that the new day was Saturday. There had been little sleep in the bay for any of them. The very poorly lady, the oxygen mask still strapped across her face, had been lifted from her bed and placed in a pillow-lined armchair. The Indian girl had suffered an emergency gall-bladder removal; she whimpered at intervals, while her mother, dressed in a luscious brown-and-gold sari and her best gold earrings, sat beside the bed and stroked her daughter's hand.

Amy sat in her armchair before the window; she ate her porridge, drank the good tea and saw the sun, pinkish-gold and huge, lift above the line of hills and moors, to touch the city roofs with silky light. She leaned forward and began for the first time to identify individual buildings. There was a lovely old church and spire only yards from the hospital car park. Streets of Victorian villas. Pubs. Pigeons flying in the cold air. The church had a patterned pantile roof. In the distance was a green park; several blocks of highrise flats; and always the long roads rising to snake away across the skyline. The sun still floated valiantly between gathering layers of dark cloud. Heavy snow, said the night nurse, had been forecast by Radio Sheffield; she hoped to reach home and bed before the downfall could begin. She said, 'If Dr Hassan says it's okay, they'll be taking your throat drain out this morning.'

Dr Hassan was surprised at her good progress. He ordered the removal of the throat drain. He said, 'All being well, I think you might go home tomorrow afternoon.'

The portable telephone stood in a distant corridor. Amy sat on the chair provided by a thoughtful member of staff and punched out her home digits but no one answered. She tried Lali's number; there was no reply. Saturday. They would be shopping, visiting friends. Perhaps they were having lunch with Michael, who was, she reminded herself, not the jet-setter of her imagination, but domiciled where he had always been, in London. The walk back to her bay seemed longer; where nursing staff were absent she leaned against the wall until the trembling in her legs had eased. She came back into the ward to find Dom and Lali waiting beside the empty bed.

Lali had brought her mother a great sheaf of carnations in every shade of pink and peach. Dom and Lali hugged her very carefully; she pointed out the clear plastic dressing, the neat red line of scar, her unexpected ability to speak.

Dom said, 'Chris is driving up to see you in the morning. We've phoned each morning and evening.'

'The doctor says my stitches can come out tomorrow. After that, well – I can come home.' Her pleasure at their presence was so fierce that she might have been away from them for years rather than days. She smiled and smiled, praised the hospital food, the doctors and nurses; invited her children to admire the stunning and therapeutic view. She did not ask if it was true that Michael had phoned to inquire about her. How could she, when whatever Michael did was of no importance to her?

She insisted that they leave while there were still two hours of daylight driving to be had. As they walked away she had the feeling that they took with them all that was good and whole and healthy; the reality that once was hers. But they would come back tomorrow, they would collect her diminished self, transport her back to the place where the first seed of cancer had been sown and accommodated. Black humour came easily to her lately. Sometimes, she thought, life gets you by the throat, in the neck; until, if you allow it, you are choked to death.

The early Sunday-morning view from the window showed lightening skies, snow on the hills, street lamps winking slowly out all over Sheffield. The traffic in the streets was sparse. The routine of the ward continued: drips and bags, tubes and dressings, the washing of bed-bound patients, bedmaking. Amy wondered if all of her thyroid gland had been removed this time. The doubt grew large in her mind. When the staff nurse came to remove her stitches she said, 'Could you find out if they took it all? I have to know. I really do.'

The nurse snipped the thread which held one white bead in position, then she pulled firmly on the other bead and the long stitch dangled from her fingers. She handed it to Amy. 'Souvenir,' she said, and walked away. Ten minutes later she was back and smiling. 'They took it all. Every last bit.'

Maureen, dressed in a pale blue suit and pretty blouse, suggested that she and Amy might exchange addresses. They might also meet again at their first check-up in the thyroid clinic. They would not, in any case, lose touch. Amy put on the uncreased cream leisure suit, and covered her neck-dressing with the bright scarf. Except for a slight pallor, and an inability to raise her chin, no one would ever guess that she was less than healthy. The carnations, their stems wrapped in damp paper, were placed together with her packed holdall. This was the good time, the time of leaving with herself mostly intact, with hope not yet destroyed. The moment of truth would come at the check-up. The hospital Registrar came to see her.

'I suggest,' he said, 'that you have your check-up done in London. Not so far for you to travel. Less exhausting.'

'No!' she said. 'No. If my check-up can't be done here in Sheffield then I won't have one!'

Her flaming vehemence rocked the man into taking a step backwards. 'Yes,' he said quickly. 'Yes, of course. The decision is entirely yours. I'll be writing to you. Sending you a date and time.'

They came for her at six minutes to eleven. Chris and Dom. Chris smiling his relieved smile at the sight of her dressed and on her feet. He put his arms around her. They looked at one another. There were no words to name the feelings that passed between them. Amy said her goodbyes around the bay, to the nurses who had tended her, the still semi-conscious patients; the incredible view.

Dom brought the car around to the main entrance, and halted illegally before the wide glass doors so that she did not have far to walk out into the bitter day. Even so, she paused, held on to the passenger door and breathed in the icy cold, the revitalizing air. They drove slowly through the Sheffield suburbs of fine old stone houses, leafless trees and interesting shops.

He said, 'We're taking the scenic route back. We'll go through the Derbyshire Peaks. I've checked on the state of the roads, and there's little or no snow.'

The car bonnet pointed upwards as they took the rising road across the moors. Amy had the strange disembodied feeling of one who travels now inside a distant and recently observed view. Like I had died, she thought, and gone to heaven, only to find that paradise was, after all, on the Yorkshire heathland.

A glittering crust of snow lay across the country, but as Dom had promised, the roads were clear and dry. A fierce longing for survival gripped her. She said, 'A nurse told me – more than once – that your father had phoned.'

The purr of the engine was loud in the silence. Dom eyed

his brother through the driving-mirror. She could not begin to interpret the look that passed between them.

'Well,' she said at last, 'say something – somebody – anybody. Did he, or didn't he?' She caught herself, just in time, from adding, 'And all the way from Rome, too.'

Chris said, 'We had to tell him what was happening; where you were, and why.' He was partly defensive, partly apologetic.

Dom said, 'Phoning the hospital was all Dad's own idea. Nothing to do with any of us.' He made it sound as if the call had been a mild obscenity, a heavy breather who had not actually spoken.

She would, at that moment, have given everything she owned just to be alone in some quiet place, to think about the confirmed significance of Michael's call; his first attempt at any contact with her in almost five years. She tried to close her mind off from her sons' perception, but her illness, her recent helplessness, had thinned the parental veil, brought about a role reversal. She felt like a child whose every little ploy and subterfuge is plotted by a watchful parent.

Chris said, 'You don't have to think about it now. Just concentrate on getting better.'

They stopped for lunch in Bakewell. This pub too offered giant Yorkshire puddings filled with hot-pot. Amy, who had thought herself faint with hunger, could eat only slowly.

Dom said, 'We'll take a walk along the river while you finish.' Once alone, she paddled hot-pot back and forth inside the golden pudding, and watched the hill-walkers at the bar, young and fit in their heavy boots and rucksacks. The hospital food, although well-cooked and sufficient, had not been ample. Faced with superabundance she now felt queasy, disinclined to swallow. There had been a time, many times in fact, when a phone call from Michael would have transformed her whole world. Now that the miracle had happened, now that he had stepped across the line between total rejection and partial recognition, she was no longer sure that a return from exile was what she wanted; needed.

Because of their implied denial she was quite sure that her sons were in close touch with their father, and in ways that had nothing to do with the furtherance of their furniture-restoring business.

Sometimes she liked to imagine herself as more interesting than she really was. The delusion was not deliberate, more like a gentle infiltration of confidence, a sprinkling of stardust which made her younger, dynamic, a character in a major film, a heroine abandoned by an insensitive husband. In the summer months after last year's operation, lying on the sunbed among the flowers, she had managed to sustain this role for whole days, and sometimes longer. She could, if she really tried, make it all seem like someone else's nightmare. It was hard to believe that life, as she had known it, was now over.

At other times, when she was forced to consider reality, she feared that she had lost her bearings in this never-ending time of probings, diagnoses, surgical interventions. All her absolutes were shattered; she trod on broken glass. There was greenfly on the roses, a wasps' nest in the attic.

In February she had come home to a garden closed by winter. The comfort of the house lapped all around her; she walked on soft pale carpets, slept in pastel-coloured sheets, arranged Lali's carnations in a cut-glass vase. She missed the hard white certainties of hospital living. She needed somebody to confirm her belief that the very worst that could strike her had already happened; that her guilt, her obligation to the aunts had been a lifelong error of false accounting. That cancer cancelled all debts. But whenever she thought about her aunts, about Michael her husband, the anger came back, like no anger she had ever known before.

*

Lali took to dropping in with a frequency that was unsettling. She brought small, thoughtful gifts. A box of out-of-season strawberries, a casket of handmade chocolates; the kind of glossy magazine Amy never purchased for herself. The shameful part of Amy's mind that could not trust Lali wondered why she came so often, what she was up to. Was she Michael's emissary, the thin edge of some conciliatory wedge? And if she was, how did Amy feel about it?

Her doctor came, entering the room on a sort of mental tiptoes; he sat on the edge of the chesterfield and did not smile.

'Well,' he said, 'so how was it? How are you feeling?'

'It was a great improvement on last year's experience. My voice came back almost at once. They tell me I was on oxygen for ages. But I feel exhausted. All the time.'

'That doesn't surprise me. You've had major surgery twice within six months.'

'Only because,' she snapped back, 'the job was half-done in the first place.'

'We don't know that.'

'*I* know it. Would you care to lay bets on what they find in the Sheffield Path. Lab?'

'When is your check-up?'

'Next month. On the first day of spring.'

The house was very clean; cleaner than it had been since the time when she had kept a shining home because that was the way Michael wished it to be. Amy moved from room to room; all the carpets had been recently shampooed, all the windows polished on both sides. She stood on a stool and ran her fingertips over surfaces, like some Victorian chatelaine checking up on a lazy housemaid. Someone had wiped the dust of the past three years from the tops of wardrobes and high cupboards. It could only have been Lali, who was, now that Amy thought about it, by nature and inclination, domesticated.

Without effort Lali was all the things that Amy had striven unsuccessfully to be. Her beauty was sculpted in the bone, in the delicate planes of cheek and jaw, the small fine nose. When Lali was very old, when her pale matt skin was wrinkled, the blonde hair silvered, she would still be a beautiful and notice-able woman. She had taken everything from Michael, and nothing from Amy, which seemed only fair in the circum-stances. Amy had not much wanted this third child. 'I'll be thirty-eight,' she told Michael, 'I'm too old to start again. I simply can't face it.'

'I'll help you. It won't all be on your shoulders this time.'

'Oh,' she had said. 'So you do actually remember the last time, do you? That highly forgettable occurrence – the births of your sons? You were so determined not to get involved I began to wonder if I'd had an Immaculate Conception.'

He'd had a trick of looking hurt that was supposed to shame her. 'Don't do this to me, Amy,' he pleaded. 'Let's just be happy about it.' Then he had spoken the unforgivable words which proved that he was without a trace of insight into her feelings. 'It might actually be a girl this time.'

'Oh, really!' She had spoken on a rising note. 'You didn't even want to look at your first daughter. So tell me, why should you be any different now, Michael?'

'I was younger then. I couldn't cope.' He looked away. 'And anyway, you always had your aunts.'

Her voice grew dangerously quiet. 'I was also young, remem-ber? Younger than you were. I was eighteen years old. I had just given birth to a dead child.' She raised her hand as if to strike him. 'Where were you, you bastard? Laying-off bets in some back alley? Propping up the bar in the Prince of Wales?' She placed the threatening hand across her eyes, forcing the tears hard back and downwards into her throat. Having lost a child that she had so desperately wanted, she would never contemplate abortion. Believing as she did that every child, once conceived, should be wanted and welcome, Amy stitched

PATRICIA WENDORF

a silk-and-lace layette for her summer baby, and tried without much success to think good thoughts. But the morning sickness persisted for every single day of that nine months.

He had promised her that it would all be different this time. And so it was. Chris and Dom, who had lived the ten years of their lives with only the minimum attention from their father, and who were, in any case, sufficient unto one another, now found themselves hauled off unwillingly at weekends on fishing expeditions and camping trips. Their mother, they were told, needed rest and quiet. Their father found them polite and well-behaved, but distant.

'What's wrong with them? It was never like this with Fin and me. When I was their age Fin and I were real pals.'

'You've left it a bit late,' said Amy. 'Fatherhood begins at birth. Fin kept you close to him always, and anyway, twins are not like other children. If you'd bothered to look at them for even ten minutes you would have seen that they're more like one person in two separate bodies. You and I are not of prime importance to them. They have each other.'

'*I* am of no importance, that's true. I might as well not be there with them. They have this special language that they use only to one another. When they need to quote a higher authority, yours is the name they always mention.'

Amy said, 'I'm sure they respect you.'

'I don't want their bloody respect, what I want is their . . .'

Amy smiled thinly. 'You can't bring yourself to say it, can you? Is love the word you're looking for? Sometimes,' she said, 'you have to give love, Michael, before you can receive it.'

Chris and Dom had never strayed far from one another. Since Dom had returned to the family home, Chris came around almost every evening. They took turns to buy take-away food: Indian, Thai, Cantonese, Italian. Amy's kitchen smelled spicy and exotic; the contents of her dustbin were lately cosmopolitan, filled with polystyrene trays and cartons smeared with coloured sauces and bits of boiled rice. She would sit at the far end of the table with her home-made vegetable soup, her low-fat cheese and salad, her wholemeal bread. Her greatest pleasure was the same as it had always been: to watch her sons talk and laugh together, the two halves of one amazing whole. It was only when in his brother's company that Chris came truly alive. Away from Dom he tended to be solemn, quiet, a little withdrawn. On these February evenings Amy studied Chris more closely than was usual. Under the fluorescent strip-light his hair was a brighter russet red, his eyes a gentler shade of hazel. The skin of his face was fine-grained, high-coloured, his features regular and handsome. He was a big man, almost bearlike. A memory came back to her mind. She had once known a man who looked a lot like Chris. But then, people often looked like other people.

Every morning she resolved to lay aside the housecoat and slippers, to wash her hair, put on some make-up, get dressed. Dom brought her early morning tea and biscuits, and she listened to the weather forecast on her bedside radio with as much attention as if she had a trip planned; then she read the papers, did the crossword. The midday soup and sandwich were eaten at the kitchen table. By the time she had washed and stacked the saucepan and dishes it hardly seemed worth the effort of getting dressed. At four every afternoon she took a bath, put on a clean nightdress and settled down to await the arrival of her children.

There were times in the afternoon when she had sufficient energy left over to take her wandering again through the house. She had said thank you to Lali for the pristine state of things, and Lali had smiled and said nothing, but Amy knew that her daughter was pleased that notice had been taken. They had never been close; not in the way that Amy had secretly expected they might be. Not in the way that Amy had been close to Aunty Belle and Mimi. (Too close for comfort. Too close for safety.) It was, she thought, a bitter irony that Lali's present devotion was all that Amy had longed for in the years before the illness. Now she felt pain at each fresh proof of her daughter's unsentimental caring. It was easier when Lali had been entirely Michael's child.

The photographs were stored in old chocolate boxes, and stacked high inside the spare bedroom wardrobe. She lifted out the boxes one by one and placed them on the bright patchwork of the quilt. She removed the lid of the largest box, the one which had a picture of puppies on it. The photos spilled out, the early black-and-white shots, taken when their only camera had been an old box Brownie which belonged to Fin, showing the boys at every stage from birth to twelve years. She had studied the chapter in each baby book which referred to twins. Every care must be taken, she learned, to preserve their individuality. They must never be dressed in matching outfits, each child must have its own bedroom. But Dom had screamed and wept when parted from Chris; at one in the morning Michael and she had been forced to move back the divan and bedclothes, to promise that never again would Dom and his brother be separated. From the time when they were old enough to recognize colours it had never been wise to dress one in green, the other blue. She remembered Chris, plump and solemn, his face reddened by the effort of articulation. 'Same – him,' he had shouted at Dom's different-patterned shirt and shorts, and she had learned the lesson while an amused young shop assistant had packed identical outfits, sun hats and sandals.

There were photos taken in Aunty Belle's garden. Chris, his small arms filled with forbidden flowers, Dom on tiptoe behind him, waiting for the rebuke from Mimi that was never uttered. Another picture showed Dom taking his first unaided steps on Aunty Belle's lawn. She remembered the suspense of that moment, the yellow knitted suit he had worn, the white leather shoes which Mimi had bought.

Then a good camera had been purchased in Torquay. A whole reel of that first colour film had been used up on the beach. Chris and Dom, smart in red shorts and white T-shirts. In navy-blue swimming trunks, running into the sea. In white sun hats, licking ice-creams. The two of them riding in tandem on one sad-looking donkey.

The photos of Lali were all in colour. The lid of the chocolate box showed a picture of a ballerina, wearing a pink tutu. Michael had taken almost every shot. Lali serious or smiling, laughing at her brothers' antics; Lali, believing herself unobserved among Amy's newly planted flowers. She recalled that sunny Sunday morning, Michael loading the camera, herself watching from the kitchen window. The smells of roast lamb and chopped mint.

The child was wearing a blue dress; her soft blonde hair, which had grown in a fluffy halo when she was tiny, now at the age of seven hung waist-length and was streaked with every shade of fair from dark honey at the crown out to pale flax. Lali walked slowly in the brilliant sunshine; she halted before the tubs and window boxes and reached out both hands, moving from vine to trailing fern and ivy geranium, always touching, stroking, seeming to need the physical contact to enhance her visual delight. She had leaned down and laid her cheek against the flowers of an azalea, gazing with such tenderness at the delicate pink that Amy herself was moved to rare tears. Michael caught the moment; when the film was developed he had re-ordered a copy of that one shot. He carried it always in his wallet.

She put the photos back into the boxes, replaced the lids and carried them towards the wardrobe. Aunty Belle and Mimi had been more methodical in their preservation of Amy's childhood. Nothing so casual as chocolate boxes with sentimental pictures on the lids. In a dark corner of the cupboard stood the leather-bound, expensively boxed set of albums presented to Amy on her sixteenth birthday. She had still never so much as glanced into a single album, had not removed even one from its dark blue box.

Pain itself, she had thought, was surely pain enough. She had never felt the need to study a celluloid record of it. The sound of car engines took her to the window. Dom's black MG pulled into the drive, followed closely by the sparkling white of Lali's Mini. Two car doors slammed. Sister and brother greeted one another. Dom laid a casual arm across Lali's suede-clad shoulder. They walked companionably together. Lali did not shrug the arm away, but smiled up into Dom's face as they walked towards the house. Amy felt herself excluded in a most poignant and unreasonable way; she stood at the window and remembered other times. Chris and Dom coming back from school together. Michael, holding Lali's hand, bringing her from ballet classes, music lessons, birthday parties. She counted all the computations of togetherness that are possible between five people. The only gathering that seemed hardly ever to have happened was the five of them together at any one time. She had never really thought about it until now. Never found it extraordinary that they had not sat regularly as a family at breakfast or dining table. Even at Christmas. Especially at Christmas.

Lali called out from the hallway, 'Mum! Where are you?'

Light from the open kitchen door spilled into the hall. She stood at the top of the stairs, her arms wrapped around her body. 'I'm here,' she called out. 'I'll be down in just a minute.'

One of them had unpacked the shopping. She heard the fridge door opening and closing. Water splashed into the kettle.

Chris (when did he arrive?) said, 'It's cold in here. I'll turn up the thermostat. Hard frost is forecast for tonight.'

She wanted so much to go down, to be among them, feel a part of something. But she was still trapped in the world of the

158

old photos: doomed to walk forever on those sunlit beaches of
their childhood; to watch Michael as he caught a single
moment of Lali's sweetness; to recall the daily visits made to
Aunty Belle and Mimi who loved her children in a way they
had never quite managed to love her. She remembered how
Mimi waited for them at the garden gate; Aunty Belle, thin-
lipped with disappointment, rattling teacups in the kitchen.
'Wherever have you been? We were getting so worried in case
anything had happened.'

'We're only twenty minutes late. Dom walked through a
puddle. I had to go back and change his shoes and socks.'

'They need wellingtons. How often have I told you?'

And Mimi's soft voice. 'We'll buy some tomorrow, Amy.
They make them in such pretty colours lately. Now what
colour would you like, boys?'

She heard Lali say, 'I'm worried about Mum. She's been out
of hospital for two weeks now, and is still in slippers and
dressing-gown.'

'It was summer last time.' This was Chris, logical and calm.

Dom said, 'She looks pretty awful. The operations seem to
do more damage than the actual disease.'

There was a silence, then Chris said, 'Is the oven hot enough
yet to cook these pizzas?'

There were times when she thought that she didn't know
them. Any of them. It was as if when they were not actually
within her sight they turned into strangers. She had tried to
imagine their lives, their separate ways, but all she could really
know was the version which they chose to show her. What
did they talk about, this girl, these men, when they were not
discussing her? She had grabbed at crumbs of reportage. She
heard from Dom what Chris was thinking on some subject.
Lali sometimes repeated the more outrageous statements made
by Dom.

She stood in the shadows of the staircase and shivered. They
were right. The house was cold. It was time that she got

dressed; time to accept that she had entered a new state of being, that her life was a limited resource. Time to wash her hair, put a face on. The sound of their voices drifted upwards but she no longer listened. She could know them only as a mother knows her children. Their respective roles were handed out at the moment of conception. They were not, had never been, nor ever should be, all-in-all to her. (Not as she had been to Aunty Belle and Mimi, she thought.) To attempt to reverse the roles of child and mother would be to connive at a disaster. Their disaster. They were her children. They were not her best friends.

Spring rushed to meet her before she was ready for it. There was a feel of sunlight just behind the grey cloud, and no wind; snowdrops scattered under trees and a haze of green in the far distance. It was a day for walking in the woods, but St Gilda's Gardens was safer and nearer. March had come in like a lamb.

Amy wore the scarlet duffle coat and black trousers; the white fleecy scarf wound about her neck reached up to cover her chin and ears. She walked, hands pushed deep into her pockets, past the bandstand and the miniature lake and towards the café. The shaky feeling in her legs and stomach was to be expected. Three weeks cocooned inside the house had been unwise. A few more days of helpless living and she would have slipped into the passive role of permanent invalid. She breathed deeply in the cold air and the muzziness in her head began to clear. There were catkins in the hazel bushes, neat green spears of daffodils pushing through the dark brown soil of formal flower-beds.

She had forgotten to look at the flowers she had planted last autumn, the pansies and bushes of pink heather, the exotically named bulbs which she had planned to admire through the kitchen window. She had become apathetic, or was it pathetic? She leaned against the parapet of the stone bridge and thought how sick she was of all this bloody preoccupation with her

body: her twice-cut throat, the way it kept on aching, the stiffness
of it. Her time, her single precious limited resource, was being
mopped up by the routines of tablet taking, by the labour involved
in the preparation of a healthy diet. She must already have scraped
a hundredweight of carrots, cooked a bushel of brown rice. She
thought about the hours in which she had meditated, relaxed,
visualized her cancer and wished it gone, and she knew that the
disruption of her normal life was total now. Was it worth all the
effort needed just to keep upright and moving?

The café's patio had lost its continental aspect; the white
chairs and tables had been put away until the summer. The
white-framed doors, which in fine warm weather stood open
to grass and flowers, were closed against the cold spring air.
Amy went inside and ordered lemon tea and a fruit scone; the
scone was not quite within the strict limits of her diet, but
today she felt rebellious. She sat at a table which gave a view
of winter trees and the copper-domed carillon. The café was
warm; it smelt pleasantly of toast and brewing coffee. The
apricot-painted walls held advertisements for ice-cream, glossy
posters which offered Cornettos and Chunkies, Tangle-Twisters
and Magnums. The green-and-white striped parasols, which
gave shade to summer customers, were stored beside the ice-
cream cabinets. Young women came here with their children.
Grandmothers pushed prams and baby-buggies. Amy wondered if she would ever have a grandchild. If she would live
long enough to see a grandchild. She did not want to think
these thoughts, but the thoughts came to her all the same.

Her mind was like a clenched fist, a fist that had, long ago,
closed itself around something very nasty. She need only relax
her fingers just a fraction, and all the awfulness came leaking out.

Cousin Rose brought Aunty Belle to see her. Finding her still
in dressing-gown and slippers seemed to persuade them, finally,
that something was, after all, seriously wrong. Mimi too, they

said, had not been quite herself just lately. A neighbour had offered to sit with her while they made this mercy visit. They sat stiffly among the soft cushions of the sofa. Cousin Rose looked unnaturally pale; she looked like someone with matters on her mind that she was not at liberty to divulge. Aunty Belle had that tight and shuttered air which she remembered from her childhood. They talked about Cousin Rose's children and grandchildren. Since she had rarely, if ever, met any of the people mentioned, her mind began to wander. She was back in the ugly house of yellow brick, standing with Belle and Mimi in the master bedroom. Mimi was touching the torn silk of the bedhead. 'Dr Hartley taught me how to inject the morphine. But, as you can see, in the end, morphine couldn't kill the pain. Poor mother.' She moved across the room to the wide sash window. 'She tried to jump out, you know. Several times. I was on my own here with her. All those months. Right up to the end.'

She was seven years old, but she had known what Mimi meant. She recognized an accusation when she heard one.

Aunty Belle had smiled that blank smile she always showed when she was not about to acknowledge guilt, or any obligation.

She came back to her own pleasant lamp-lit room. She said to Aunty Belle, 'Tell me about my grandmother's cancer.'

'She'd had some sort of internal trouble for quite a long time. She went into a private clinic. They did some tests and told her that she needed an operation. She refused, came home, went to bed and never got up again.'

She knew then by the way she spoke that Aunty Belle had loathed her own mother.

'She lived for another fourteen months. Your grandmother made a slave of Mimi.'

The first official day of spring was colder than January. Bitter winds roared across the high peaks of Derbyshire; the sky had a look of approaching snow. She wore the warm cream leisure suit and a bright scarf, which had become required garb for hospital appointments. Chris and Dom took turns at driving. They travelled the M1 motorway until they reached Chesterfield, and then detoured into the hills.

Her appointment was for two o'clock. 'Let's call it a day out,' Dom had said. 'We'll make an early start. Take it slowly. Stop for lunch along the way.' They found a pub called The Peacock, a squat greystone building, miles from anywhere, among the heathland. Brown rice and salad was not included on the menu. Chris ordered three portions of game pie which came with the most delicious gravy she had ever tasted. Nobody spoke about the reason for the journey. They did not tell her this time that she had no cause to worry.

The hospital was visible from a great distance. Today those wonderful windows reflected the racing clouds and weak March sunlight. Amy counted the floors and identified fondly the window which she thought might have been hers.

The waiting area was depressing. Black chairs, grey carpet, grey walls. She gave her name at the desk and presented her appointment card. The thyroid clinic, she was told, was running very late due to the illness of two surgeons. Perhaps she would rather come back next week? Amy explained that she had travelled from London, that her sons had taken time off from their business to bring her to Sheffield. She would wait.

When her name was finally called she had already waited for two and a half hours. Chris had brought her cups of tea and slices of fruit cake sealed in silver foil. He and Dom disappeared at intervals. The only place where smoking was permitted was the Staff canteen. They returned each time from their impersonations, looking guilty but relaxed.

Patients for the thyroid clinic were now told to wait in a long cold corridor which was furnished on one side with wooden benches. Amy counted sixteen women, middle-aged to elderly, many of whom had large swellings in their necks. The queue moved very slowly. When only three patients remained still to be seen her uneasiness turned into panic. She considered going back to the waiting area where Chris and Dom were sitting, but feared to stand up in case she disgraced herself by fainting. They were leaving her until last – which could only mean –? The nurse said, 'Mrs Amy Sheldon? Doctor will see you now.'

The doctor was young, dark-haired, pale-faced. He invited her to sit down. The file on his desk was already open. He apologized for the absence of her surgeon, but assured her that he himself was a part of the same team. He sifted the multi-coloured papers of her reports and notes. He asked how she was feeling since the operation. The apprehension on his face must, she thought, be a mirror-image of her own expression.

She said, 'I know I have cancer. I've known since the very beginning. Just tell me what you have to tell me. I promise I won't fall to pieces!'

His hands became still. She thought, it's not fair. He's too young for all this. He left me until last deliberately. She said, 'It's all right. Really it is. You found some more cancer, didn't you.'

'It was very small. Very small. Your first tumour was much larger.' Once started, his face lit up with a professional interest. 'You see – your tests had led us to expect extensive trouble. We were most pleasantly surprised at what we found.'

'So what happens now?'

'Your thyroxine dosage will have to be increased. The hormone itself is a cancer suppressant. Your future check-ups will be done in your hospital in London.'

'But I need to see Mr Rhys-Jones.'

'I'm afraid that won't be possible. Not at this hospital.'

'Then I'll see him privately.' She stood up and moved towards the door.

'If you should need further in-hospital treatment, Mrs Sheldon, we would always be prepared to treat you here. You have a very rare condition.'

'Thank you,' she said, and then she smiled. 'There's no kudos to be had from rarity, doctor. Common or garden is so much safer.'

It came upon her like a kind of madness, the impulsion to be somewhere else; to be any person but herself. The walking began each day soon after daybreak – the route planned with care so that she might rest along the way, eat breakfast in an early morning café, and not exceed her physical limits. She could no longer bear to be inside the house in the hours of daylight. Sometimes she took the car, drove to a distant town and roamed the unfamiliar streets. At night she fell down into sleep like a woman drowning, never lifting an arm to attract a rescuer.

The first days of April were very cold. The fallen almond blossom looked like snowdrifts. She was finding it difficult to conceal her anger. There were whole hours when she was in a state of constant rage. Her dreams were untellable. In spite of her fears, her instinct for disaster, she had not really believed that they would find a second cancer.

She kept her bright face for her children; bought a brilliant lipstick in a shade called Grenadier, which helped to keep a smile pasted on her face. She needed help, knew that she needed help; knew that there was one place only where that help was to be found.

There were clubs in America, she had once read, which awarded membership exclusively to those who had performed some amazing feat of survival or effrontery. There were regular meetings of these men and women whose only link was that of reaching the peak of a certain dangerous mountain, or of having been shot through the head several times, and survived.

Amy, who had not experienced chemotherapy or radio-therapy, had thought that her single cancer and its surgical removal must look pretty run-of-the-mill to the other patients in the Group. Hardly a case for the award of a Gold Star of Merit. But now two cancers, two operations, must surely grant her increased status. Not quite a veteran at the game, but almost.

Nothing had changed in the James Johnson Community Centre. As she passed through the ground floor area, the members of the Bridge Club still sat in an awesome silence, their cards held close to their chests, waiting for the world's end.

Walking in from the cold dark night, the heat and light of the building was intense. She climbed the stairs feeling nervous but elated, and paused in the doorway of the room. Here was the brown carpet, the stripy orange curtains, the grey uphol- stered chairs, the candle not yet lit, standing on its tin tray. So here I am again, she thought. Last room. Last chance.

Jan was setting out the books and tapes. She turned from the table, said, 'Amy!' and held out her arms. The hug held elements of healing, as if Jan in some mysterious way had become a refuge, a family.

'So how are you?'

'Pretty well,' said Amy. 'Getting better all the time.'

'Have you had your first check-up?'

Amy knew what Jan meant. 'They found more cancer. But only very small this time. They advised me to forget about it.'

The other healers came to greet her, Diana, Val, Rachel; and every greeting was a benediction. The circle of chairs was filling up with patients and their carers. Amy studied faces. John, who had looked pale and strained was laughing now, a good colour in his face, his eyes bright. Janet no longer wore a wig. To her amazement, after the chemo her straight brown hair had grown back curly and black as jet. She touched a curl occasionally as if to assure herself of its permanent presence.

Kathleen came in. She sat down beside Amy. 'Nice to see you back. How are you?' The soft Irish voice brought back memories of Fin; and encouraged a deeper affinity with Kathleen.

'They found more cancer,' Amy said, 'but only as big as my little fingernail.' She could hear the doubt in her voice. 'They behaved as if it was not important.'

'I know. I know exactly what you mean.' Kathleen's perception was acute. Amy wondered, if she asked questions, would Kathleen be prepared to answer. She said, 'How did you feel when they first told you it was cancer?'

'Angry. I kicked and thumped the walls. I thought, "Why me?" and then, "It's not fair. I haven't done anything bad enough to deserve this." I thought about how my family would cope without me. I really wanted my younger son to reach adulthood with me still around. My elder son was about to take his A-level exams. He was wonderfully supportive. He told me he had decided that he wouldn't use my devastating news as an excuse to do badly. In fact, he did very well!' Kathleen paused. She said, 'I thought that my husband might not cope very well on his own account. And then there was my elderly mother over in Ireland. I arranged for my brother and sister to go and tell her. She took it well.'

Amy thought about Aunty Belle and Mimi who had not taken well to her own bad news.

'My sister-in-law,' said Kathleen, 'is an oral surgeon. She was great, always seemed to say the right thing, and supported me in all the things I was doing with this Group.'

Amy said, 'But how did *you* feel?'

'I had panic attacks that first weekend. I had been told at the hospital that the doctors would need to have a meeting to decide who should treat me! I had cancer and nobody was doing anything about it! I felt as though a thick black blanket had been put over my head and I was suffocating. I was walking the streets at four in the morning. In the end my husband called the doctor. I was given Valium, and continued to take it until I joined the Group.'

Amy said, 'Thank you for telling me all that. It helps to know that my own reactions are not unique. In spite of the contrary evidence here in this room, I am sometimes still in danger of thinking that I am the only person in the whole world who has cancer.'

Kathleen smiled. 'Have you ever considered seeing Dr Quinn?'

'Is he the psychotherapist who works with this Group?'

Kathleen nodded. 'He's helped me enormously.'

'I don't know. Well, of course I've thought about it. I certainly need help. But I don't feel strong enough yet to face up to all that probing into the past.'

'It might well be,' said Kathleen, 'that a few sessions with Dr Quinn would actually give you the sort of strength you need.' She opened her handbag. 'I've got his card here somewhere. Yes, here it is. Take it. Think about going. You've got nothing to lose and everything to gain.'

The arrival of her visitors was almost always signalled by the sounds of brakes and roaring exhausts. Tim came in silence. He stood in the front porch, tall and stooped, and too thin in a bright green track suit and yellow oilskin, his pale hair slicked with rain. His bicycle leaned up against the sycamore tree.

Amy could not recall a time when Tim had come to see her on his own. Before standing aside to let him enter she said swiftly, unflatteringly, 'There's nothing wrong with Lali, is there?'

'No,' he said, 'at least nothing that need concern you.' Even as he spoke, Tim's thin face reddened at the abruptness of his words. 'Sorry,' he said. 'That's not exactly true.'

Amy laughed. 'Come in. Let's have a cup of tea and begin again, as if we had never spoken on the doorstep.'

He followed her into the kitchen. While the kettle boiled, she assembled mugs, milk and sugar and a plate of biscuits. Tim pulled out a chair and sat down at the table. He said, 'How are you?'

'Improving, slowly but surely.' She paused. 'So how are you, Tim?'

'Oh, me? I'm okay.'

He neither looked nor sounded okay. She made tea in the old brown pot she always used when Chris and Dom came to talk. For this was Tim's sole reason for coming – what other reason could there be? Her mind roved across the possible disasters. Lali had also visited frequently just lately. She set the teapot in the middle of the table and sat down to face him. He had draped the yellow oilskin across a kitchen chair. Together they watched the beaded moisture run down and drip on to the white tiles of the floor.

He said, abstractedly, 'I'll mop that up before I go.'

'No need,' she said. She looked at his face, the thin, almost elegant gauntness of him. He had a strong resemblance to Michael. To Michael as he had been when she first met him. There was a theory that devoted daughters selected lovers who looked a lot like their own fathers. So where did that leave Amy, who had never possessed a blueprint from which to choose? She poured tea while Tim worked upon the biscuits as if he had not eaten for some time. When the plate was empty she replenished it with the teatime doughnuts meant for Chris and Dom. Tim seemed to be regressing now into childish mode. He hunched above the mug of tea, his elbows on the table, and dunked the doughnuts absent-mindedly, a habit forbidden to him long ago by Lali. He licked the sugar crystals from his fingertips, spinning out time. He could hardly be expected to start talking with his mouth full, could he?

The kitchen was warm. Amy sipped her tea and nibbled on a gypsy-cream. The drips from the oilskin continued to fall mesmerically upon the floor. She began to think about Michael. About Michael as he had been at the age of twenty-five; how passionately she had loved him without ever knowing exactly why she cared so fiercely. She could more easily have cata- logued his faults: his lack of commitment; her suspicion that he could be unprincipled in business matters, that, if necessary, he would quite happily tell a profitable lie. So what was it about Tim that had first drawn Lali to him, that had held them together for three years?

The doughnuts were all eaten, the oilskin no longer dripped. Amy, teapot poised, said, 'More tea?'

Tim pushed his mug towards her. He said, 'Has Lal told you that I've left her?' A stream of amber-coloured liquid shot across the table. Amy fought to control the teapot. She said in her most level, conversational tone, 'No, Tim. She hasn't told me.'

'Well, it's not so much that I've left her. She threw me out.'

'Why?'

'Because she's pregnant.'

Amy set the teapot down with great care. 'That hardly seems like a reasonable move on her part.'

'That's exactly what I told her. You'll need me, I said, just you wait and see.'

Amy realized with horror that Tim was weeping. The tears of men unnerved her. Don't cry, she thought (but did not say it), you know it only upsets *me*.

'Tim,' she said, 'Lali's been disturbed for some time now about our family problems. There's trouble between her father and me; and then there's my illness.' Amy moved to where Tim sat, put an arm around his shoulders and felt his bones relax at her touch, so that he slumped sideways against her. 'It's hardly surprising if she's confused.' Amy hesitated, hardly knowing how to phrase the question. 'Did – you – she – intend to get pregnant?'

'I did. She didn't.'

'Ah.' Amy set Tim firmly back into his chair. She sat down beside him. 'Do you think that was a good idea?'

'I want her to marry me. She won't, so I tried to force the issue. It was a mistake. Now I don't know what to do.' He gave her the same shamed half-glance she remembered from long ago when the twins were small and naughty. 'I got her a bit drunk,' Tim said, 'on her birthday, on Bacardi. Well, I might as well tell you exactly how it was!'

Amy counted swiftly backwards, and then forward. 'Christmas,' she said. 'A Christmas baby.'

Tim nodded. 'If she goes through with it.'

'Where are you living?'

'I've moved in with Chris. Well – his flat has three bedrooms – and now that it's all over with him and Camella – he needed some company and help with the rent.' Tim sighed. 'We're keeping the third bedroom vacant until Dom can join us.'

'What do you mean, *until* Dom can join you?'

Tim's pale face burned a painful scarlet. 'Well,' he said, 'we thought – they thought – you really oughtn't to be on your own. Not just yet. Not until you're stronger.' His tone became severe. 'You have been very ill, you know.' The scarlet colour deepened into crimson. 'In fact, I really shouldn't be here now, giving you this worry, but I didn't know what else to do.'

'It's all right, Tim. I'm very glad you came. That you felt able to trust me. My children don't seem to tell me much, do they? I'm really grateful to you.'

The red receded from his face leaving it waxen. She could see a few dark freckles on the bridge of his nose. He wants me on his side, she thought. He's promising me a grandchild. Trouble is, he's chosen to enlist with the wrong parent. 'Tim,' she said, 'until Lali herself comes to tell me about this, there is nothing I can do. If she does come – and there's no guarantee that she ever will – I'll do my best to give her wise advice. But you should really be talking to Lali's father, she's much closer to him than to me.'

'And that's another thing!' Tim said. 'He doesn't like me. I can tell by the way he looks at me. As if I don't quite measure up.'

'Michael? Why should Michael dislike you?'

'You tell me! I'll be taking my finals in a few months, then I'm to go into my father's business. I'm pretty steady, usually – except for what happened on Lali's birthday. What does the man want for his daughter, I'd like to know? Would he prefer a skinhead with a pin through his nose? Or a New Age traveller leading a mangy dog around on a bit of string?'

Amy closed her eyes and summoned up the alternative suitors Tim had just described. She remembered the black trench coat which in the fifties had swung from Michael's shoulders; the floppy too-long hair and silk socks. Michael in his time had made the small rebellious statements of his generation. Who knows? He might actually approve the safety-pinned nose, the mangy dog?

'Tim,' she said, 'I'll speak to Lali straight away.' She touched his shoulder and the gesture made her a conspirator. 'You're sure about this baby? It's not just a ploy to bind Lal to you?'

'I'm sure. I want them both. Never wanted anything so much in all my life.'

She watched him ride silently away between the dripping trees. She went back into the kitchen and began to clear the table. He had eaten all the biscuits and all the doughnuts. If she phoned Lali's office right away, a meeting with her might be arranged for tomorrow evening.

Lali looked preoccupied (as well she might). She sat, as she always did, in the button-backed chair which had once been Michael's, a cushion placed carefully in the small of her back as if she were someone in pain, or very old. Amy studied her daughter with new insight and recognized now the new sharpness of features, the shadowed eyes, the hasty refusal of food and drink.

Amy said, in a voice which was gentler than she felt, 'How are you feeling?'

Lali lifted her head, suddenly amused. 'Hey! You're stealing my lines. I'm the one who's supposed to . . . Oh no! Oh God, he's been here, hasn't he?' She stared around the room, examined the carpet closely, as if Tim might have left his spoor. She studied Amy's face. 'That bastard,' she said quietly. 'He just had to come whining to you. I shall probably kill him.'

Amy said, 'I expect you've already told your father the good news?' She could see that Lali wanted to lie. Possibly to protect Amy, but more likely to protect herself.

'Lali,' she said, 'I don't mind if you choose not to confide in me. But don't blame poor Tim because he came to see me. We all need to talk to somebody, sometime.'

'Mum! I don't need to talk about things to anybody. In fact, I'm sick of talking.'

'You seem to have forgotten that I'm your mother. Surely at a time like this –?'

Lali leaned forward in her chair. 'Keep out of my affairs! You've never been good at the all-girls-together sort of thing. It's too late now for you to start taking an interest in my life: and anyway, you're not equipped.' Her antagonism was naked, burning. 'I'm not like you. I don't have the same needs, the same compulsions. I have no intention of ruining my life in the way that you have ruined yours.'

'My life isn't ruined. I intend to be around for quite some time.'

'Oh, I don't mean the cancer. Your life fell apart long before the illness. I doubt if you ever really got it together.'

'What on earth do you mean?'

'You and Dad. You can't really believe that yours was a normal kind of marriage? Haven't you ever, just for a minute, wondered why he left you? Men don't walk out, after all those years, unless they're thoroughly fed-up.'

'I was always a good wife.'

'No, you weren't. You were an excellent housekeeper. Didn't you ever see how lonely he was? And now, you're as lonely as he is. They don't want you up at The Avenue these days, do they? Now that you're no longer useful to them.'

Anger boiled in Amy's veins; the scar in her neck began to

ache and throb. The mockery in Lali's voice destroyed her; she had that knowing wide-eyed stare that Amy had so detested in her daughter's teen years but, having once started, Lali was finding it impossible to stop. 'I'm surprised Dad stayed with you for as long as he did. Oh, they had you on a piece of elastic. Amy, come here! Amy, do this! Amy, we can't possibly manage without you. My God! Did you think we children never noticed?'

'I had to stay near them. I was all they had. They loved me, which was more than Michael ever did.'

'Oh, he loved you. You just never seemed to see him.'

'How dare you! You have no right to say such things to me. I would never have spoken in such a way to –'

'– Belle and Mimi? Of course you wouldn't. You're too frightened of them. I'll bet you always have been. Manipulation is selfishness of a very wicked kind. If I have this child – and if I do it will be *my own* decision, and not in order to give you a Christmas present – I swear I will never do to it what has been done to you.'

Amy said, 'I have never tried to tie you to me; or the boys.'

'No,' Lali said, and Amy could see that for her this was a new thought. 'That's quite true, you haven't. Which proves, of course, that you subconsciously knew what your problem was, and chose not to repeat it with your own children.'

'Well, thank you, Sigmund Freud, or should I say Claire Rayner?'

Lali said, 'You know why you got ill, don't you?'

'No, I don't know. Because I was unlucky.'

'Cancer, in the case of some people, is an acceptable way of committing suicide. So think about it!'

'. . . an acceptable form of suicide,' she had said, 'So think about it.'

A great silence fell across us. I could not bear to look at her, my child, my daughter, who had just rent asunder the temple veil, invaded the inner sanctum; desecrated something, I was not sure what. She and I had spoken about my life in the past tense, as if I was already dead. She left me sitting on the sofa; she did not say goodbye but slammed the front door and her car door, and raced the Mini's engine out of sight and hearing.

'Lonely,' she had said. 'You're as lonely as he is, these days. They don't want you, do they? Now that you're no longer useful to them.' Well, she would think that, wouldn't she? She was young; of a different, less loyal, more selfish generation. And anyway, how dare she! If anyone is going to be critical of Aunty Belle and Mimi it certainly shouldn't be Lali, who is unmarried and pregnant, and does not know her own mind. When Dom comes home this evening I shall tell him I am feeling stronger, ready to resume my life; that it is time for him to make a move, to put his own life into order; to join Chris and Tim in Boys' Town.

'They had you,' she had said, 'on a piece of elastic.'
'They loved me,' I had said. 'I had to stay near them.'

The storm began soon after midnight. Forked lightning split the darkness of the June night, thunder boomed directly overhead. The wind got up, roaring through the tops of the sycamore trees. When the rain began she went down to the kitchen and heated milk. She drank it seated by her bedroom window. She had not slept, could not sleep; doubted she would ever sleep again.

So it had to be Lali in the end, who held up the Camelot mirror; who showed Amy to Amy. As others saw her. As Michael must always have seen her.

Some good friend might possibly, over the years, have warned her; have pointed out where she was going wrong.

If she had ever had a good friend.

Or just a friend.

But there had been no space for friendships.

There had been neighbours, acquaintances. Lately, a few clients had become sufficiently well known to meet her in the town for morning coffee. Sometimes people said they wanted life, said they fought to live. But all the time, deep down, they had long since given up. When had she reached the point where she believed that nothing good could happen? That she was doomed for ever to waken in the night because Michael was not there beside her? Cancer, Lali had said, is an acceptable form of suicide for some people.

Dr Quinn lived in a windy northern town that stood among green hills. Amy took the morning Intercity Train; she bought tea from the buffet and attempted to read the daily paper. She wore the smart green suit and matching sandals.

Her appointment was for two o'clock. She wandered in pleasant unfamiliar streets until her legs ached, ate a sandwich and drank more tea in a café. The taxi took her out of the town into tree-lined avenues of large old houses. A nameplate set into a stone wall confirmed that she had come to the right place. Her finger on the doorbell committed her irrevocably to an hour of Dr Quinn's time.

He possessed the most beautiful speaking voice she had ever heard. Whenever Amy thought about him it would always be his voice that echoed first in her mind. His wife had welcomed her into the house; he had welcomed her into his study. He asked first about the site of her cancer, its duration and treatment; she pointed out her scarred neck.

Amy said, 'I think I know what my other problem is. I just don't know what to do about it.'

'Tell me,' he said, 'about your life in the two years before your cancer was diagnosed.'

Amy told him, and the hour passed as if it were five minutes. They had obviously, said Dr Quinn, a considerable amount of future work to get through. He would like Amy to return in two weeks' time.

*

In St Gilda's Gardens the roses were in full bloom. In the afternoons a carillonneur played 'Greensleeves' on the tower bells.

Amy walked slowly past the swings and seesaw; she peered intrusively into passing prams. Young women, many of whom bore a striking resemblance to Lali, chatted on benches and watched their children as they played. Amy imagined herself, next spring, pushing one of those brightly coloured prams. Perhaps she too would sit on a bench in the sunshine. 'My grandchild,' she would say to the young mothers. 'Her birth weight was eight pounds. She sleeps right through the night, you know. Never any trouble.' For the child would be a girl, no doubt about that, Lali's daughter. A blonde and blue-eyed child. A reason to go on.

The flower-beds around the bandstand were filled with pink impatiens and waxy-white begonias. Amy gazed at them until her vision blurred. Dom had moved out at the weekend, had gone to share the flat with Chris and Tim. She had not allowed him to feel guilty at what he saw as a too-soon departure. 'I want my house back to myself,' she had told him. 'I've been grateful for your care, but now I'm ready to be on my own. I also have some sorting out to do.'

Even so, she missed him. Missed ironing his shirts, grilling pork chops for his supper; the sound of doors opening and closing, all the little signs of life he brought into her dead house.

She walked past the aviary of exotic birds; the parakeets dozed on their perches, silenced by the heat of afternoon. She ordered tea in the café. A swift glance around the patio tables confirmed that all the occupants were strangers to her. Amy relaxed into her chair; she had, just lately, a desperate need to be *among* people but not *with* them. But then, what else was new? Sometimes she thought that her whole life had been lived among strangers.

'Do you cry much?' Dr Quinn had asked.

'No. I never cry.'

'Not even when you were told the nature of your illness?'

'Especially not then.'

'You need to be able to weep. It's dangerous to keep the tears inside. The energy of grief can get stuck in that part of the body used to express it, and this can cause the beginnings of malfunction. I want you to cry!'

'I'll try,' she had said, smiling.

Lali came round unexpectedly. She looked thinner – her pallor alarmed Amy; the honey-gold hair had lost its sheen. This time she appeared deliberately to avoid sitting in the button-backed chair, and instead sat on the sofa.

'I've come to apologize. I said things I had no right to say.'

'You spoke your mind, which is a very good thing to do within the family. Bottling up emotions and resentments can actually damage your health.'

Lali's eyes came wide open; she looked searchingly at Amy, but said nothing.

Amy said, 'You look dreadful.'

'I feel dreadful. Sick all the time. Can't eat. Can't seem to concentrate on anything.'

'You'll feel better when you've made your mind up. One way or the other.'

'I almost have.'

'And –?'

'I want to have the baby, but not by myself; not in the flat.'

'Well, you and Tim can get a house.'

'No. Tim's out of all this. I'm finished with him. All his life he's had everything he's wanted. Well, this time it hasn't worked. He tried to trick me into marriage. He's weak and immature and utterly disgusting, and I don't have the time to wait for him to grow up.'

'Are you sure about all this?'

'Oh, I'm sure. There was never really any option.' She

looked swiftly at Amy and then away. 'I want to come home, Mum. I know it's a lot to ask, and if you think it'll all be too much for you, then I can make other arrangements.'

Amy wanted to ask what other arrangements, but thought that she already knew. Where else would Lali go but to her father?

'Of course you can come home! How could you ever doubt it?' Amy spoke gently, carefully, as if the faintest intonation of reluctance on her part could cause something vital to collapse in Lali.

'Thank you. I won't disrupt your life, I promise.' Lali struggled to keep a light note in her voice. 'We might even get on better together, second time around? Which reminds me; Dad is very anxious to come and see you. How do you feel about it?'

Amy longed for the Monday evening meetings; for the healing, for the easement of mind which came from the facility to talk without the pretence of perfect health and stoicism. The feelings she now had for the other members of the Group were very close to love.

The room where healings were performed was small and quiet. From the window she could see the autumn-coloured trees, the blue mysterious dusk which softened the sharp outlines of the carillon tower. On this particular evening Amy's thoughts were all with Lali. When her healing ended she returned to the main meeting room. She sat down beside Louise whom she knew as both a patient and a healer. They smiled at one another.

Amy said, 'It's funny, isn't it? When you get cancer you think oh well, the very worst thing that could happen has already happened. After this, nothing else will ever seem as bad.'

'Doesn't seem to work out that way though, does it? Disaster is still disaster after all.'

Amy said, 'My daughter is pregnant. She won't marry her boyfriend. She wants to come home to have her baby.'

Louise sat very still. She looked down at her hands, then clasped them tightly together. 'The most devastating news I ever had was when my teenage schoolgirl daughter told me she was pregnant. That was a real body blow. It took two weeks to sink in. It was springtime.'

Amy turned to face Louise; she recognized a style that was only too familiar; the matching violet shades of sandals, dress and earrings, the neat dark hair. She began to admire the calm and deliberate way in which Louise catalogued her troubles.

'When the baby was six months old my daughter left home. She took the baby with her. It was a wrench. But it had to be. My cancer was diagnosed soon after.'

'What happened?'

'Well, I had been to the City Breast Clinic twice with lumps which, when drained, turned out to be harmless cysts. Now another small lump had appeared. Some fluid was removed and sent for testing. When I went back for the result I was not shown into the usual clinic room but into an office. I was given the bad news by the professor himself, and in the presence of the Breast-Care sister. I remember wondering if she was present in case I dissolved into a gibbering heap.' Louise unclasped her hands and flexed her fingers. She began to turn her gold wedding band, first one way and then another. 'The Professor looked uncomfortable about having to tell me. I felt really sorry for him. He had such soft hands and a gentle manner.' Louise paused. 'Imagine having to tell literally thousands of people over the years that they have cancer.'

Amy thought about her own experience of bad news. 'I wanted to kill the messenger,' she admitted.

Louise said, 'Well – the result was what I had expected, really. It's funny how sometimes you just know, don't you? It was bad – but not as bad as what had happened with my daughter. I asked a few questions and then left the clinic. I had a lumpectomy two weeks later.'

'Is that the removal of just the growth and not the whole breast?'

'Yes – but after that was done, they said I would need another operation. I said, well, all right – but can I go on holiday first? After all that had happened that year I really needed a holiday. My husband did a wonderful job of arranging a trip at short notice. He spent a whole day going around the local travel agents. He and I, and our eighteen-year-old son, went off to Paris. It's a city I have always loved.'

'Yes,' said Amy softly. 'I have happy memories of Paris.'

'I returned fit and well for my next operation, which turned out to be more serious than I expected. On the morning of the operation I was told that the Professor had decided I should have a mastectomy because of the nature of my cancer. I asked the ward sister how painful it would be. She said more soreness than bad pain.' The long, slim fingers no longer turned the wedding band. Louise spread out her hands, palms upwards. 'So there I was. Within the hour I would have the Big Op. I had breast-fed both my children. I have this belief that when we die we are made whole again. I looked at the breast I was about to lose. I thought, you have served me well, so goodbye until we meet again. I was forty-four years old. Both of my children were grown-up. I had lived to know my grandchild' – she smiled – 'which was good; and in any case I knew I couldn't die. It wasn't my time.'

Amy said, 'How could you possibly know that?'

'When my children were quite small, a Gypsy came to my door selling lucky lace. Rather nervously I bought two yards. "You will have two children," she told me, "your husband will be faithful to you, you have a good fate and destiny. And you will live to be ninety-two." There have been times when I have wished that she hadn't promised me quite such a long life. But since all her other predictions have come true, I think – well, I can't die yet, the Gypsy said so.'

'So how did you come to join this Group?'

'A few weeks after my operation, a breast counsellor from the hospital came to see me. I said that I thought I should be doing something to cut down on the stress of living. She told me about the Group and gave me a number to ring. I phoned, and spoke to Gill. We talked for a long time. One month after my mastectomy I came to the Group, and have come regularly ever since. That was almost five years ago. Since then I have had three operations and radiotherapy.'

'How did you become a healer?'

'After my last op I had a special healing. When it was finished I was told that I could, if I wanted to, also be a healer. I mulled it over for a long time. When I was about thirteen years old I wanted to donate my eyes. I discovered recently that if you have had cancer you can't donate any organ of your body. I thought about it; another forty-one years of living still to go, and I have to do something useful with all that time. The healers say that all you need to be a healer is to *want to be one*.'

Lali moved back in late September, into her old bedroom with the pink-flowered bedspread and curtains, and the ballerina pictures hanging on the walls. Amy polished the pale wood furniture, and on the window-sill she set a pink azalea in a white pot. Chris and Dom transported Lali's suitcases and the few items she had retained from her life with Tim.

Tim himself appeared on the doorstep late that evening.

'She won't see you,' Amy said, sounding apologetic although she knew she shouldn't. 'She's angry now, Tim. Very angry, and resentful. But it won't last. You'll see. Give her time.'

She closed the door gently on his vulnerable face, but she could still feel his agony through the oaken panels. Her own resentment towards Michael had lasted forty years. She had worn her anger like a suit of armour. She hoped that Lali's intransigence was not so durable. But in her heart she feared it might be.

*

At the end of a week in which Amy re-discovered all those things about Lali which she had always found irritating, it became clear to both of them that changes needed to be made.

They drove out to the woodland pub and sat in a high-backed settle, close to the log fire. Amy thought about the last time she had come here; how easily she and Dom had talked together. She wrapped her arms about her body and shivered inside her warm tweed suit. Lali's closed and private face was bent to the menu card with the same look of indifference which she now turned on Amy. The drive to the pub had been made in silence. Lali laid down the menu card.

'I'm not really hungry.'

'You must eat something. I could ask them to make you some dry toast.'

'Don't fuss, Mum.'

'It'll be a girl. I was sick all the time when I carried girls.' Amy breathed deeply, in and out to calm her tension. 'Look, Lal. I've been thinking. We could make a few changes in the house. Make life more – well – pleasant for you. Chris and Dom are settled now in their own place. We could clear out their bedrooms, have them redecorated, and make one into a sitting-room for you, and the other could be a nursery for the baby.'

'Babies.'

When Amy did not answer, Lali said, 'Twins, Mum. So how do you feel about that? Double trouble, eh?'

'Are you certain?'

'I had a scan. Two girls, they said. No shadow of a doubt.'

Amy said, 'Oh,' and then, 'Oh, Lal! That's wonderful!'

'I'm glad *you*'re pleased. It came as a bit of a shock to me.'

'It shouldn't have. Twins seem to occur frequently in my family.'

'You've never talked about your parents.'

'I don't have anything to say about them.'

'Your mother must have been Belle and Mimi's sister?'

'I suppose so. I was always discouraged from asking questions. I think something pretty shameful must have happened. I decided long ago that I didn't want to know about it.'

Lali looked into her coffee cup. 'That's just you, isn't it? Passive. Accepting. Never doing anything about anything. I look at you sometimes and wonder what goes on inside your head. What about your father? You must have had one. Don't you ever wonder?'

'It's not something you should be concerned about. Especially now.'

'There you go again. Telling me what I should think. You're my mother, for God's sake. I'm authorized to worry about you!'

'Don't, Lal. Please don't. This is not what we came here to talk about.'

'Just one more thing, Mum. When you were talking about being sick all the time you said it happened to you when you carried girls. Does that mean that I was a twin and the other one died?'

Amy leaned her head back against the settle cushions. 'It won't do you any good to know this.'

'It will do me considerable harm if I'm left to wonder about it.'

'All right. You want to know, so you shall know! Your father married me because I was pregnant. The baby was stillborn. Perfect in every way, but she never breathed.'

Amy felt Lali's gaze fall upon her like a blow. But when Lali spoke her voice was soft. 'You would never have told me that if I hadn't forced you. Oh, Mum. Why can't you trust me – anybody? How many more secrets are there in this family?'

Chris and Dom brought a van and took away the contents of their bedrooms, including the carpets and the curtains. Tim came with them, arriving at a time when they knew that Lali would be absent. He seemed less gloomy. Amy longed to tell him that he would soon be the father of twin girls. He had, she thought, a right to know; but hers was not the right to tell him. There was a lot of laughter as they wrestled beds and wardrobes down the stairs. Tim might have already been a brother-in-law, their sister's husband. Chris and Dom, Amy now realized, were not as clear-cut in family matters as she had once taken them to be.

Chris came into the kitchen before they drove away. 'We found a lot of old photograph albums in Dom's wardrobe,' he said. 'I've piled them up in a corner of the room.'

Sometimes people died.

If she had really thought about it she should have known that such a probability was high: that death for some members of the Group was an inevitable outcome; that the most to be hoped for by any patient was to live longer than the medical prognosis – to astound some authoritative hospital white-coat, to be able perhaps to say the magic word CLEAR for at least six months, a year, five years.

Claudia had been with them at the meeting on the previous Monday. True, she could no longer climb the stairs, but she used the lift. True, she was very pale under skilful make-up, but her hair had been cut in a new style and given highlights. She had smiled as she always did; had told Amy about the anniversary trip to Spain planned by her husband. Claudia, Jan told the Group, had died that morning. Her husband had telephoned with the sad news.

On the other hand, a letter had come from Patricia, to whom the surgeons had recently said, 'We'll do our best – even if it's only palliative.'

Jan read it aloud. 'Right – now it's out! I've seen it in black and white. IT'S OUT. Now it's up to me. Body has been done, now it's up to me to do mind and spirit. Must put into practice all the good things I know about from the Group. Having prepared for death, having persuaded myself life isn't much cop anyway, I now find I'm cancer-free. The surgeons "were surprised". I'll bet! Didn't they realize I'm a special person? Didn't they know they were dealing with *me*?

'So, now I just watch the sunset. I lose all need for my erstwhile hustling, bustling, dashing, whizzing, buzzing life. I desire less. I want a quieter soul, a stiller being. This is a message to me, this cancer. And a very rudely worded one. It's *for* something; telling me to slow down, allow only funda-mental necessities.

'It'll be very difficult not to let my old ways creep back; hard not to keep practising my mistakes. If the telephone rings – leave it! Cut out all the crap and just BE.

'This is the second chance I have been praying for.'

Visits to Belle and Mimi were leaving her increasingly drained and disturbed, so that she had barely recovered from the last meeting with them when she presented herself at their door for yet another ordeal.

Dr Quinn advised that she should, for the present, cut off all contact with them. But Amy could not bring herself to close that particular door. And so she compromised, talked inanities, kept the visits short.

Mimi's confusion of mind was growing deeper. Aunty Belle's inability to cope with Mimi was painful to observe. Amy, heartsick and overwhelmed with guilt, and yet knowing that there was nothing she could do to change things, walked away from the house in The Avenue one October morning and met Chris, whom she had not seen since Lali had moved back in. He looked at her face, took her arm, and steered her firmly into the lounge bar of the Prince of Wales. He sat her down on the green mock-leather of a comfortable bench; Tiffany-style lamps shed pools of light into the gloom. Behind the mahogany bar a young man polished glasses. He and Chris seemed to know each other. 'Your dad was in a few minutes ago,' said the barman. 'He was looking for you. Said to tell you he'll be back at lunchtime.'

Amy half-rose from her seat, but Chris told her to sit down;

he placed the brandy glass before her. 'Drink that,' he said. 'I know you don't like the taste, but it's what you need.' He was drinking something dark from a tall glass. Guinness, she guessed. Like Fin, like Michael. She knew then just how careful she would need to be when talking to Chris. She could no longer assume that because she loved him he would agree with every word she spoke.

'Why do you do it, Mother?'

'Do what?' She wondered why he always called her 'Mother', when Dom and Lali called her 'Mum'.

'You know what.' His tone was indulgent but he did not smile. And Chris, in general, was a smiler.

'Belle and Mimi?' she said. 'I can't seem to help myself. I have to – oh, I don't know – keep the contact.'

'It's not good for you.' His voice shook a little. She knew how difficult he found this sort of conversation.

'I know. I really do know. I'm working on it, Chris. The habit of a lifetime can't be broken all at once.' The smell of the brandy nauseated her; she took it in small sips, and then was surprised at the warmth spreading in her chest and stomach.

'Camella came back.' His voice was dreamy, his eyes soft.

Amy was unsure if she was supposed to have remembered that Camella had departed. The life of an air hostess was bound to be unsettled, and Chris was so secretive about his love life.

'You'll be regretting the presence of Dom and Tim in your flat now.'

'Not really. We plan to buy a house. We're getting married. All her relatives are coming over from Italy. She's giving up the air-hostess job. She'll work on the airline desk in future.'

It was the most information about his life that Chris had ever volunteered to her. She reached for his hand and held on to it.

'I'm so pleased for you,' she smiled. She thought, I wonder if twins can be transmitted through the male line of the family?

*

187

Shopping with Lali was exhausting. That old childhood need to look and look, to touch and test had increased rather than diminished. Amy had watched her daughter stroke a dozen sofas, set innumerable cradles rocking before she herself admitted weariness.

'You should have said,' Lali scolded. 'You always pretend that you are capable of doing more than you really can.' In the restaurant Lali drew plans in black felt-tip on a yellow paper napkin. The nursery was to be all white with touches of gentian blue (why should boys always have the nicest colours?). Lali's sitting-room was to take its colours from the faded pink and gold upholstery of a wing-chair donated by Tim's mother. (So you are in close touch with his mother, are you, Lali? Close enough to accept a little gift or two?)

In this seventh month of her pregnancy Lali wore baggy denim overalls of a kind that were once used for protection by men who swept the streets and cleaned out drains. Amy had offered to buy her pretty maternity wear but Lali had said it was hardly worth it. Twins, she said, would take some accommodating towards the end, and the overalls had special gussets. Surely Amy remembered how it had been with Chris and Dom? On the other hand, she said, since she was still finding it difficult to eat, the babies might be very tiny. No, said Amy, babies were clever, they stole all the nutrients they needed from those stored in the mother's body. It was more likely to be Lali herself who ended up depleted.

It was at the very end of the meal when Amy, from habit, was piling dirty plates and cutlery together, that Lali opened her handbag and took out the little package. She handed it over, making a small ceremony of the transfer. 'Open it,' she said. 'I'm longing to see what it is.'

'Isn't it from you, then?'

'Sorry. But no. It's from an – an old admirer, you might say.'

Amy stripped away the wrapping paper and removed the lid

of a small box. Nestled in cotton wool lay a dark-blue glass bottle with a silver top and label. Evening in Paris. She read the tiny gift-card. 'I promised you this when you were eighteen, and never gave it to you. Is it too late for me, Amy?'

The bottle was one-third full of perfume. Lali reached out a hand for it and unscrewed the top. She sniffed and said, 'Why, it's lovely! After all this time! Oh, Mum, why won't you just see him? Talk to him. That perfume hasn't all evaporated. Perhaps his love and your love haven't either.'

She couldn't believe that Lali had said those words. Those romantic words. She sounded like virtuous Melanie in *Gone with the Wind* talking to poor limp Ashley Wilkes. Amy wanted to answer like Scarlett O'Hara, oh, don't be so silly, Melie. Men don't think like that.

But suppose they do? Some of them. One of them. Michael. Evening in Paris. When Amy was seventeen, eighteen, that small phial was the ultimate sophistication. And he did promise her a bottle; and never kept his promise.

Lali's eyes were full of tears. The tears were brimming over, dripping down those awful denim overalls. Don't, Lal. Please don't. We are not worth your tears, Michael and I, she thought. And you have troubles of your own.

The transformation of the bedrooms into sitting-room and nursery was accomplished in the space of one weekend. Dom came early on Saturday morning. He brought Tim with him. They laid new carpet and hung new curtains. Amy, in the kitchen brewing coffee, felt excluded. She eavesdropped from the hall. Lali spoke exclusively to Dom, punishing Tim, forcing loneliness upon him. Amy poured coffee into three mugs, put biscuits and doughnuts on a large plate. Tim collected the tray. His colour was bad, his face drawn. He said, 'Thanks for letting her stay here, Mrs Sheldon. I feel better just knowing she's with you.'

'This is her home, Tim. It's a big house, too much for one person. It's giving me something else to think about, to plan for.'

He picked up the tray and then put it down. He said, with the first real flare of anger she had seen in him, 'It's such a bloody stupid situation! I don't know why she's doing this. I admit I made a big mistake, but we'd planned to have a child quite soon, and it's surely not a hanging matter?'

'Like I said before, Tim, you'll have to be patient for a few months.' She wanted to comfort him but could not. She remembered the time after she had lost her first child. How she had almost gone back to Aunty Belle and Mimi. Instead, she had stayed with Michael, refusing to sleep in his bed, not speaking to him; punishing him, forcing loneliness upon him. For what had surely not been a hanging matter? She began to call up other times, other tenderly nursed resentments. In her head she heard Dr Quinn's deep and beautiful voice. 'Anger,' he had said, 'is so extraordinarily energetic, it involves the body from top to bottom. Under the influence of anger all the chemistry changes: tensions arise, pulse rate rises, blood pressure goes up, pupils dilate – and if this energy is not released, if it is held back in the body, then it starts off by causing malfunctions, and ends by causing structural damage.

'Let the sun not go down upon one's wrath,' he had said, 'is an aphorism one really must take to heart.'

She had let many suns go down upon her wrath, had so often swallowed the hard words she had not dared to utter, because if she spoke her thoughts aloud the person who had caused the hurt would withdraw love: and this she could not face. But love had been withdrawn anyway.

Michael had walked away, never to return. Aunty Belle and Mimi seemed hardly to remember who she was. She believed her children cared about her; even Tim who confided only out of desperation. But they were young – and yes – she must face the truth about them. They were *naturally*, *normally*, *blessedly* SELFISH!

And thank God for it.

She walked slowly up the stairs, and stood in the doorway of the room that was to be a nursery for her granddaughters. Her fatherless granddaughters.

There they sat, munching biscuits and sipping coffee, Tim and Dom on the almost-laid blue carpet, Lali in a white wicker nursing chair. Amy studied them, unobserved: the silent misery of Tim, the embarrassed Dom, the smug, self-satisfied pout of Lali, who appeared to be enjoying the situation she had herself created.

Amy said sharply. 'A word with you please, Lalique. In my room.'

Lali stared, hardly able to believe that it was Amy who had spoken.

Dom said, 'Something wrong, Mum?'

Tim looked away, seeking uninvolvement.

'It is healthier,' said Dr Quinn, 'to be assertive; it is healthier to please oneself; to say no when one means no; and to say yes only *when it pleases us*.

'And it will frequently occur that pleasing *us*, pleasing *ourselves*, also means pleasing others. When the smiling yes-sayer takes courage and dares a no, to his or her surprise he finds, if it is done properly, then the other person fully understands the reasons for the no, and is *not at all upset*.'

She came into my bedroom promptly, the same apprehension in her face as long ago, when her childish touching and stroking of inanimate objects had sometimes been too enthusiastic. But this time it was different. She did not hold bits of broken china in her hands, or an armless doll which had been too much cuddled. What she carried was beyond my power to protect or repair. Yet I knew that I would try.

She sat down in the chair beside the window; her movements

were heavy, graceless. Her hair hung in strands around her head and shoulders, her eyes were puffy. The denim overalls and T-shirt were unattractively, necessarily baggy. I could not stop myself from looking at them, making the outfit a focus for my wrath.

I moved the dressing-table stool closer to the window. We faced one another, the silence thick between us. We were good at these silences, Lali and I. We used them both as a defence and as a weapon. Sulking, Michael had called it.

'I know what you're going to say.'

'Well, if you already know, what do you propose to do about it?'

'I can't forgive him. You have no right to expect me to. He's an absolute bastard. I could never trust him after what he's done.'

'In that case, perhaps it would have been better if you'd had a termination.' I could hear myself saying the terrible words and could not hold them back.

She pulled herself upright in the chair. 'Oh no! I could never do that – well, *you* didn't, did you?' Lali paused, then said with satisfaction, 'I'll bet Aunty Belle gave you seven sorts of hell when you told her you were pregnant.'

'Yes. She did rather.' For the first time in forty-two years I allowed the memory of those words to surface. 'You're worse than your mother, Amy. At least she was well acquainted with your father!'

Lali said, 'Don't look like that, Mum. I didn't mean to –'

'Long time ago,' I said. Long time ago, I thought, and still it has the power to hurt, to awaken my resentment.

'Resentment,' Dr Quinn had said, 'is the first cousin of anger, and possibly the most dangerous of the emotions. We need to be very much in touch with our resentments. They lie hidden in the depths of the mind like coiled springs, exerting their effects upon us.'

I gazed out at the leafless trees, the grey skies, and then back at my daughter. I was old enough to be her grandmother. Perhaps that had always been the problem.

As if she read my thoughts, Lali said, 'What is it with us? You get along fine with the boys – you can even make allowances for Tim. I think I shouldn't have come back here. I had this stupid idea that maybe – just maybe – we could get closer.' The old knowing look was in her face. 'You thought if I didn't come to you, I would go to Dad. And you didn't want that, did you? He still keeps trying to reach you – reach out to you – but you can't stop punishing him, can you?'

I smiled and nodded, and I saw her thoughts click into place, making the inevitable connection.

'My God!' she whispered. 'I'm exactly like you, aren't I?'

'No,' I said, 'not exactly like me. A little bit perhaps. But in the ways that will only cause you pain.' I went to her then, knelt down before her and held her hands. 'You love him, don't you?'

'Yes.'

'Well then –?'

'No. Not yet.' She gazed down at her unwieldy body. 'Let him sweat for two months longer. I expect I shall forgive him. But in my time, not his.'

She stood up and so did I. She touched my shoulder briefly and then walked away. Almost at once I could hear her issuing instructions. 'Not there! Put it over here, next to the window.' I heard their laughter, even Tim.

Dom said, 'What are we supposed to do with these old photo albums and chocolate boxes?'

'Put them in Mum's room,' Lali said.

Dom had a new lady. 'Nice,' Lal said, 'very nice. In a different league altogether from that brainless clothes-horse Chantal.'

They were eating supper without benefit of tablecloth, their yoghurt pots and malted-grain rolls, their goats' cheese and salad-makings dumped anyhow at one end of the kitchen table. 'Her name is Verity and she's heavily into culture. You know – opera and ballet, and the sort of books that are too heavy to carry home from the library.'

'How is Dom coping with all that?'

'Why ask? He's going around with a big fat grin on his face – so something must be going right between them.'

Most of the time she was glad of Lali's presence in the house now. They spent one whole evening up in Amy's workroom sorting through materials and patterns for christening gowns, petticoats and baby dresses. Lali, she was finding out, walked a fine line between outrageous modernity and old-fashioned conventionality. It was not at all clear yet who was taking care of whom.

But there was still those times when the house closed around Amy; when the walls shuffled inwards, the ceilings zoomed downwards, everything folding endlessly in upon her like the aftermath of earthquake, captured on slow-motion film. These were the days when she took flight, left a note on the kitchen table to whom it might concern, and got into her car and drove.

On this quiet November afternoon she travelled with the photograph albums beside her on the passenger seat, and the old, gold-rimmed magnifying glass which had once belonged to Fin.

The quality of time had altered. The diagnosis of that first doctor (get that lump cut out of your neck before it kills you), had been a summary of her personality, as well as a cancer verdict; something lodged in her throat, an obstruction that would, in time, have cut off air and sustenance; something that had already placed her among the walking dead, unaware of what was happening around her. Other people's agonies.

And then there was guilt. Somewhere she had read that the ability to accept blame was the ultimate proof of a mature mind. If this was true then her mind was more mature than antique wine; and just as pointless.

'Do you cry much?' Dr Quinn had asked her.
'I never cry,' she had said. 'It only upsets other people.'
'Then upset them!' he had shouted.

She had known where Michael lived since the day after his departure; which proved that she was capable of lying when it came to saving face. It had been so easy. She had parked in a side street close to Angel Row, had watched while Michael treble-locked the heavy oaken door of Sheldon Antiques. In the gathering dusk of the November evening it was unlikely that he would recognize her old black Metro. She had slotted into traffic several cars behind his, had followed him into a part of the city which was unfamiliar to her. He had driven to an area which had been badly run-down, but was rapidly coming up. She watched him park before a large, partly renovated building, saw him tread warily among heaps of sand and cement, then walk, first under one builder's ladder and then another. She had wondered at the risks he took.

She waited until lights came on in the ground-floor rooms, had seen the wary, hunted look on Michael's face as he twitched heavy curtains across the windows; almost as if he had known that she stood in the darkness, watching.

She had thought then, driving back through the dark night, passing Guy Fawkes's bonfires on the Heath, seeing rockets arc and glow and fall to earth, that Michael would tire long before she did of the single lonely life. Home before Christmas, she had foretold. But it never happened.

Five years on and she drove again through unfamiliar streets. She at first hardly recognized the renovated house which had lost its angular greyness beneath a rendering of soft-pink stucco. There were new, white-painted windows and matching double entrance doors. Window-boxes at the lowest windows (Michael's windows) held yellow-and-purple winter pansies. On the paved area around the house dwarf conifers grew in low stone tubs. She could just make out four bell-pushes with the appropriate names slotted in beside them. Which meant that the whole of the ground-floor area was in Michael's occupation. She parked in a facing side street in a spot which gave her a full view of the house, switched off the ignition, and reached for the first of the photograph albums. She sat very still, the album propped unopened against the steering wheel, and gazed at the place where Michael lived.

When I first knew him, first knew that I loved him, it was enough to breathe his air, to walk in his shadow, to sit where he had sat, to touch where he had touched.

I was transparent, without guile; and men always know when they are too much loved.

Except that I was not entirely his.

I denied it. Well, I had to. Most young women, when first married, make the transition from parents to husband without too much pain. New loyalties replace old ones. The cut cord scarcely bleeds. Except in my case. And Michael knew it.

The albums creaked open like old, unused doors. The pages were of stiff, dark grey paper interleaved with sheets of tissue. The photos had been glued firmly into place, and lovingly arranged according to age. The first showed a young woman, posed beneath a silver-birch tree. She wore the loose, low-belted coat that was the fashion of her time, and a small cloche hat with a feather in it. Her state of pregnancy was well advanced. The printed name beside the photo said MARGUER-ITE, but the young and pretty face could almost have been Mimi.

The baby appeared in subsequent photos, a round-faced hairless infant either yawning or sleeping. AMELIA AT THREE WEEKS. TWO MONTHS. FOUR MONTHS. Amelia sitting up in a large dark pram, wearing a bonnet heavy with pom-poms. Amelia standing, unsteadily, holding on to the fingers of someone just out of shot. The same pose, same child, but this time the man was in the picture; and the man was Chris. Could not be Chris, not in 1932. The words beneath the photo blurred. DADDY AND AMELIA ON HER FIRST BIRTHDAY.

Amy felt the vomit rise, hot and bitter in her throat. She pushed open the car door and gulped in cold air. Slowly the nausea receded. She forced her gaze back to the albums to Archie, who in 1932 would have been the age that Chris was now. So Archie, whom she had loved, had been her father, and the gentle, smiling girl called Marguerite, who looked a lot like Mimi, had been her mother.

She leaned back in her seat, pressed her head into the headrest and closed her eyes. What had she expected to discover? She had sensed, for as long as she could remember, that they were lying to her. The best she could have hoped for was to find out that she was the child of strangers. But the most heinous lies, it was said, were almost always told within the family.

She sat upright. Her hand, her independent hand, began to turn more pages. The black and white pictures were extraordinarily clear. But still she viewed them through the magnifying glass, seeking confirmation of what she already knew to be the truth. Page after page showed the same three faces; the handsome burly man who was almost Chris, the pretty girl who was almost Mimi; and the solemn child who did not, in any feature, resemble either of them.

There was a feel of sunshine in the sharpness of the black and white. Someone had posed the child carefully, lovingly, as if she were a jewel deserving of a quality setting; her head bent to an arrangement of sweet-peas; sitting motionless among daisies on a wide lawn; holding a toy watering-can waveringly towards the trunk of a rowan tree. There were walls of weathered, mellow stone up which honeysuckle climbed; another background showed a bandstand, uniformed musicians. On a separate page, right at the back of the final album, an elderly white-haired couple held the baby called Amelia.

Grandparents; and Amy recognized the background, the conservatory, and the tiny garden where orange lilies grew.

The house was the ugly house of yellow brick where she had once lived with Archie and Mimi.

She wondered how many people had guessed the truth. The albums had not answered all her questions. Fin had known. Mimi must have told him. She remembered the final minutes of his life, holding his hand, trying to decipher the words he muttered. Fin, long-lapsed Irish Catholic, had said 'Father – father', and she had thought it was a priest he called for. If Fin had known that Marguerite was Mimi, then so did Michael. They had no secrets from each other.

She sat very still, knowing there was only one place left for her to go. The pink house, even in November, had a warm continental aspect. She could imagine it perched high on a Spanish hillside, or set among trees in a village of the Dordogne.

Darkness gathered quickly; when he finally came, the night was well established. She watched him check the locks on his car, walk quickly across the paving and go in through the white door. Lights and lamps went on in the flat, illuminating every room within her view. He does what I do, Amy thought; light makes the place appear less lonely. This time he did not at once pull the curtains across the windows. She could just make out the silver of his hair, the gold rims of the spectacles she had not known he wore. There was an unbearable poignancy about her monitoring of him. She had never really wondered about Michael alone.

She packed the albums into their case, checked her hair and make-up in the driving mirror. Lali had persuaded her to buy a long loose coat of tangerine wool; the effect of the colour upon her was remarkable. Wearing it made her feel optimistic even when, deep down, she wasn't.

She locked the car carefully, emulating Michael, and walked the short distance to the pink house.

*

So there I was ringing his doorbell, doing what I had sworn I would never do. He took his time in answering. Perhaps he needed a minute or two to hide the whisky bottle, or turn down the heat underneath his pan of baked beans? Through the frosted glass panel of the outer door I could see the approaching outline of him. Tall, too thin, a little more stooped than I remembered. It was then that I wanted to run.

He opened the door and we stared at one another. I thought at first that he did not quite know who I was. I said, 'Michael', he said, 'Amy'. We were like actors who had not only forgotten their lines but mislaid the prompter. He shook his head as if to clear his thoughts. He said, 'Come in', and stood aside for me to enter.

I walked into a room which was as close a replica as he could make it to that first home we shared in Angel Row; but untidy! The same cabinets and sideboard, dining-table and chairs; the blue, velvet-covered sofas, the long swagged curtains, the Tiffany lamps. He observed my shock with satisfaction. I sat down on the edge of a sofa cushion. Directly in my view was a glass-fronted cabinet which contained a single object. The Lalique girl.

The room was warm but I pulled the wool coat tight around me. I had, of course, known the figurine was here – where else would it be? But to see it, in his sole possession, was still shocking. But then, I thought, so what? I have the living breathing Lali, soon to be the mother of twins, in *my* house, in *my* care.

I looked at him and saw that he also studied the figurine, and I knew then why he had sought a reconciliation. He wanted to be where Lali was, to be a father, a grandfather, back on the inside, warm and involved and looking outwards.

He said, polite as ever, 'Can I get you anything?'

'A pot of Earl Grey tea and directions to your bathroom.'

He grinned, knowing me as only a husband or lover could.

'You've been sitting a long time in your car, waiting.'

When I came back into the room a tea-tray stood on a low table. He had made an effort; the china matched, two pink paper napkins lay folded beside a plate of gypsy-creams. We sat on facing sofas, the tea between us.

He said, 'I never really thought you'd come.'

'I almost didn't.' I poured tea and handed him a cup. We sipped the Earl Grey, but left the gypsy-creams untouched. He looked much older. There were new lines in his face; his hair was thinning on the crown. The professorial gold rims suited him, but I assumed he knew that.

When the silence had stretched to an unbearable length he said, 'How are you, Amy?'

I could hear the reluctance in his voice, sense his unwillingness to acknowledge an illness he had been fortunate enough not to have witnessed at first hand.

I said, 'I am exactly as you see me. I have good days and bad days.'

'Are you cured?'

I smiled at the naivety of him, the well-meaning, clod-hopping naivety that meant he was as ill informed as most. 'No, Michael. I am not cured. The wise person never thinks or speaks in terms of cancer being cured. On the other hand, I am not *dying of* cancer, I am *living with* it. There is quite a difference.'

Once again his head gave that brief shake. 'You've changed. You sound like – well, like somebody I've never known.'

'And does that bother you?'

'Yes. Yes, it does.' He pushed the slipping gold rims back up to the bridge of his nose.

'Surely you didn't think that you could disappear for all this time and find nothing changed?'

'I didn't disappear. You always knew where you could find me.'

'*You* always knew where *I* was. Which hospital. The children kept you well-informed. You never got in touch.'

'I phoned. Phoned the ward. They always said stable or comfortable.'

'They always say that. Right up until you draw your final breath.' I stopped, listened, heard the echoes of my words. We were back in the old pattern. He defensive. I accusing.

I set my teacup down upon the table. 'Why did you leave?'

He rubbed the heel of his hand across his chin, the way he always did when words were difficult to find.

'Because I had to.'

'Belle and Mimi?'

'That. Other things.'

'What things?'

He drew his breath in sharply and I braced myself for some awful accusation.

'It sounds so trivial just to say it.'

'I have to know.'

'It sort of built up gradually over the years. You ironed my socks. You hung my shirts on hangers. You gave me cravats and cuff-links for my birthday. I felt impelled to live up to your expectations.' He sighed. 'It got very wearing, Amy.'

'But you wanted me to do those things. Right from the beginning, when I first met you, you had this superior air, as if you were a special person; only the best was good enough for Michael Sheldon.'

He smiled. He said softly, 'If you had been abandoned, in your pram, outside a Dublin pub, you'd have also grown up wondering who and what the hell you really were. We invented Michael Sheldon, Fin and I. He sent me to that bespoke tailor. It was like a game we played. "Look the part," Fin said. "Wear the good clothes, put the style on. Sure an' you can be anything you choose to be." And so I did. And it worked. I landed this classy girl who worked in the solicitors' office, the one who lived with her aunts in the big house in The Avenue; the treasure that was guarded day and night. I won you, Amy, although it was a near thing sometimes. Time and again I thought you'd see through me.'

'You didn't love me, did you?'

'No. Not then. Not the sort of love you mean, the sort of love you wanted. Think about it! What could I have known about love between a man and woman, growing up with Fin who had affairs but never married? As for you – Belle and Ken were hardly a prime example of a happy marriage.'

I leaned back into the sofa, the strength drained out of me as if a plug had been pulled.

He said, 'What's wrong?' and then, 'I keep forgetting you've been ill.'

'Yes,' I said, 'well, I can understand that. It must be difficult to believe in an illness you haven't actually observed.'

'I'll drive you home.'

'I'll drive myself.'

'You can't. You're in no fit state –' As he stood up the spectacles again slid down his nose.

'Oh, get those bloody glasses fixed!' I shouted.

He drove me home. As I left the car he said, 'We can't leave things like this.'

'No,' I said.

'I'll ring you. First thing in the morning.' He waited until I had entered the house and closed the door, then he drove away.

He didn't phone. I slept little and rose very late. I was grilling bacon for Lali's breakfast, a special brand of oak-smoked that I hoped might tempt her into eating. It was she who answered the sharp ring of the bell. She came into the kitchen, a wide grin on her face. 'It's Dad. He's brought your car back. He won't come in, he's standing in the front porch.' She took the grill pan from my hand. 'Go on then! Get your coat. He wants to take you for a walk.'

There was colour in St Gilda's Gardens even in November; beds of winter-flowering pansies, chrysanthemums and Michaelmas daisies in herbaceous borders; the deep pink of heathers in the rockery beside the gate. We followed the stream down to the stone bridge.

'We brought Lali here,' he said, 'when she first learned to walk.'

'Mostly you,' I said. 'I hardly ever came.'

'No,' he said, 'you didn't, did you? You spent your time with the boys.' He rested his elbows on the parapet and looked down into the water. 'Since I left,' he said, 'I've become very close to my sons. I've really come to know them.'

'It's the same with Lali and me. I was very touched that it was me she turned to.'

'Checkmate, Amy,' he said softly.

I turned and walked quickly away towards the café. He followed with that old loping stride that I remembered. I could almost see the black trench coat swinging from his shoulders, the fair hair flopped across his forehead. Facing him across the café table, I took in properly for the first time his changed style of dress. The corduroy trousers and Aran sweater, the heavy brogues, the olive-green waxed jacket. The thick brown woollen socks.

He became aware of my observation. 'Yes,' he said, 'a change of style is beneficial sometimes.'

I was wearing the tangerine wool coat over the cream leisure suit, trainers on my feet, a band around my hair. The thought crossed my mind that for the first time ever we looked right together; and yet I felt uneasy in his company. We had never, since Paris, sat idly at café tables, expending time on one another. I was unsure of what was expected of me.

He said, 'Where did the years go, Amy?'

It was the wrong question at the wrong time. 'I wasn't keeping count. And now it doesn't seem to matter.'

'I couldn't have built the business up without you.'

'Or had three children.' I smiled. 'Or at least, those particular three children.'

'True. But what about us? The two of us.'

PATRICIA WENDORF

'There never was an "us", Michael.'

'And whose fault was that?'

'Mine.'

He spooned sugar distractedly into his coffee. 'I never thought to hear you say that.'

I imagined, for a moment, that the hand which held the spoon shook a little. 'No,' I said. 'I've done a lot of thinking lately. My life is very different these days. I've become quite selfish, really.'

'Are you sure?' The concern in his voice, the belated concern, made me angry.

'Of course I'm sure.' I could see the doubt in his eyes. I stood up. 'I'll have to go now. Thank you for the coffee.' I walked out of the café, and through St Gilda's Gardens, and did not look back. Nothing changes, I thought. Give him an inch and he'll still take a mile.

I began to meet Michael on a regular, mid-morning-coffee basis, which felt more like an old-fashioned assignation. I bought two cowl-necked angora sweaters, one in emerald and one in gold; they helped to soften my bony angles and conceal the scar on my throat. I considered the purchase of an olive-green waxed jacket, but decided that would be taking compromise a touch too far. To begin with we spoke to one another in the manner of people who were losing the ability to communicate with their own kind. I arrived in the café at ten-thirty every morning; he was almost always there before me. On the days that he was not, I felt bereft until he came. The silences buzzed with our unspoken thoughts, words too dangerous to be uttered. I ventured the occasional disinterested question. 'Can you really spare the time to be here?'

'I'm already semi-retired. I plan to retire altogether at Christmas.'

I wanted to say he wasn't old enough for that, but of course he was. 'What will you do then? Will you sell the business?'

'Chris and Dom are taking over.'

'I didn't know.'

'They didn't know how to tell you.'

'That's ridiculous.'

'I know.'

'You'll have time on your hands.'

'I already have.' He smiled. 'It's greatly overrated, leisure. Especially when it's spent alone.'

'Yes,' I said.

'Do you go out much in the evenings?'

'Only on Mondays. I go to a Cancer Self-Help Group.'

'And does it? Help?'

'It's turned my life around. Changed everything. Changed me.'

'But you were never a joiner.'

'Depends how great the need.'

'I let you down. I failed you.'

I thought about my answer; he might get up and walk away. Forever. I said it anyway. 'Yes, you did. Not a sign that you even knew what was happening to me. I would never have done that to you.'

He was quiet for a long time. I ordered more coffee. We drank it, and still he did not speak. At last he said, 'Truth was, I couldn't face it. Couldn't begin to cope with what was happening to you. It felt like a reproach. As if you were doing it on purpose, to get even with me.'

'It was not a form of revenge I would have deliberately chosen.'

'I can see that now.'

'If it's any consolation, the causes of my problems go back further than my years with you.'

'Yes,' he said, and did not seem surprised.

*

In December there was hoar frost in the mornings; later on in
the day there was sunshine and blue skies. We drove out most
afternoons to the woodland pub. The coffee breaks had begun
to stretch into lunch breaks, into afternoon teas, occasionally
evenings spent in Michael's flat.

It was not always good between us, and never easy.

Chris and Dom came often to the house to spend time with
Lali. Verity and Camella now fulfilled the role of sisters to her.
For a banished suitor and redundant father-to-be, Tim was
looking pleased with himself. I would meet him on the stairs
or in the kitchen. He would greet me with fond amusement; in
fact they all had a way of looking at me as if I was a
precocious child about to perform a party piece. They were
waiting, I suspected, for some late-in-life romantic develop-
ment; willing me to tell them all about it in my sweet old-
fashioned way, and to the sound of violins. Well, to hell with
them!

It was none of their business, anyway.

For the first time in my life I began to wish that I was Irish,
or Italian or French, or any nationality except this English
woman of rectitude and deep restraint who still found it
embarrassing to argue, rock the boat, jump the queue. Even
so, my children, my liberated children, had their own taboos.
Sex was discussed among them in the easy, casual way that my
generation might have talked about cricket, or long-distance
running, or the merits of a good book.

Love was their banned word.

They had relationships. Sometimes they mentioned
commitment.

I had said to Michael, 'You didn't love me, did you?'

'No,' he had answered, 'not then', which allowed me to
imagine that he might have come to love me later. But how
much later? And did he still? And could I ever bring myself to
ask him? For to ask was to admit need. And to admit so much

neediness was to confess to failure. The failure to be self-sufficient. In control. English.

'Now love,' Dr Quinn had said. 'Our love may frequently be held back by our fear of hurt. So we then have a building up inside us of the positive energies associated with loving, but unable to be expressed by the results of our early experiences. Thus, if we have difficulty in loving, we need to understand that we are *practising a mistake*. Developing our self-awareness is really the only way that we can begin to initiate a change. If we convict ourselves of not displaying our affections we perhaps can then determine to begin to take some risks. We can perhaps say to ourselves, well if I love someone, it would be nice if I told them, and not expect them to know I love them by thought transference. The ability to love,' said Dr Quinn, 'surely is the light within us; perhaps the most important element of our human nature.'

He asked me to go away with him, for a long weekend, to an auction of paintings and fine prints to be held in a remote corner of the Peak District.

'I can't possibly.'

'Why not?'

'Lali's near her time.'

'I'm sure she'll manage to give birth without your presence.'

His tone was sharp, his words disturbed me. So much so that I at once agreed to go with him.

'We'll leave them our hotel phone number,' he said. He made it sound as if we were doing our children a favour; making a concession they had no right to expect.

'I wonder what they'll think?'

'For God's sake, Amy, who gives a bugger what they think?'

'Well, we are still married,' I conceded, 'so I don't suppose they'll be too surprised.'

He took off the gold rims and treated me to a myopic stare. He said, 'You're nothing like your mother, are you?'

I said, 'Whoever she was.'

'I think you know,' he said. 'I think you've always known.'

'Leave it,' I warned him. 'I don't want to talk about it.'

The bright cold weather held. After London, Derbyshire was wide and green and almost empty. We stopped for lunch in Bakewell. I told him how Chris and Dom had brought me from the Sheffield hospital by this same panoramic route.

He said, 'I'd like to go with you when you have your next check-up.'

I stared into my giant Yorkshire pudding. 'Yes,' I said, 'I think I'd like that.'

We walked around Bakewell. In a shop which sold boots and clothing suitable for hill-walkers, he bought me an olive-green waxed jacket. We looked in on the auction of paintings and fine prints. We stayed for ten minutes. He did not make a single bid.

The hotel was comfortable and warm. Our room was chintzy. A bowl of bronze chrysanthemums stood on the windowsill. The bed was soft and wide. I remembered Paris, how young we had looked then, how sure we had been that life and love were promised indefinitely; perhaps for ever.

He came out of the bathroom wearing blue and white striped flannel pyjamas and a thick brown dressing-gown. He grinned when he saw my old-fashioned, cream-coloured, long-sleeved Viyella nightgown. He took off the gold rims and placed them on the bedside table. He held out his arms and I went to him. I cried a little, and so did he. We leaned into each other like winded runners.

'We've been such fools,' he said.

'I know.'

'It's not all sorted yet, is it?'

'No. But I expect we'll manage.'

We made love gently, kindly, like old friends long accustomed to one another's needs. I woke towards morning; I listened to his quiet breathing, was achingly aware of the sweet familiarity of his body. He lay with his back towards me. I reached out my hand and touched his shoulder, and he was instantly awake. He switched on the bedside lamp and turned to look at me. I wondered how I appeared to him; perhaps I looked younger when he viewed me without the aid of the gold rims? He said, 'I love you, Amy.'

'Likewise.'

'Say it!'

'I love you, Michael.'

On Sunday we walked beside the river. We wore our waxed jackets. He held my hand. I stifled tears. Happiness made me confidential. I said, 'I found out who my father was. I looked in some old photograph albums. His name was Archie. Chris looks exactly like him.'

'They've waited years for you to say something about those pictures. To ask questions. When you didn't, they assumed that you were too upset to talk about it all, or that you had simply never made the connection.'

'You seem to know an awful lot about it.'

'Fin and Mimi were very close.' His words confirmed all of my suspicions. I released my hold on his fingers and pushed my hands into my jacket pockets. I walked a pace apart from him.

'What are you saying, Michael?'

'Mimi told things to Fin.'

'And Fin told you.'

'He thought that you should know the truth. He never understood the peculiar ways of English families. He wanted me to tell you about your father.'

'Why didn't you?'

'Why didn't I?' There was sadness in his voice and a bitterness I had never heard before. 'Think about it, Amy! Remember the way we were then, caught in a marriage that was never quite right from the beginning. Each nursing our own little resentments, neither of us capable of understanding or forgiveness. What do you think would have happened if I had dropped it casually into the conversation? Oh, by the way, dear, I've just found out that you've been lied to all your life. Your aunt is really your mother, your father was her long-time lover. Your parents never died in an accident after all.' He paused. 'It's often the messenger who gets shot, and you were always so devoted to Belle and Mimi.'

'I never really thought my parents died in an accident. Even quite small children know when adults are lying to them.'

'So what have you believed all these years?'

'I've tried not to think about it. I've told myself it didn't matter. When I was ten – eleven years old, I asked some awkward questions. Like – why did I say "Aunt" to Belle and not to Mimi?'

'What did they say?'

'Mimi said it would make her feel frumpish if I called her Aunty. She certainly didn't look much like anybody's aunt.'

'*I* know why you called her Mimi.'

I began to walk faster. He lengthened his stride. 'You called her Mimi because, when you first started to talk, you couldn't quite pronounce "Mummy". Her given name is Marguerite, but then, you know that too, don't you?'

Tears burned behind my eyelids. My hands clenched into fists inside my pockets. Michael said, 'Are you okay?'

'No,' I said. 'I'm not okay. I don't know why you're subjecting me to this.'

'It was you,' he pointed out gently, 'who raised the subject. I think you – we – should have talked about all of it long ago.'

I found the words difficult to utter, but we had come too far now for prevarication. 'Children,' I said, 'have a need to conform, to be like other children. I wanted a family, a mother and a father. What I actually had was Belle, the upright respectable one, whom I resembled so closely that people often thought I was her daughter. And then there was Mimi, pretty, unreliable, and loving. Men never stayed very long in that household. They either died or ran away.' I halted on the river path. I watched the children at the water's edge throwing bread to swans and mallard ducks; I saw their vigilant fathers.

I said, 'You know what they've done to me, don't you? They've robbed me of Archie!'

Michael said quietly, 'He was married when he met Mimi. His wife would not divorce him.'

'That's not the point! I needed to *know* that he was my father. When he died I was told that I mustn't talk about him any more, in case it upset Mimi. But what about me? What about my feelings? I loved him too.'

I looked at Michael's face and saw surprise and guilt. 'You're right,' he said. 'I should have – they should have – told you about him long ago.'

I said, 'Identifying my mother wasn't too important. Belle and Mimi were twins; they complemented one another. You've seen how that works between Chris and Dom. In a way, I think I sort of wanted Belle to be my mother. I often resented the things she did and said, but I always felt safe with her; and oh, how I needed to feel safe! From Mimi I had the treats, the spoiling, the sharing of secrets, the fun, the love. Looking back, I can see that I was very lucky. It hardly mattered which of them had borne me.'

I remembered Mimi as she had been on my last visit, the inch of henna still bordering her white hair, the scuffed blue carpet slippers, her uncertainty as to who I was; and I thought my heart would break. I recalled Aunty Belle, standing sentry over Mimi, fierce and protective. And that, of course, was how it had always been with them. The strong one had protected and defended the weak one, and neither of them had ever spoken about any of it. Everything that could be shared had been shared. Even me.

I said to Michael, 'I love them. Both of them.'

'Yes,' he said. 'I know you do.'

'The ability to love,' said Dr Quinn, 'surely is the light within us, perhaps the most important element of our human nature.'

We came back to London through heavy rain and cold winds. As we entered Michael's flat his phone began to ring. He picked up the receiver. I heard him say, 'Where is she? Yes, I'll tell her. Don't worry.'

'What is it?'

'Lali. Went into labour early this morning. She's in hospital.'

'It's too soon! Something must be wrong!'

'Hey, hey! Twins are often early. Don't you remember?'

I picked up his car keys from the coffee-table. 'Take me to her. Now, Michael!'

He walked through to the kitchen. I could hear him filling the kettle, rattling cups. I shouted at him. 'What do you think you're doing? Who wants coffee at a time like this? Michael – are you crazy?'

His eyes, behind the gold rims, were no longer kindly. He took me by the shoulders and propelled me back towards the velvet sofa. 'Sit down, Amy. Sit down and listen. You are *not* going to that hospital until you are requested so to do. Neither am I. It is Tim's place to be with Lali now. Not yours. Not mine.'

And then I remembered. Belle and Mimi, first into the ward when Chris and Dom were born. First to hold them. 'Michael,' they had said, 'we saw him as we were coming into the hospital . . . not to speak to . . . he rushed past us without a word.'

'You're right of course. I just wasn't thinking.'

'There's something else,' he said. He sat down beside me, but did not hold my hand. 'I don't want you to go back there.'

'Where?'

'The house. The place that was once ours, but is now, as far as I can see, in the occupation of our children and their partners.'

'But where else should I go? I thought that you would –?'

'No. I shall never move back.' His gaze roamed around the room, and came back to me. 'Stay here, Amy.'

It was not what I had expected. 'I don't know. It might not work. I couldn't go through a second parting.'

'There won't be one.'

'I'm not the woman you walked out on.'

'I'm not the man who walked out.'

There were things that still needed to be said. 'I thought you were planning to come back because Lali would be there.'

He looked away towards the cabinet which held the Lalique girl. 'I won't lie to you. That was my first intention.'

'And now?'

'I want it to be just us.'

'"Just us" might not be quite what you had in mind.'

'You're talking about your illness.'

'As I told you, I'm not cured of cancer. Oh, it's no longer this insurmountable barrier shutting out the sunlight. I have it whittled down to size. It was like a door opening, first a crack and then wide open. I've established a relationship with death; learned the limits of my fear. But it's my fight. Not yours.'

'Do you think I haven't thought about it?'

'Well – have you?'

'I've thought about the good years that we've missed, that we can still have if we want them. I still want it to be *us*.'

We came like thieves into the empty house. Already the rooms showed signs of their careless, multiple occupation. I began to wipe sticky rings left by mugs on the kitchen table. Michael pulled the cloth from my hands and threw it into the sink. I took only leisure suits, the scarlet duffle coat, the boots and trainers.

I left my house keys on the hall table and a note which said: GONE TO START A NEW LIFE. WITH MY HUSBAND.

READ MORE IN PENGUIN

In every corner of the world, on every subject under the sun, Penguin represents quality and variety – the very best in publishing today.

For complete information about books available from Penguin – including Puffins, Penguin Classics and Arkana – and how to order them, write to us at the appropriate address below. Please note that for copyright reasons the selection of books varies from country to country.

In the United Kingdom: Please write to *Dept. JC, Penguin Books Ltd, FREEPOST, West Drayton, Middlesex UB7 OBR.*

If you have any difficulty in obtaining a title, please send your order with the correct money, plus ten per cent for postage and packaging, to *PO Box No. 11, West Drayton, Middlesex UB7 OBR*

In the United States: Please write to *Consumer Sales, Penguin USA, P.O. Box 999, Dept. 17109, Bergenfield, New Jersey 07621-0120.* VISA and MasterCard holders call 1-800-253-6476 to order all Penguin titles

In Canada: Please write to *Penguin Books Canada Ltd, 10 Alcorn Avenue, Suite 300, Toronto, Ontario M4V 3B2*

In Australia: Please write to *Penguin Books Australia Ltd, P.O. Box 257, Ringwood, Victoria 3134*

In New Zealand: Please write to *Penguin Books (NZ) Ltd, Private Bag 102902, North Shore Mail Centre, Auckland 10*

In India: Please write to *Penguin Books India Pvt Ltd, 706 Eros Apartments, 56 Nehru Place, New Delhi 110 019*

In the Netherlands: Please write to *Penguin Books Netherlands bv, Postbus 3507, NL-1001 AH Amsterdam*

In Germany: Please write to *Penguin Books Deutschland GmbH, Metzlerstrasse 26, 60594 Frankfurt am Main*

In Spain: Please write to *Penguin Books S. A., Bravo Murillo 19, 1° B, 28015 Madrid*

In Italy: Please write to *Penguin Italia s.r.l., Via Felice Casati 20, 1–20124 Milano*

In France: Please write to *Penguin France S. A., 17 rue Lejeune, F–31000 Toulouse*

In Japan: Please write to *Penguin Books Japan, Ishikiribashi Building, 2–5–4, Suido, Bunkyo-ku, Tokyo 112*

In Greece: Please write to *Penguin Hellas Ltd, Dimocritou 3, GR–106 71 Athens*

In South Africa: Please write to *Longman Penguin Southern Africa (Pty) Ltd, Private Bag X08, Bertsham 2013*

READ MORE IN PENGUIN

A CHOICE OF FICTION

Asta's Book Barbara Vine

In 1905, Asta and her husband Rasmus came to East London from Denmark with their two little boys. Over seventy years later, Asta's diaries are published ... 'Barbara Vine has once again done her readers proud ... for a good, absorbing, well-told story, you could hardly better the unveiling of Asta's secret' – *Sunday Times*

Peerless Flats Esther Freud

Lisa has high hopes for her first year in London. She is sixteen and ambitious to become more like her sister Ruby. For Ruby has cropped hair, a past, and a rockabilly boyfriend whose father is in prison. 'Freud sounds out as a clear, attractive voice in the literary hubbub' – *Observer*

One of the Family Monica Dickens

At 72, Chepstow Villas lives the Morley family; Leonard, the Assistant Manager of Whiteley's, his gentle wife Gwen, 'new woman' daughter Madge and son Dicky. Into their comfortable Edwardian world comes a sinister threat of murder and a charismatic stranger who will change their lives forever. 'It is the contrasts that Dickens depicts so rivetingly ... she captures vividly the gradual blurring of social divisions during the last days of the Empire' – *Daily Mail*

Varying Degrees of Hopelessness Lucy Ellman

'Funny and furious ... what the author is interested in is the hopelessness of life. Her merry little novel is a vehicle for disgust. Lucy Ellman is clever, and very angry' – *The Times*. 'An irresistible cocktail of satire, slapstick and tenderness' – *Cosmopolitan*

The Killjoy Anne Fine

Nobody has ever treated Ian Laidlay in a natural way. Presented with his hideous facial scars, everyone he meets falls back on distant courtesy to hide pity or disgust or shock. But then someone laughs ... 'A wonderful and original piece of work ... a horror story which rings absolutely true' – Alan Sillitoe